STRANGLE A LOAF OF ITALIAN BREAD

AN ELLIE BERNSTEIN/
LT. PETER MILLER MYSTERY

STRANGLE A LOAF OF ITALIAN BREAD

DENISE DIETZ

FIVE STAR
A part of Gale, Cengage Learning

GALE
CENGAGE Learning™

Detroit • New York • San Francisco • New Haven, Conn • Waterville, Maine • London

GALE
CENGAGE Learning

LIBRARY OF CONGRESS CATALOGING-IN-PUBLICATION DATA

Dietz, Denise.
    Strangle a loaf of Italian bread : an Ellie Bernstein/Lt. Peter
Miller mystery / Denise Dietz. — 1st ed.
        p. cm.
    ISBN-13: 978-1-59414-760-9 (hardcover : alk. paper)
    ISBN-10: 1-59414-760-4 (hardcover : alk. paper)
    I. Title.
PS3554.I368S77 2009
813'.54—dc22   2009001222

First Edition. First Printing: May 2009.
Published in 2009 in conjunction with Tekno Books and Ed Gorman.

Printed in the United States of America
1 2 3 4 5 6 7 13 12 11 10 09

This book is dedicated to Eleanor Estill Congdon Putney
(1912–2007),
an extraordinary woman who spent a goodly portion of
her life teaching people to read.

ACKNOWLEDGMENTS

I'm grateful to The Muses—Lillian Stewart Carl, Annette Mahon, Sherry-Anne Jacobs, Mary Jo Putney, Garda Parker, Harriet Pilger and Terey Ramin—for keeping me on track.

I would like to thank my editor, Alice Duncan, and acknowledge the Five Star copyeditor, Vicki Kupferman.

A big hug to Lynn Whitacre, who was there from the beginning . . . when Ellie Bernstein was spawned.

I'm very grateful to the CSPD. Without them, Peter wouldn't be a viable character.

As always, I owe a huge debt of gratitude to Jean Neidich, founder of Weight Watchers. As a teen, I "bussed it" to Little Neck, N.Y., where Jean inspired me to become thinner and healthier. Eventually, I worked for the organization as a group leader.

Last but definitely not least, I'm incredibly grateful to my best friend and soul mate, Gordon Aalborg, who ignores "deadline dust bunnies" and is responsible for my romance scenes.

For those who want to read the entire novella, *Dream Angel,* it's on my Web site: www.denisedietz.com.

"Eating is self-punishment; punish the food instead. Strangle a loaf of Italian bread. Throw darts at a cheesecake. Chain a lamb chop to the bed. Beat up a cookie." —Gilda Radner

ONE

Wednesday

Members of the jury had been chosen from a box of crayons, with colors ranging from Burnt Sienna to Laser Lemon to Fuzzy Wuzzy Brown. The jury's foreman, a woman of indeterminable age, wore a somber pantsuit, enhanced by tummy liposuction, and a somber, surgically enhanced face. Her skin tone was Crayola Peach (formerly known as Flesh). The diamond on her third finger was as big as Poland, and she looked as if she was about to hype the benefits of a miraculous arthritis capsule whose side effects might be nausea, diarrhea, insomnia, memory loss and erectile dysfunction.

Instead she said, "We the jury find the defendant—" she paused for dramatic effect "—*not* guilty."

With a triumphant smirk, the racist defendant turned and shook his black lawyer's hand.

Ellie Bernstein turned from the TV to Jackie Robinson. "I'll bet you a can of albacore tuna that the racist defendant will be shot on the courthouse steps," she said, "or killed in his sleazy apartment, gunned down by the victim's husband, father, brother or fiancé."

Her regal black Persian continued tongue-bathing his ears with one padded paw, as if he couldn't believe his human was dumb enough to think he'd take that bet, so Ellie smiled at her cat and rested her eyes.

When she opened them again, the *Law & Order* rerun was

over and the peachy jury foreman was touting the benefits of a miraculous arthritis capsule with an X in its name. Only this time she was a soccer mom.

Ellie sat at the kitchen table. Her left hand cradled the side of her face. Her left elbow anchored a free weekly paper, *The Big Mouth Shopper*, whose pages were chock-a-block with discount coupons and classified ads. In her right hand she held a pair of scissors like a weapon, the twin blades positioned downward, their sharp points embedded in a prominent display ad for used pickup trucks. If her hair had been blonde rather than red and she had lost eighty-five rather than fifty-five pounds, she could have doubled for Grace Kelly in *Dial M for Murder*.

Still half asleep—or, technically, half a doze—she stared at the scissors. Had Eleanor Bernstein, diet club leader and trivia maven, subconsciously wanted to stab the jury foreman/soccer mom?

Oh, God, it was tempting. If incapacitated, the aging actress would stop popping up on a different TV show every week and driving Ellie nuts with the itchy notion that she'd seen the jury foreman/victim/bereaved relative/judge/perp/soccer mom before.

With an unrepentant smile, Ellie placed the scissors on the table, picked up the remote control, and aimed it at the small TV that perched atop an old, pre-divorce, faux-cedar microwave cart. She usually ate her supper while watching *Jeopardy!* or *M*A*S*H* reruns or Sunday/Monday night football, but on this cloudy Wednesday afternoon, alone in her kitchen, she had opted to have detectives Briscoe and Logan keep her company while she clipped coupons.

Ordinarily, during her downtime she'd be reading a book, preferably a complex mystery novel. However, she had to admit that she derived pleasure from clipping coupons. Not that she ever used them; three or four months later she'd clean out her purse and trash the outdated vouchers. But clipping coupons gave her a weird sense of purpose.

Or maybe it was simply osmosis. Her mother had always been, and still was, a copious coupon clipper. Mom even had a "coupon organizer" that she carried around in her seemingly bottomless handbag. Often, she'd spend a hundred dollars to save five.

Ellie's brother was even worse. At thirty-eight, three years younger than Ellie, Tab "temporarily lived at home." He had tanked at three commercial ventures and nobody in their right mind would lend him the money to invest in a fourth flop. Tab did, however, have access to Mom's credit cards, and if Ellie had a dollar for every time he'd held up a new shirt (sweater, shoes, CD, Harley accessory) and said, "I couldn't pass this up, it was such a bargain at 20% off," she could retire from the diet club business. Not that she wanted to retire. And even if she did want to retire and finish writing the mystery novel that lurked inside her head, she had an inheritance from her grandmother Eleanor—for whom she'd been named—that would keep a dozen Jackie Robinsons in albacore tuna for a long, long time. Tab, who had charmingly and smarmingly sponged off Grandma Eleanor for years, had not been "bequeathed" one red cent. *Quid pro quo.*

On the last classified ads page Ellie struck gold: a fifty-cents-off coupon for a giant bottle of Hellmann's Light Mayonnaise. Surrounding the coupon, like Indians circling a wagon, were a chimney sweep ad, a "free Corgi-Shepherd puppies to good home" ad, a coupon for a free appetizer at Uncle Vinnie's Gourmet Italian Restaurant—with the purchase of two entrées—and a personal ad that extolled "romantic candlelight dinners and long walks along a moonlit beach."

Beaches in Colorado Springs were a tad difficult to find, Ellie thought with a grin. Long walks along a moonlit mountain trail or along a moonlit, boulder-strewn path would be more apropos. She, herself, liked early morning jogs along an aspen-strewn footpath. She loved to watch tie-dye colors sluice the horizon. In the spring and summer, when her heart was high, Disneyesque birds chirruped "Whistle While You Work," or even better, the upbeat opening to the rondo of Beethoven's "Violin Concerto in D, Opus 61." In the fall, gaudy leaves fragmented like the inside of a kaleidoscope. In the winter, shrubs sported white tonsures while tree branches boogied at a skeletal extravaganza, a Bare Branch Ball aptly chaperoned by Mother Nature and her Greek chum, Boreas.

Often, while taking her crack-of-dawn treks, Ellie pictured a dog by her side. Lassie or Rin-Tin-Tin. Or, even better, an Irish setter, color coordinated to match her hair. "Accessorize," she could hear her mother say. "A lady should always accessorize. It's even more critical when you're fat."

Someday, Ellie thought, she'd stop wincing over matriarchal memories. Yeah, and someday pigs would fly.

"Don't worry," she told Jackie Robinson, just in case he could read her mind. "Even if I *were* crazy enough to adopt a dog as an accessory, it would be smaller and probably thinner than you. At any rate—" she glanced at her watch "—we'll soon have a chance to try one on for size. A dog, I mean. A guest. A *short-term* guest, so don't get your tail in a twist."

Jackie Robinson responded with a pointy-toothed yawn, not unlike a miniature, landlocked, furry feline shark, so Ellie refocused on *The Big Mouth Shopper.*

Above the "Chimneys R Us" ad was an open-auditions announcement for the John Denver Community Theatre's production of *Hello, Dolly!*

Ellie thought about trying out—briefly.

Only one thing would impede her audition.

Actually, two things.

She couldn't sing and she couldn't dance.

Two

Sara Lee—nee Sarah Leibowitz—liked to tell everybody that she was a cold-blooded killer. "I killed the 'h' in my name when I was thirteen," she liked to say. Then she'd laugh. She had a unique laugh—a cross between a puppy's playful growl and wind chimes. Her laughter was contagious. Nobody ignored it and most people joined in—laughing with her, not at her.

Her smile was contagious, too.

A month or so ago she'd bumped into one of her regulars at the Safeway. He had said, "You're not smiling, Sara Lee," and she had replied, "I'm off the clock."

Although she hadn't clocked out yet, Sara scowled. Damn Trent and his phone calls! If he called during a busy shift again, she'd be off the clock for good.

Her hand shook as she fished her compact from her apron pocket.

Ignoring the compressed powder, she stared into the little round mirror and saw Barbra Streisand. Oh, she didn't have Streisand's magnificent nose or sky-blue eyes. But the rest of her face was comparable, especially her mouth. Lips that looked vulnerable and kissable. Lips that opened up to pour forth Broadway show tunes, R&B, country-western, punk rock, acid rock, you name it. Everything but rap. Sara couldn't get a handle on rap. "Obscene poetry," she told her husband Trent, who couldn't get a handle on anything except Elvis.

Last week Trent had seen The King at a truck stop outside

Denver. The week before, at a carwash in Colorado Springs. Elvis had been kidnapped by aliens then brainwashed, Trent told Sara. Uh-huh, she said. Sure. Whatever.

Twenty-three years ago she'd been adopted; there was no doubt in her mind. Sandwiched between kid number three and kid number five (total seven) she was the only Leibowitz who could sing. The others were tone deaf—excruciatingly tone deaf.

Mom said no, Sara hadn't been adopted. Mom said, "Are you out of your freaking mind? Why would Daddy and me adopt when we breed like rabbits?" Mom wanted "her Sarah" to become a world-famous singing star and support her family, like Shania Twain. Instead, Sara had cashed in Uncle Ira's high school graduation gift—a U.S. Savings Bond—then flown to Vegas and married stud-muffin Trenton Zachariah. A big mistake.

Trent had a temper. Trent had a jealous streak a mile long. Trent didn't believe her when she said she had to work double shifts at Uncle Vinnie's Gourmet Italian Restaurant. Trent liked to use her body as a punching bag. Sometimes, depending on his mood, all he had to do was fist his slab of a hand and hum the theme from *Rocky* and she'd obey his every desire. Trent had a voracious appetite. He liked food, too.

If everything went according to plan, Trent would soon be roadkill.

Returning the compact to her apron pocket, Sara retrieved a mangled pack of cigarettes. She was on a smoke break. Vincent, the gourmet chef who owned Uncle Vinnie's Gourmet Italian Restaurant with his brother Al, didn't allow his waitresses to smoke inside the building. So she stood outside, in an alley behind the kitchen, sharing her small weedy patch with two puke-green Dumpsters. She smelled rotting lettuce. And tomato sauce. She hated the smell of tomato sauce, and was always tempted to shout "Hooray!" and perform her most provocative cheerleader's routine when one of her customers ordered shrimp scampi or fettuccine Alfredo. One of her *guests,* that is. Vincent insisted his wait staff call the customers "guests."

The cheap guests ordered spaghetti and meatballs. With a side salad and garlic-buttered Italian bread, it was the lowest-priced entrée on Uncle Vinnie's overpriced menu. Sara had nothing against spaghetti, although the price of one Uncle Vinnie's spaghetti and meatballs dinner would feed a family for a week, assuming they ate spaghetti and meatballs. But the cheapies drank water with lemon, rather than wine or beer or soda, keeping the tab—and tip—to a minimum.

She desperately needed every cent she could scrounge. Money for her thrift-shop clothes. Money for cigarettes. Money for her secret singing lessons—if Trent knew about the lessons he'd slice her throat. Money for a hush-hush plan she called "America the Beautiful." *Let freedom ring!* As Sara Lee, actor and vocalist, she'd wave so long to Colorado Springs. Her game plan was to take Broadway or Nashville or Hollywood by storm. And if her scheme to eighty-six her husband hit a snag, she'd shove off anyway and hire a Kevin Costner clone.

A girl can always use a bodyguard, she thought, Whitney's signature song on the tip of her tongue. "I Will Always Love You" was, in fact, Sara's favorite karaoke song. Every time she sang it, she got a standing ovation. She loved karaoke, loved to enter karaoke competitions and win tacky trophies. Her only rival was the insufferable Angel Pitt. Under different circumstances—*very* different circumstances—she and Angel could have been friends, even though, standing next to each other, they'd look like Mutt and Jeff. Sara was five-three while Angel was nearly six feet tall.

Schemes and daydreams were sanity savers, Sara mused, but before the dreary waitress could Cinderella herself into a brightly plumed songbird, she needed a grubstake, the bigger the better.

One of her fellow servers always earned big bucks. She had asked him how and, for weeks, he refused to tell her. When she finally wheedled it out of him, his fail-safe scam wasn't exactly legal. It wasn't exactly fail-safe, either, even though he said restaurants never prosecuted because of the bad publicity.

If things didn't pick up, she'd try his scam. Except, with her luck, she'd probably get caught. And prosecuted.

Sara heaved a deep sigh. She climbed on top of the sturdy wooden crate that short waitresses used when they tossed bloated trash bags into the Dumpsters. As she tap danced in place, her cigarette punctuated the sky with exclamation points. She mentally shed the black slacks that didn't show stains and the starched white shirt that did. In her mind's eye, she unknotted the skinny strings that kept her cranberry-colored apron moored to her waist and the tie that strangled her throat like a noose. Vincent left the choice of necktie motifs up to his waitresses—waiters wore black bowties—and Sara had opted for whimsy. Today: Daffy Duck.

Still pensive, still fully clothed in her server's uniform, she closed her eyes and imagined her supple body sheathed by a long, glittery gown. She added a tight corset so that her ample breasts threatened the gown's low-cut bodice. She hid her blonde-streaked ponytail underneath an elaborate wig. What else? Jewels. At her ears and throat. How about a diamond choker? She'd seen one in Wardrobe. The fake diamonds would sparkle and draw attention to her bosom, assuming the person who worked the spotlights knew the difference between up and down, left and right.

In an obvious, kiss-ass attempt to secure a part, Ray Morass had volunteered to help with the lighting for the John Denver Community Theatre's production of *Hello, Dolly!* But as a member of the JDCT theatre committee, Sara had nixed his request. Ray was a klutz.

During the JDCT's production of *The Pajama Game,* Sara had soloed with "Steam Heat." Clothed in black tights and leotard, she had thought herself sexy, seductive, cute. Unfortunately, Ray's focus—and spotlight—was still on "Hernando's Hideaway," an earlier production number. What a bonehead!

She had altered her choreography, scrambling to stay in the light's beam, and one nasty newspaper critic had called her performance "awkward."

Ray Morass reminded her of Walter Matthau. Not physically. For one thing, Ray was much younger . . . and alive; Walter Matthau had died in 2000. But Sara had read somewhere that Matthau detested Barbra Streisand and, during the *Hello, Dolly!* shoot, would only go near her when they had scenes together. Sara had also read—or heard—that on a break from filming, Matthau and Michael Crawford, who played Cornelius Hackl, had visited a nearby racetrack. There they saw a horse named Hello Dolly. Matthau refused to place a bet on the horse because it reminded him of Streisand, but Crawford thought it an omen. After Hello Dolly won the race and Crawford collected a sizable payoff, Matthau would not speak to Crawford for the rest of the shoot unless absolutely necessary.

If that anecdote wasn't an urban legend, Matthau had behaved like a mean-spirited curmudgeon, while Ray Morass was merely a moronic crosspatch.

"Crosspatch," Sara said, enunciating both syllables. She loved the word, which always made her think of Disney's spunky Br'er Rabbit and his briar patch, and she often murmured crosspatch under her breath when Trent was in a surly mood. She didn't want to whisper anything more profane, like bastard, just in case it came out too loud.

Ray Morass reminded her of Walter Matthau because she was

certain Ray hated her guts as much as Matthau had purportedly hated Barbra Streisand's guts.

Uncomfortable with the thought, Sara pushed it to the back of her mind.

Tomorrow night she would audition for the starring role of Dolly Levi. She had every song down pat, sounded more like Streisand than Streisand. She'd get the part, and while she was strutting on stage, the perfect alibi, a stranger with no discernable motive would ambush Trent and—

Her eyes snapped open. Come to think of it, she could have planned the hit for tomorrow night. Her audition would make a good alibi, too. She shook her head, her long ponytail whipping like a scourge. She didn't want to know when it happened. She would take her curtain call and sing an encore and the cops would be waiting in the wings, looking sorry-ma'am-solemn, and she'd play the grieving widow with nary a pause. After all, Dolly was a widow and Sara, who believed in omens (bet your bottom dollar, *she'd* have placed a bet on Hello Dolly to win the race), took that as a good o—

Lord have mercy, her tie was *killing* her! Her friend Nico had perfected a Windsor knot that pressed against her throat. And her buttoned shirt collar felt way too tight. She would have to buy more shirts at the Salvation Army's thrift shop.

Maybe, on her way home, she'd stop at the supermarket. She didn't have to work tonight, thank goodness, so she'd cook up some pork chops. Trent liked pork chops, the swine. She had tried to leave him once, but he said he'd kill her if she tried again. He'd get away with it, too. Trent was a good ol' boy, an ex–football player, the quintessential personification of an adorable redneck. He coached a kids' football team and made sure every kid played—as long as his team was ahead by fifty points. He hawked used cars at one of the dealerships owned by a retired Denver Broncos quarterback. Everybody loved Trent Zachariah.

Turning her face away from the Dumpsters, Sara tried to do a Baryshnikov. She had watched *White Nights* a bazillion times, watched Mikhail—in sneakers!—dance on his toes. However, her sneakers gave way at the last minute and she landed, flat-footed, on top of the crate. She glanced around, hoping no one had caught her "awkward" performance.

Uncle Vinnie's Gourmet Italian Restaurant anchored a pet supply store, a beauty salon, a sports equipment store, a video rental mart and, at the end of the small strip mall, an overpriced consignment shop called The Merry-Go-Round. Uncle Vinnie's was easily seeable from the Interstate, and easily accessible if one exited the Interstate and/or drove east along Austin Bluffs Highway. Across the highway, golden arches pierced the vista, and Sara, who swore she'd never eat pasta again as long as she lived, was addicted to Ronald McDonald's fries. A temptation-laden breeze carried the succulent scent of seasoned grease. Maybe tonight she'd—no!

Trent would skin her alive if she served him fast food.

Instead, she'd cook up some Rocky Mountain Chili, her own original recipe. It was easy to prepare and she could rest her aching feet while it simmered. All she had to do was brown a pound of ground beef in a large pot, adding onion, garlic and pepper when the meat was half cooked. Then, later, after a soak in the bathtub, she'd add a cup of warm Coors, two bouillon cubes, a chopped green pepper, a minced banana pepper, kidney beans, canned tomatoes, basil, oregano, thyme, and a cup of ripe, chopped olives. What made her chili special—and moist— was the beer. And, God knows, there was plenty of warm Coors hanging 'round her kitchen.

Yes, chili made more sense than pork chops. Her chili tasted even better the second day, and Trent could scarf it down while she was at the *Hello, Dolly!* auditions. Too bad she couldn't add rat poison.

As Sara's mind wandered, she loosened the Windsor knot at her throat, wriggled the necktie free from her collar, and flung the arrow-shaped end over her shoulder. She lit a second cigarette, then shoved the pack and lighter inside her apron pocket where it joined car keys, pennies, nickels, dimes, quarters, pens, her compact and a corkscrew. *And a partridge in a pear tree,* she thought, her Streisand lips morphing into a Cheshire cat grin. She unbuttoned her shirt collar and—with profound relief—inhaled. She sucked in the smell of pungent tomato sauce, gagged, and felt the osso bucco tidbits she had snitched during her lunch shift tickle her throat.

She coughed, swallowed, and glanced toward the restaurant's back door. She really should go inside before Micki Mouse, the tattletale hostess, ratted on her.

First, she'd finish her cigarette and practice one song.

Nico—fellow waiter, friend, occasional lover—was keeping an eye on her last two tables. After her guests paid their tabs, she could clock out.

"I'm the greatest stah," she sang in a New York accent, mimicking Barbra in *Funny Girl.*

Sara felt arms encircle her waist. Leaning back against a body that smelled of hairspray and mousse, she said, "Darling, we don't have time."

One arm draped her chest like a beauty contestant's banner.

"Darling, you're baaaaad," she said, thinking she sounded more like a sheep than a flirt. She'd have to work on her inflections. Nuances were so important, the difference between success and failure.

She felt something press against her throat.

Not diamonds . . .

Not even a fake diamond choker . . .

The necktie she had flung over her shoulder!

Dropping her cigarette butt, Sara clutched at her throat. She clawed at the tie but couldn't get a fingerhold. She waved her hands, as if she were a mime pressing against an imaginary piece of glass.

Her motion slowed, grew sluggish, as if she waved from a parade float.

Sara Lee—nee Sarah Leibowitz—did not see her life pass before her eyes. All she could see, in her mind's eye, was Daffy Duck's loony smirk.

THREE

Ellie Bernstein thought she'd die laughing.

On the other end of the phone, in his office, in his precinct, Lieutenant Peter Miller said, "What's so funny?"

"Ssssscout," Ellie managed, hissing the word in between giggles.

"Gesundheit," Peter said.

"No, no, honey . . . Scout . . . dog." She flapped her free hand in front of her mouth, trying to control her laughter. "I told you about her . . . about Scout . . . last night."

"Right. You're dog-sitting. For one of your diet club members. And she just did something funny." Peter's last six words sounded triumphant, as if he had solved a *Murder, She Wrote* rerun before the first commercial. "The dog did something funny," he amended, "not your Weight Winners member."

Ellie stopped waving at her face and swallowed her last chortle. "An hour ago I drove to Rachel's house and picked Scout up," she said. "I told you about Rachel, didn't I?"

"Sure. Rachael . . . Ray?"

"Rachael Ray is the food guru, Peter, the one you think is so pretty. My diet club member is Rachel . . . R-a-c-h-e-l . . . Lester. She's very quiet, very shy. I think she has marital problems, but I could be wrong about that." *I'm not wrong; all the signs are there.*

"Rachel one 'a' Lester. Right. Now I remember." Peter sounded uncertain. An attentive bedmate, he wasn't always an

24

attentive listener. On a scale of one to ten, Ellie's offer to dog-sit for a week was a nine, the toppings for his greasy pizzas a two.

Unfair, she silently chastised. Peter tended to focus single-mindedly when she was in peril, especially if it was a life-and-death situation, and in the short stretch she'd known him, she'd encountered three such "situations" and lived to tell the tale—obviously.

"Scout was fine in the car," Ellie continued. "Very conscientious, as if I were a dognapper and she wanted to map the route in her canny canine brain. She peed in the front yard, marking her new territory, I suppose, or simply leaving a smelly telegram for cats, birds, squirrels, and any dog foolish enough to jump over or dig under my fence. Then she sped into the house." Ellie slanted a glance at an old patchwork quilt, scrunched near the fireplace. "Rachel gave me a quilt. And dog toys. Scout curled up on the quilt and—"

"Jackie Robinson," Peter guessed.

Ellie nodded then realized Peter couldn't see her nod. "Before I could close the door to the kitchen," she said, "Jackie Robinson pranced into the family room, king of the manor. Have you ever seen a long-haired, black Persian cat do a double take?"

"I don't think I've ever seen any cat do a double take. Is it different from a human double take?"

"No. Exactly the same."

"So . . . Jackie Robinson hissed? Clawed? What?"

"At first he looked as if I'd plugged his tail into a light socket. Then he looked like Elsa Lanchester as Frankenstein's reluctant bride. Then he stared. Scout stared back. They've been like that for fifteen or twenty minutes. Staring at each other. Both waiting for the other to make the first move. It's really funny, Peter, but I guess you'd have to be here."

"Why don't you make the first move, sweetheart? Take Scout

by the collar, or by the scruff of the neck, and gently but firmly lead him—"

"Her."

"*Her* into the backyard. It's fenced, too," he added, as if she hadn't lived on the same street, in the same house, for twenty years.

Ellie blurted the first thing that came to mind. "Scout's a guest."

"Scout's a dog!" Peter groaned. "Please don't tell me you think dogs are furry little people."

"No. Of course I don't. They're furry little animals." Even to her own ears, her voice lacked conviction. "I've never owned a dog, Peter. My mother *said* she was allergic. Mick wanted a dog in the worst way. 'Mom,' he begged, 'you can use my allowance for dog food and I'll never ask for anything again.' I said okay, but—"

"Your ex said no."

"Tony liked the image: man, dog, very macho. But he thought a dog would be too much of a responsibility, would restrict our freedom, meaning *his* freedom." She sighed. "You've owned dogs."

"Dozens. When you grow up on a ranch, dogs multiply like rabbits. In fact, I had a terrier named Rabbit. His brother— same litter—was named Hare, as in 'hare of the dog.' " Peter chuckled.

"I'll need your help, please, until I get the hang of it."

"The hang of taking care of a dog? You walk it, feed it, pet it, and teach it not to beg."

"Beg?" She stared at Scout staring at Jackie Robinson. "Beg for what?"

"Food."

"You're kidding. You're not kidding." She held her breath, waiting for him to make fun of her diet club. After all, she had given him the perfect cue line. When he didn't tease, she let out her breath and said, "Will you train me to train the dog?"

"Sure."

"Let's start with this stupid staring contest."

"Okay. Carry Jackie Robinson into the kitchen. Shut the door between the kitchen and the family room. Are you writing this down? There'll be a test later."

"Very funny. I'm having a major crisis here and—"

"Hold it, sweetheart. My other line's buzzing."

Ellie cradled the receiver between her ear and shoulder. Afraid to move and disturb the peaceful standoff between her black Persian and Rachel Lester's black-and-white border collie, she tapped her fingernails against the polished wood of the telephone table. At the sound of her finger tapping, both animals focused for a microsecond on her hands. Then they went back to staring at each other.

She pictured Peter at his mahogany desk, inside his office, off the main precinct's main corridor. His wall held two framed diplomas from the Law Enforcement Officers Training School—one for general law enforcement and a second for police management—and three framed movie posters: *Notorious*, *The Third Man* and Gilbert and Sullivan's *Pirates of Penzance* with Kevin Kline and Linda Ronstadt, the love of Peter's life. His iconic adoration had begun when he first heard the 1968 Stone Ponys and "Different Drum." He loved everything about Linda Ronstadt, above all her lips. Especially when those pouty lips were projected onto a theater screen.

Toward the back of the room, a wooden shelf held several equestrian ribbons, rosettes and trophies.

In the eleven months they'd been together, Ellie had made a few office décor changes. Nothing as drastic as lace curtains at the window. For one thing, she wasn't a lace-curtains-at-the-window kind of gal. Her own windows were curtained by plants:

Philodendron, spider plants, English ivy and snake plants, also
known appropriately as "Mother in Law's Tongue." Each plant
she nurtured helped remove harmful chemicals from the air,
but she didn't dare suggest Peter follow her example. She knew
if she did, it would be as bad as covering his window with lace
curtains, and there was always the chance one or two redneck
cops would dub him Girlie Man—a misnomer they'd eventually
come to regret.

On Peter's bookcase, in between his CD player and a stack of
country-western CDs (topped by the Dixie Chicks), she had
placed a statue of the god Ganesha, who possessed an elephant
face and the huge, pot-bellied body of a human being. The lord
of success and destroyer of evils and obstacles, Ganesha was
also worshipped as the god of education, knowledge, wisdom
and wealth. Peter's bookcase statue had been a six-month anniversary present from Ellie, even though a statue of a Granny
Smith apple would have been more apropos.

She had first seen Peter in the hallway of the Good Shepherd
church, where she held her diet club meetings. He had been
investigating the murder of one of her members. Mesmerized,
she had watched him carve an umbrella above and below the
apple's seeded middle. Ellie's mother thought the meeting an
"intervention by God," and likened it to Adam and Eve in the
Garden of Eden, conveniently forgetting that the consumption
of an apple had led to the loss of a bunch of nifty things, including paradise.

But then, Eve had never bitten a Granny Smith.

Ellie had a similar Ganesha statue at home, only her statue
showed him riding a mouse, "the lowliest of all creatures." She
knew that there were at least two versions of the Ganesha story.
She liked the one where the goddess Parvati, while bathing, had
created a boy out of the dirt of her body and assigned him the
task of guarding the entrance to her bathroom. When her

husband Shiva returned, he was surprised to find a stranger denying him access to the room, and, enraged, struck off the boy's head. Parvati grieved, and to soothe her, Shiva sent out his *gana* to fetch the head of any sleeping being that faced the north. The company found a sleeping elephant and brought back its severed head, which was then attached to the body of the boy. Shiva restored its life and made "Ganesha" the leader of his troops. Shiva also bestowed a boon that people would worship Ganesha and invoke his name before undertaking any venture. Ellie sincerely doubted that Peter invoked Ganesha's name before undertaking any venture, but—like chicken soup for the dead person—Ganesha's godly presence couldn't hurt.

A framed photo of Peter's teenage niece, Jonina, graced his cluttered desktop. The picture had been taken a few months ago, at a dude ranch outside Aspen. Since then, Jonina had become a frequent visitor—to all intents and purposes, a member of the family.

Before Jonina, Ellie had not known her neighbors very well. In fact, her adjoining property owner might have said, "Ms. Bernstein? She was so quiet, so well mannered, so inconspicuous, I never dreamed she'd shoot up that sushi bar with an Uzi."

Jonina had the kind of exuberant, puppy-dog personality that drew total strangers together. She had organized a three-family garage sale, and her next project would probably be a block party where Peter would play the guitar and the whole neighborhood would sing Peter, Paul and Mary.

Ellie was humming an off-key rendition of "Puff the Magic Dragon," making the song her own, when Peter returned to the line.

"Gotta go," he said. "See you tonight. Love you. Will you marry me?"

"Will you marry me?" had become Peter-speak for "have a

nice day." Ellie usually replied with "I'll think about it" or "not yet," but he had already hung up the phone.

She shook her receiver as if by that action she could reconnect the fragile, albeit cordless, lifeline to her significant lover. At the same time, a proverbial goose walked across her grave and the hairs at her nape prickled. She shivered. She wasn't the least bit chilled, but Peter's abrupt hang-up could only mean one thing: a mystery to solve.

Her brother Tab called her a bush league sleuth, a designation Ellie loathed. She considered herself minor league rather than bush league, and she fully intended to work her way up to the majors.

One of her diet club members, originally from Tasmania, had nicknamed her "Stickybeak."

She deemed that a compliment.

Stickybeak was so evocative.

And so true.

Four

Denver's documented felonies fattened the national stats, but Colorado Springs had been on cruise control. No one had robbed any banks or convenience stores. Gangs had apparently signed, initialed, or spray-painted a truce. To tell the God's honest truth, it was as though the month of September, rather than January, had ushered in a new year. Dreamt up, trumped up, cooked up, ripped-from-the-headlines TV shows, and a plethora of hot-off-the-press whodunits by her favorite authors, were the only mysteries Ellie had encountered lately, if one didn't count a three-point Denver Broncos loss to the Chicago Bears.

"It's not that I want to see anyone hurt or, God forbid, murdered," Ellie told Jackie Robinson, uncontested winner of the cat–dog staring competition. "But if someone has been knifed, shot, strangled, or bashed over the cranium with a blunt instrument, it's only fair that Peter consult me. Two heads are better than one, especially if one of the heads has been solving fictitious mysteries her whole life. And the reason the Broncos lost to the Bears is because the coach called a quarterback sneak on fourth down when the obvious call was a slant pass over the middle, followed by a quick spike."

Ellie's NFL-sanctioned Denver Broncos T-shirt, tie-dyed orange and blue, was neatly tucked into a pair of faded-from-washing designer jeans. Her waist pressed against the kitchen counter as she attacked a chopping block. Her knife's honed blade left scars in the wood, but somehow her carrots and celery ended up diced, her fingers intact.

She had always been a good if lazy cook, forsaking health for convenience and, admittedly, caloric gratification. Her ex-husband Tony and son Mick never minded her excess sugars and carbs, especially when she served potato pancakes and homemade peanut brittle. But Tony more often than not ate out with his playmate-of-the-month, and Mick metabolized by running up and down a basketball court, or by hula-hooping his hips while he strummed a guitar, shedding sweat and pounds until he was as thin and wiry as his idol, Mick Jagger.

Ellie—also known as "Big Mama" and "the little woman"—did not believe in waste. Most of the time she couldn't remember swallowing, much less tasting, leftovers. Despite several quick-fix diets, her weight had ballooned, until she looked like the turkey that flew above the Macy's Thanksgiving Day Parade, assuming the turkey was stuffed with something other than helium.

Last she'd heard, Tony had turned vegetarian, more into tofu than toffee. Married to an ex–Dallas Cowboys cheerleader who subsisted on low-fat cottage cheese—when she wasn't binging and purging—Tony had packed up his Armani suits and his young wife's pom-poms and moved to L.A.

Following her divorce, Ellie had joined Weight Winners and lost fifty-five and a half pounds. Hired as a group leader, her leftovers now traveled from table to garbage disposal. Or when waste-management kicked in, the freezer.

Her cooking skills had improved as well. It was much more difficult to cook healthy meals, but much more gratifying, and her favorite accolade had come from Mick. "Hey, Mom," he had said, gobbling down her Weight Winners–sanctioned Short Ribs Borscht and Judeo-Christian Coffee Ring, "you should open a franchise."

Ellie slanted a glance at the kitchen clock. As she added her carrots and celery to the transparent onions that sautéed on top of her stove, she said, "Of course, the Broncos wouldn't have been three points behind if their lamebrained coach hadn't called for a prevent defense. Which, by the way, never, ever works."

Creasing the cushion of a kitchen chair and looking like a black wreath, Jackie Robinson lifted his furry head and yawned. He wasn't into football. He wasn't into baseball, either, even though he had been named for one of the greatest baseball players of all time.

Tempted to hum Simon and Garfunkel's "Mrs. Robinson"—her cat's favorite song—Ellie hummed "Homeward Bound," instead. Soon a minced garlic clove, oregano, thyme, rosemary, basil and one teaspoon of chili powder joined her onions, celery and carrots. Then she scrubbed preparation dishes while the hands on her clock inched, second by second, toward the five-minute mark.

"Homeward Bound . . . I wish Peter were . . . homeward bound," she sang, her hips swaying like Elvis at a county fair. Fortunately, her hips didn't know that she couldn't carry a tune in a bucket.

Enticing aromas filled the kitchen as she added canned tomato sauce, mushrooms and three tablespoons of honey to the concoction inside the pot. She stirred vigorously, then turned the stove to simmer. Later she would cook six lasagna noodles and spread a thin layer of her seasoned, simmered sauce over the bottom of an oiled pan. She'd add layers of noodles, cottage cheese, Cheddar cheese, and more sauce, ending with mozzarella and a little sauce on top. Her directions said to bake for fifty minutes and cool for ten—more than enough time to interrogate her homeward-bound lieutenant, assuming he *was* homeward bound. "Gotta go . . . see you tonight" could mean 11:59 p.m.

Peter would also play guinea pig, since the simmering sauce was a brand-new recipe donated by Charlene Johnson, one of Ellie's diet club members. If it tasted as good as it smelled, Ellie would type up the recipe and thumbtack it to the "inspirational" bulletin board at her Weight Winners meeting site. Charlene, who had lost forty pounds, regressed, regained, rejoined, and re-lost twenty-one pounds, called the dish "Veggie Lasagna." Ellie had renamed it "Honey Lasagna." Peter would never touch anything that included the word veggie, not even vegetable oil. However, in all likelihood her carnivorous detective would detect a lack of meat. If he did, she had microwavable pork sausages on hand.

She heard Peter before she saw him. He had been trained by his Nana to take off his shoes before entering a home. He didn't remove his shoes inside a crime-scene house, of course. Instead, he shrouded his shoes with paper booties. But at the start of his career, he'd automatically bend to one knee and reach for his laces. Some of his colleagues still called him Shoeless Pete.

Lieutenant Shoeless Pete.

Lieutenant Shoeless Pete, *sir.*

Strolling into the kitchen, he straddled a chair catty-corner to Jackie Robinson and said, "Something smells good."

"Sauce, Peter. For a new recipe called *honey* lasagna. You're playing guinea . . ." Ellie paused. She eyed Peter's gray sweatshirt, jeans and white tube socks as if they were sprayed with luminal. Then, using her brilliantly honed deductive powers, she said, "You changed your clothes."

He pressed the heels of his hands against his bleached-to-an-almost-white blue denim thighs. His hands anchored his legs and butt. He was trying really hard to appear relaxed, Ellie thought, but his hands betrayed him. So did his tense shoulders.

"These are my 'locker clothes,' " he said. "I decided to leave the precinct early for a change. I was about to tell you that when a call came in . . ." He clamped his mouth shut. His gaze touched upon Jackie Robinson, the stove, the sink, the refrigerator, and the refrigerator magnet that stated: PEOPLE WHO ARE FORCED TO EAT THEIR OWN WORDS WILL REDUCE THEIR BIG MOUTHS. Opening his mouth again, he said, "Where's the dog?"

"Outside. In the backyard. Staring at a squirrel." Ellie strolled over to the stove and stirred her sauce with a wooden spoon. "Tell me," she said, making an about-face.

"Your spoon's dripping," Peter observed.

"Jackie Robinson will clean it up. He loves tomato sauce, the spicier the better. Tell me."

"I should introduce myself to what's-her-face. The dog."

"Scout. She was named for the little girl in *To Kill a Mockingbird*. Played in the movie by . . . Mary Badham."

"How do you remember things like that?"

"Trivial Pursuit should have been called Eleanor Bernstein."

"Hah! I bet you can't do that Kevin Bacon thing with Mary what's-her-face."

"Badham, and I bet I can." Ellie had introduced Peter to the game that linked actor Kevin Bacon to just about any other actor. Not that Peter could link anybody to anybody, except maybe Roy Rogers to Trigger, or Clint Eastwood to Dirty Harry Callahan. But Ellie, a movie buff, had a mind like a blotter, or as her son Mick put it, a self-stick notepad inside her head. "If I can link Badham to Bacon," she said, "you owe me dinner and a movie at any restaurant and theatre I choose. If I can't, you choose and I'll pay."

"Deal."

"Sucker!" She grinned. "Mary Badham was in *Our Very Own*

with Faith Prince. Faith Prince was in *Picture Perfect* with Kevin Bacon."

"What about Atticus Finch?"

"Gregory Peck? That's too easy. Peck was in *Mackenna's Gold* with Eli Wallach. Eli Wallach was in *Mystic River* with Kevin Bacon."

Ellie placed her wooden spoon on top of the chopping block, and splayed her hands across her hips. "Now . . . tell me."

"Tell you what?"

"Don't play innocent, Lieutenant. You were talking to me on the phone when you got another call, and . . . ?"

He ran his hands through his thick, dark hair, a stall tactic.

"Don't you know," she said, "that running your hands through your hair like that will make you bald?"

"Says who?"

"Says my mother. She also says overweight people should starve themselves to death so they can live a little longer."

Peter rose from his chair and strode across the kitchen. Squeezing his eyes shut, he lightly scuttled his fingertips across her breasts. "And according to your mother, messing around in the bathroom will make you blind."

"My brother Tab has twenty-twenty vision," she said as liquid fire shot through her belly.

Peter's silver-streaked mustache grazed her forehead. His blue-gray eyes, when open, usually sparkled with tender mischief. His nose, once broken then reset incorrectly, angled toward the left of a mouth that enjoyed kissing. Those same lips that could caress her into a kaleidoscope of oblivion could assume a frowning line of professionalism while announcing, "You have the right to remain silent."

"My brother doesn't even need reading glasses," she added, breaking the silence, "which proves my mother doesn't know everything, even if she thinks she does."

"Forget Tab. Forget your mother." Peter opened his eyes and grinned. "*Jeopardy!* is about to commence."

Peter liked to neck, or as he put it "canoodle" in front of *Jeopardy!* For some incomprehensible reason, the sound of Alex Trebek's voice turned him on. The fact that Ellie knew ninety percent of the questions to the answers stoked his flames. She had tried to explain that she had always been a walking, talking trivia machine and that she was a complete dud when it came to geography, but it didn't matter. During the diet club murders they'd made love in front of *Jeopardy!,* and now it was a ritual.

"Tell me about the phone call first," she said. "The call that interrupted my dog-training lesson."

"People-training lesson," he amended.

"If you don't," she threatened, ignoring his modification, "I'll turn the channel to a local news station."

He started to run his fingers through his hair again. Then he stopped and said, "A waitress was murdered."

"Holy cow! I had hoped for something less . . . irreversible. Where?"

"In an alley, behind the restaurant where she works."

"And that restaurant is?"

"Why do you want to know the name of the restaurant?" he asked, his voice filled with suspicion.

"The local news will tell me if you don't," she said, her voice smug.

"Uncle Vinnie's."

"Uncle Vinnie's Gourmet Italian Restaurant? Holy cow! I've eaten there. Their lunch salads are good but the shrimp scampi is to die for." She winced at her choice of phrase. "Time of death?"

"Sometime between two-thirty and three-fifteen."

"Two-thirty and three-fifteen? No one noticed she was missing?"

"The deceased had finished her clean-up—they call it side-work—and during her absence a waiter collected her tips and stuck the money in an envelope. The owner and chef, Vincent, said the deceased often left spur-of-the-moment."

"Was he terribly upset?"

"Who? Vincent? Yes. But he seemed more upset over the loss of two waitresses than he was over the death—"

"*Two* waitresses?"

"May I taste your sauce, Norrie?"

That brought a smile to her face. Peter had nicknamed her Norrie, short for Eleanor. Because, he said, she ig-*nored* his advice. "The sauce isn't done yet, honey. It still has to simmer for a while. Why was Vincent upset over the loss of *two* waitresses?"

"One's dead. It's a bit difficult to wait tables when you're dead, Norrie, unless you're Tom Hanks."

"Tom Cruise, if you mean *Interview with a Vampire,* and please don't ask me to connect Tom Cruise to Kevin Bacon. I can do it easily, one movie, but not right this instant. What happened to the second waitress?"

"She found the body and lost it."

"She lost the body?"

"No. Her marbles. Vincent said the customers at the Mc-Donald's across the highway could hear her screams."

"Where was the body found?"

"I told you. In an alley behind the rest—"

"On the ground? Hidden behind trash cans?"

"Nope, but good guess. The deceased's body was found inside a Dumpster. The waitress who lost her marbles was standing on top of a wooden crate. She wanted to trash some trash. Her eyes were half-shut and she held her breath, hoping to expunge, or at least dissipate, the smell of the garbage. She opened her eyes, glanced into the Dumpster, screamed bloody murder, fell off the crate, and suffered a slight concussion. She'll be out of commission for a couple of days, but Vincent doesn't think she'll come back. He says waiting tables is a killer job to begin with and murder puts a strain on . . . employee relationships."

"He suspects another employee?"

"I didn't say that."

"You didn't have to."

"Vincent thinks the deceased was messing around with a waiter named Nicholas. Nicholas vehemently denies it."

"Of course he does. What's her name? The second waitress? The one who found the body?"

"Theodora something . . . Mallard, I think, like the duck. Why?"

"No reason. Curious."

I know her, thought Ellie. *Her nickname was Tad, she was a cheerleader in high school, and she went steady with my brother Tab long enough to confiscate his basketball jock jacket. I think they broke up because of name confusion: Tab and Tad.*

Peter said, "Stay away from this case, Norrie. Leave it to the CSPD. We're dealing with a cold-blooded killer and—"

"What was the murder weapon?"

"Daffy Duck."

"Excuse me?"

"The deceased was wearing a Daffy Duck necktie."

"Stop calling her the deceased." Ellie glanced at the kitchen clock. "You've got less than eight minutes if you want to scurry to the bedroom and watch Alex Trebek."

"I don't want to *watch* Alex Trebek," Peter said with a Groucho leer and the flick of an imaginary cigar. "Okay, here it is in a nutshell. Sara Zachariah, also known as Sara Lee, was taking a smoke break. The restaurant's owner doesn't allow his waitresses to smoke inside the building. Someone crept up behind the poor kid and strangled her with her Daffy Duck necktie—the tie is a part of her waitress uniform. We figure she was standing on top of the wooden crate."

"How do you know that?"

"She lost control of her sphincter muscles and—"

"I get the picture."

"So unless the murderer was standing on a second crate, he was fairly tall. And before you say 'or she,' that's the empirical he."

"*Was* there a second crate?"

Peter shook his head. "There's a stepladder—"

"In the alley?"

"No. The kitchen."

"Could two people fit on top of the crate?"

"Yes, but it would be a tight squeeze. And if the deceased . . . if Sara Lee struggled, one or both would fall off."

"When the wind blows," Ellie murmured, "the cradle will rock."

"What?"

"Nothing." She glanced toward her window. Outside, the wind had begun to blow and the café-curtains above her aloe and herb plants were dancing a Judy Garland–Mickey Rooney jitterbug. Maybe she should let Scout inside.

"We don't know yet if Sara Lee was raped," Peter said, "but I doubt it since the murder occurred in broad daylight and the alley is usually populated with smoke-breakers from the other establishments. And that's all I'm going to tell you."

"Fair enough, honey. Was the motive robbery?"

"Nope. She had sixty-some-odd dollars in her pants pocket."

"Her tips," Ellie said, "and her bank."

"Bank?"

"My brother Tab waited tables one summer. He was forgetful and clumsy. He was also cute and charming, so he did okay, gratuity-wise. People always asked if Tab was his real name.

He'd say yes, he was named for Tab Hunter, which is true. Then he'd schmooze his tables with Tab Hunter movies, especially *Battle Cry* and *Operation Bikini*. A bank is the money you start your shift with—short for bankroll. At the end of the shift, you turn in everything to the manager or the owner, except your bank and tips. Do you have a key suspect, other than Nicholas?"

"Nope. Everybody liked Sara Lee. And that's all I'm going to tell you."

"*Everybody* didn't like Sara Lee. Is . . . was she married?"

"Yes."

"Zachariah . . . *Trenton* Zachariah?"

"Yes. How'd you know that?"

"He used to play for the Kansas City Chiefs. He was traded to the Broncos, lasted one season, and was dropped from the team. No other team would touch him with a ten-foot pole. He wasn't a bad player, but he kept piling up penalties for personal fouls like late hits, unnecessary roughness, face-masking and roughing the passer. He could have carried that attitude off the field, Peter, and roughed up his wife."

"We're checking that out, sweetheart. There were no emergency calls to 9-1-1, but we'll talk to the deceased—to Sara Lee's family. And the neighbors. And that's all I'm going to tell you."

Ellie opened her mouth to ask another question, but Peter scooped her up into his arms and gave her a kiss that left her gasping for breath. His motion was aggressively tender rather than rough, and had she been an NFL referee she wouldn't have thrown a flag. Not that she possessed the strength to throw a flag. Peter's second kiss had jelly-fished her whole body. She could almost smell her desire, musky and warm.

Peter scaled the staircase, two steps at a time, like Rhett Butler on a mission from God.

In the book, Rhett takes a breather to kiss Scarlett.

In the movie, Clark Gable didn't waste time on kisses.

Peter compromised by kissing Ellie breathless, inhaling between kisses, and climbing nonstop.

He entered the bedroom and transferred her from his arms to the bed. His face was tense with arousal. As he turned on the flat-screen TV, a nine-month anniversary present, Ellie heard the familiar music, heard the announcer say, "This . . . is *Jeopardy!*"

FIVE

Rachel Lester stared at the mountains through the cabin's plate glass window. Like millions of other children, she had been taught that George Washington could not tell a lie. Neither could Rachel. If she tried, her lips would quiver, her pinch-me-please cheeks would flush, her cornflower-blue eyes would tear up, and her voice would stumble over the simplest syllable. Even the forehead beneath her bangs and the scalp beneath her perky pageboy would sweat.

"I cannot tell a lie," George Washington had purportedly said when confronted with his hatchet job. At age sixteen, Rachel had listened to a classmate tell a somewhat risqué joke that incorporated the F-word and a sexual innuendo about the cherries in George Washington's cherry tree. If she recalled correctly—she never *could* remember punch lines—the tasteless shaggy dog story had something to do with three presidents who walked into a bar. Or maybe they fished from a rowboat. Or sat in a cherry tree. At any rate, one of the Sacred Heart High School sisters, a math teacher, overheard the joke and freaked out when Rachel got the giggles.

Incensed by Rachel's nonstop laughter, the nun roughly pushed her to the ground and dragged her—by the hair—into a classroom. Rachel's school jumper bunched up, displaying her safety-pinned-at-the-waist, hand-me-down, practically transparent underpants. Her thinly clad butt scraped up splinters from the scuffed wooden floor, and in no time her incessant giggles had become uncontrollable sobs.

But that didn't dissuade the nun. Upon reaching her desk, she grabbed a ruler, yanked Rachel to her feet, and rapped her knuckles so many times and so hard, three fingers broke. Rachel's parents didn't have the money for intense physical therapy, so over the years her right hand had curled into a claw. During moments of stress she could actually *feel* it stiffen and coil. Although the sadistic nun was long-dead, Rachel's husband had adamantly insisted she call Jonah Feldman, the famous—some said infamous—attorney. Jonah Feldman had filed a class-action lawsuit. Apparently, Rachel wasn't the only student crippled by sharp rules and razor-sharp rulers.

Outwardly, Rachel had survived that horrendous experience. Her mother even insisted that the teacher the students called Sister Vicious was in the right, that exorcising Rachel's "profane evil spirit" was a blessing in disguise. But Rachel knew, or at least suspected, that inside her placid exterior lurked a raging beast—a killer dragon with its nostrils unlit.

Comfortable with the knowledge that *she* was in the right, that the knuckle-rapping and broken fingers had *not* been her fault, Rachel had finally fabricated a falsehood and gotten away with it—"gotten away" being the operative words. At age thirty-seven she had, at long last, lied. She had cooked up a teensy distortion, a little white lie that couldn't possibly hurt anyone, and—miracle of miracles—everybody believed her.

So why did she feel so conscience stricken, as if she had been caught with her hand inside the cookie jar?

Because Ellie Bernstein had believed and, worse, trusted Rachel, that's why. When Ellie liked someone, she tended to ignore a fib, even if it bit her on the butt. How many times had Rachel heard Ellie tell a Weight Winners member that he or she had hit a plateau when Rachel—and everybody else—knew darned well that the member had spent the week cheating like crazy?

Charlene Johnson was a prime example, always sucking up to Ellie by donating recipes, always cheating and bragging about it. "I lost two pounds and I cheated like crazy," she would whisper, after she stepped off the scale. Charlene cheated on her husband, too.

There was a lot of that going around. Probably because of the Internet. It was so easy to arrange an assignation on the Internet. Not that Matthew used the Internet. He liked to use the phone—land or cell—and he liked to cheat close to home. Maybe the danger of getting caught spiced his two-timing stew.

Materialistically, Matthew wasn't a bad husband. He gave Rachel a generous monthly allowance. He traded in her car every three years. He insisted she supplement her wardrobe with the latest styles. He didn't want kids but he had no objection to a dog, although he would have preferred one with a pedigree.

Believing herself privileged to have acquired such a charitable provider, Rachel had ignored Matthew's "little indiscretions" for years.

But this time he'd gone too far. This time three so-called friends had cornered Rachel. Chittering away, starting every sentence with "We thought you should know," they had given Rachel lurid details she preferred not to hear.

Last week her three so-called friends had been lunching at Uncle Vinnie's Gourmet Italian Restaurant and they'd seen, with their own six eyes, the way a drop-dead-gorgeous waitress named Sara Lee had flaunted her *ass*ets. Matthew, at a nearby table, had left his business associates and wandered toward the back of the restaurant. One of Rachel's so-called friends had to "go potty." The bathrooms were located at the back of the restaurant and the so-called friend just *happened* to accidentally catch a glimpse of Matthew and the waitress in the alley behind the kitchen. The so-called friend didn't want to tell tales after school, but if Rachel really wanted to know what Matthew and Sara Lee were doing, think Monica Lewinski.

Her husband had been caught with his pants down once too often, Rachel now mused, her lips trembling. And just like her favorite country-western singers, she couldn't forgive, or forget, Matthew's cheating heart.

Not anymore. Never again.

And yet, before she accused him face-to-face, she needed to consider her options.

Which was why she had lied.

She had told Matthew that her sister Margee, who lived in Houston, was very sick, practically at death's door, and she needed Rachel to baby-sit her three kids.

To tell the God's honest truth, Margee's illness wasn't a little white lie. You could even call it a whopper. Margee, who lived in a one-bedroom Houston apartment and worked at a bookstore called Murder By The Book, was alive and kicking and healthy as a horse.

And she didn't have three kids.

During the ten years they'd been married, Matthew had never asked Rachel one question about her family. It was as if she were a puppy he'd adopted from the pound. On the day she and Matthew tied the knot—and wasn't *that* a germane expression?—she had become his property, duly licensed with a marriage certificate rather than a dog tag.

So when she told him she had to nurse her ill sister and baby-sit her sister's three kids, he simply gestured toward Scout and said, "You'd better take that friggin' mutt with you, Rachel. Don't expect me to walk and feed him and clean up after him, because I won't."

"Her," Rachel had said. "Not him, her. And I've made arrangements to leave Scout with a friend."

"I didn't know you had any friends," Matthew had said with

a nasty laugh.

Well, she did. The three so-called friends from her book club, the ones who had told her about Matthew's drop-dead-gorgeous waitress. And Ellie Bernstein, her friend as well as her diet club leader. And Cee-Cee Sinclair.

Three years ago, Cee-Cee had discovered Scout, all skin and bones, discarded like a litterbug's candy wrapper less than fifteen feet from a roadside souvenir stand. Cee-Cee ran a rescue operation for abandoned and often mistreated dogs, and she had become Rachel's friend. A good friend. Such a good friend that she'd given Rachel a spare key to her Pikes Peak mountain cabin. "Feel free to use it any time," Cee-Cee had said. "You don't even need my permission. The cabin belonged to my late husband. I stay there occasionally, when I need some peace and quiet and thinking time, but I'm not a bogtrotter and my idea of *roughing* it is to toss my credit card to the clerk at a Norman Bates motel. And I rarely, if ever, use the cabin between September and Memorial Day."

Rachel had sincerely planned to fly to Houston, but she'd put off phoning her sister. In the back of her mind she thought Margee might exclaim, "No, hon, I'm way too busy right now," and she knew that the rejection would send her into "an abyss of despair from which there is no exit," as her favorite romance author, Marty Blue, liked to say.

Due to a *real* family emergency, Cee-Cee had said she couldn't dog-sit Scout. But that meant that Cee-Cee's cabin was unoccupied, and Rachel had impulsively decided to kill her Houston visit.

Without saying a word to anyone about her change in plans, or the vacant mountain cabin, she had asked Ellie to dog-sit Scout, which in retrospect was too silly for words. She could have put her beloved dog in her rental car and driven off to Zanzibar, for all Matthew knew or cared.

By now, Cee-Cee had probably forgotten she'd given her spare key to Rachel, which was okay. Metaphorically speaking, Rachel was invisible, and the fact that nobody knew she stayed at the cabin was even more okay. She had such an incredible sense of freedom, autonomy, and *independence,* it just about made her giddy. Arms crossed, she kept hugging herself to stay anchored, but she couldn't help uttering little sounds of delight that, to her ears, sounded like a mishmash of a squeal and *wheeee.*

Scout would love it here, she thought, as her last *squee* transformed itself into a deflated, balloon-like sigh. Although she felt totally isolated, as if she'd landed on Mars or the moon, she was less than two and a half hours from downtown Colorado Springs. Her nearest neighbors were a rinky-dink gas station and a small grocery store. Both charged like wounded bulls.

Surrounded by acres of foliage and trees that touched the clouds, Cee-Cee's snug cabin was a port in a storm, a haven in every sense of the word. In Cee-Cee's words, "An accommodation that offered the most favorable opportunities."

Rachel desperately needed an opportunity to think, to reach a conclusion that was based on common sense rather than pathetic sentiment—or fear.

Cee-Cee called her cabin "nouveau rustic." Clean as the proverbial whistle, its kitchen and bathroom were up-to-the-minute, brand-spanking-new. However, the downstairs living room and the loft bedroom were straight out of an historical romance novel. A fireplace. Wood-hewn furniture. A double bed with an old-fashioned feather mattress. A sofa that looked and felt like a church pew.

The cabin had no TV or radio, but it did have a phone, and Rachel had brought her cell phone, so she wasn't wholly disconnected from the outside world.

She really should call and check up on Scout.

Whoa! Was she losing what little remained of her mind? She had only been gone a few short hours and she was supposed to be winging her way to Texas.

Inside the cozy kitchen, inside a copper-bottomed Revere saucepan, a couple of all-beef kosher hot dogs boiled merrily. Rachel knew it was silly, but when she cooked franks she always pictured them as cartoon hot dogs, the kind that drive-in movies would put up on the screen during intermissions. Magnified, the hot dogs would be smiling as they merrily leapt from grill to bun.

But then, they never got burned.

Sauerkraut simmered inside a second saucepan. Rachel loved sauerkraut, the saltier the better, despite her tendency to retain water.

She felt so virtuous. Everything on top of the gleaming-white stove was "legal" Weight Winners fare, even though, technically, she could cheat. Didn't people cheat when they were on vacation? Wasn't she on vacation?

Well . . . no.

She was on a mission. She needed to write a Mission Statement. She needed to get her priorities straight. She needed to get her head on straight. As soon as her broken-fingers-lawsuit was settled, she'd have money. Granted, the lawyer would keep a goodly portion, but there'd be some left over. *And guess what, ladies and gentlemen of the jury? For reasons I'm sure you can understand, I didn't want Matthew Dillon Lester to get his dirty, cheating hands on one red cent of my payoff.*

The sauerkraut smelled delicious. The sauerkraut smelled burned!

Rachel raced to the stove and turned it off. Oh, well, she wasn't really all that hungry. Of course, she could always eat the hot dogs without sauerkraut, but why bother? Her hot dogs didn't look happy. They looked old and shriveled and dead.

Returning to the family room, she sat on the floor. Her knees supported her chin as her spinal column pressed against the pew-couch. For the umpteenth time she wondered how a girl who had been voted most likely to succeed had ended up in a time warp. Of course, no one had ever told her what she was supposed to succeed *at*. And while unfaithfulness was an old-fashioned word—and possibly an out-of-date concept—she felt like such a cliché. Maybe she'd cut her hair, get rid of the Prince Valiant bangs and June Allyson pageboy she'd worn since nursery school. That would be a good start. She even had a recommendation from one of her so-called book club friends—a stylist named Raymond, who worked in a beauty salon two or three doors down from Uncle Vinnie's Gourmet Italian Restaurant, practically spitting distance from the pet shop where Rachel bought Scout's toys and special dog food.

Next to the cabin's wooden sofa, on top of the carton Rachel had transported from home, were neatly stacked books: romance paperbacks and hardcover mysteries. Her sister Margee—alive and kicking and healthy as a horse, thank God—had boxed up and mailed some new mystery novels, but Rachel preferred romance novels, especially historical romance. She liked to lose herself in the seventeenth, eighteenth and nineteenth centuries, where women were beautiful and gutsy and slender. Where men were, for the most part, faithful to their wives.

Matthew Dillon Lester didn't know that he'd been caught with his pants down.

Rachel was a good Catholic, so divorce was not an option. *Or had the rules changed?*

Rachel was a good Catholic, so the designation "widow" was socially acceptable. *Of course, the designation "black widow"—as in spider—might not fly.*

Rachel was a good Catholic, so she couldn't kill Matthew. *Thou shalt not kill.*

But the Bible—and, as far as she knew, the Pope—had never said anything about waiting until one's two-timing husband was asleep, then cutting off his—

What did Marty Blue, her favorite romance author, call it? Oh, yeah. His "turgid organ."

Six

When Ellie awoke from her post-*Jeopardy!* snooze, a local TV reporter was asking tall, burly, thick-necked Trenton Zachariah how he *felt* when he'd heard that his wife had been strangled to death.

And Peter was nowhere in sight.

As the stoical Trenton Zachariah said he felt "bad," Ellie fumbled for the remote and pressed MUTE. Then, cocking her head, she listened carefully but didn't hear any bathroom sounds. No running water. No singing. Unless she and Peter shared the bathtub, he'd sing. Nonstop. He sang in the shower. Heck, he sang while he brushed his teeth. Privately, Peter imagined himself Mario Lanza. Too bad he sounded more like "Mario Langur." And while he didn't have the chin tufts of a langur monkey, he definitely possessed the voice.

She reminded herself that even without a certified singer's voice, Peter was Richie Blackmore and Jimi Hendrix combined when it came to the guitar, and that no Discovery Channel langur monkey played classic riffs, and that Peter—who mangled the names of most actors and TV personalities—could quote Jimi Hendrix.

Jimi Hendrix just happened to be one of Ellie's favorite philosophers. "When the power of love overcomes the love of power, the world will know peace," Jimi had said. So simple. So true.

Monkey business forgotten, Ellie saw that Peter's jeans and

sweatshirt had disappeared, too.

There would be a note downstairs.

And a missing pair of entrance-hallway shoes.

She heard branches *whap-whap* against the half-open bedroom window, stirred *and* shaken by a gusty breeze. The earlier, cradle-rocking, kite-wind had apparently swallowed a growth-hormone capsule.

Daylight was rapidly diminishing and she could smell September. There was no other smell like it. She loved September, when the iridescent aspens shimmered like gold aluminum foil and the air smelled of burning leaves, even though, nowadays, sated leaf blowers blasted one's eardrums with boisterous belches. Best of all, September ushered in a new football season. True, the Broncos had won one game and lost one game, but they had fourteen more to go before they clinched the AFC championship. Ellie was nothing if not optimistic. Peter said she was optimistic to a fault, which was his way of saying nosy to a fault, but wasn't that better than being negative to a fault?

Outside, it sounded like Tin Pan Alley. City workers had begun tarring the main boulevard's potholes, and her usually traffic-free street served as a detour route. Car horns honked like bronchial geese. Competing with the horny geese, piano music wafted from a neighbor's open window—Gershwin's "Rhapsody in Blue." Another neighbor was listening to Bette Midler belt out "Boogie Woogie Bugle Boy." Despite the miscellaneous overtures, Ellie heard the fluty whistle of the wind as Aeolus somersaulted over her roof and around her eaves. Crisp, cool draughts blew away any leftover dregs of torridity, abolishing, until next year, the lazy, hazy, dog days of sum—

Dog! Scout!

She hoped Peter had let the dog inside. She hoped Peter had fed the dog. She slanted a glance at the bedside clock. Five-forty-five. Holy cow! She was supposed to feed Scout at five o'clock.

As she clicked the remote, negating MUTE, she saw that the reporter was now interviewing two men. Both wore black-and-white, teensy-checkered pants, white chef jackets, and stiff, white, shirred-paper chef hats. One man looked droopy and mournful, the other bright-eyed and bushy-tailed, as if he planned to make the most of his fame-filled fifteen or so minutes.

Ellie clicked the volume louder.

"Tell us, Vincent," a local reporter said to the mournful man. "How did you *feel* when you heard that one of your waitresses had been strangled to death?"

Vincent and his companion stood under an awning. Both were practically plastered against the double doors of Uncle Vinnie's Gourmet Italian Restaurant. When Vincent tried to step backwards, away from the microphone, he had no place to go. The reporter waved her mike in his face until it was parallel with his upper lip. Shaded by his beaky nose, it looked like a metallic mustache.

The other man snatched the mike away from the reporter. "I'm Al, and I own Uncle Vinnie's Gourmet Italian Restaurant with my brother Vincent," he said, enunciating each word carefully. "My brother, the Vinnie in Uncle Vinnie's Gourmet Italian Restaurant, is our certified gourmet chef and tonight's special is osso bucco—braised veal shanks. Sara Lee, whom we loved dearly and will miss like a family member because we here at Uncle Vinnie's Gourmet Restaurant treat all our servers like family . . ." He paused to catch his breath and ostensibly wipe a tear from his eye. "Our Sara Lee tasted a sample of the osso bucco this afternoon, the last food she ever ate. She said it was heavenly, and it makes all of us here at Uncle Vinnie's Gourmet Italian Restaurant feel really good to know that Sara Lee's tummy was full of yummy gourmet food when she joined God's angelic choir."

Al raised his eyes heavenward. Apparently, Ellie mused, he could see God's angelic choir through the green-and-white-striped entrance awning.

"If you mention you caught my brother and me on the news," Al continued with a wink, "we'll take twenty percent off your dinner tab, liquor not included. We're located on Austin Bluffs at the corner of—"

Furious, face contorted, the reporter grabbed the microphone back before Al could finish his spiel. Almost spitting, she said, "And how did *you* feel when you heard . . ." She paused, shifting gears. "I presume you and your brother were questioned by the police."

"Of course we were. We told them the truth, that everybody liked Sara Lee, that she was one of our finest waitresses, and that she treated our customers—"

"Guests," Vincent said.

"—like family."

"And yet you plan to open tonight?" The reporter raised her eyebrows as high as they could go, which wasn't very high, considering that they had been plucked and penciled in. Her wrinkled forehead looked like a monkey's.

"We *are* open," Al said, ignoring the sarcasm. "We open for lunch at eleven and shut down at three, but we unlock our doors again at five sharp, six days a week. We're closed on Sunday. Sara Lee would want us to stay open tonight, to go on with the show. She was an actress, you know. Why, only this afternoon she was rehearsing for the John Denver Community Theatre's *Hello, Dolly!* tryouts and she sounded more like Streisand than Streisand. The auditions are tomorrow night—there's a detailed flyer at our hostess stand. Uncle Vinnie's Gourmet Italian Restaurant supports the Arts. If you buy tickets to a show and want to eat out first, we'll give you half off your second meal, liquor not inclu—"

"Tell me, Al," the reporter interrupted, her voice even more derisive. "Will you shut down for Sara Lee's funeral?"

"Absolutely. If the funeral's on a Sunday." Al winked again, but apparently decided that this time a wink wasn't appropriate, so he caught his lower lip with his teeth and wiped away another imaginary tear.

Invading the space beneath the awning, a colossal gust of wind seized the two chef hats. Vincent and Al, in unison, grabbed at their heads, then chased their paper hats down the path, away from the restaurant. The reporter could be heard guffawing rudely in the background as her cameraman zeroed in on the Buster Keaton–style pursuit, and Ellie turned off the TV.

Before she did, she noted that Vincent was tall, well over six feet, and that his hands were huge, oversized, almost clown hands—totally out of proportion to the rest of his skinny, small-boned body.

And something about Al troubled her; something other than his blatant—one could almost say flagrant—insincerity. She tried her best to focus, but couldn't quite capture the elusive whiff of an anomaly in his Sara Lee tribute. She would have to weed through his numerous plugs for Uncle Vinnie's Gourmet Italian Restaurant before she could capture the exact phraseology and run it through her mental food processor.

Maybe if she didn't try so hard, it would come to her.

SEVEN

Even though the mischievous wind mussed his mousse-spiked hair, Nicholas Vladimir Nureyev waited until the TV reporter and cameraman moved away from the restaurant's front doors.

Ordinarily he would enter through the kitchen. THE RULES said to enter through the kitchen. But tonight the alley that led to the kitchen was blocked by yellow police tape. He had a queasy repugnance for yellow, a color he equated with weakness, and would have preferred ecru or saffron. Even better, a tint from the red family. Crimson, maybe, or considering the circumstances, bloodred. Yes, bloodred tape made much more sense, although red would be harder to see in the dark.

He lurked in the shadows of the restaurant's front entrance because he didn't want to be on TV. TV was for chumps and Nico Nureyev wasn't born yesterday. He knew his tall, muscular body, his dimpled chin, and his smoldering black eyes were identifiable, especially to women, and the last thing he needed was for some jerk to look at the TV and say, "Hey, Mabel, I think I seen that guy somewhere before. Come take a look-see."

When it appeared safe to cross the threshold undetected, Nico strolled nonchalantly toward the double doors. As he did, he imagined a red carpet unfolding and trumpets heralding his approach. If you acted like royalty, people treated you like royalty, his mother liked to say. He couldn't swear those were her last words before she turned yellow and died, because sometimes he forgot things, but he thought maybe they were.

Upon entering the restaurant, he walked up to the unstained wooden hostess stand and planted a kiss on the hostess's pale, chapped lips. "Hi, Shelley," he said. "You look beautiful tonight."

She flushed beneath her acne. "I'm not Shelley," she said. "I'm Micki . . . M-i-c-k-i."

M-o-u-s-e, he sang silently.

Damn, it was hard keeping the hostesses straight, especially since they all seemed to be named Michelle. This one was young, scrawny, flat as an ironing board beneath a blue sweater that displayed sweaty half-moons at her armpits.

Hadn't she worked the lunch shift? Yes. He gave her his best smile and said, "I'm terrible with names."

"Michelle Lopez," she said, pointing to her chest like Tarzan. "They call me Micki, you know, for short?"

"Any relation to Jennifer Lopez?"

She inhaled a giggle that erupted into a piggy snort. "I hardly think so."

"The reason I asked was because you look like her. I swear you could be her twin sister."

"Aw, Nico, you're lyin'. My hair's different."

True, he thought. Micki Mouse's dark brown hair was long like J-Lo's, but coarse and dull rather than sleek and shiny. Dull as Uncle Vinnie's dishwater.

"That's because Jennifer Lopez can afford to hire a professional hair stylist," he said. "If you don't mind, I'm gonna call you M-Lo."

"I don't mind." She blushed and smiled, revealing teeth that had never met—much less had a nodding acquaintance with—an orthodontist. "You'd better get on the floor, Nico. We're really busy tonight."

He gave her a thumbs-up and bobbed his head, aware that his mousse-spiked hair was behaving nicely again. He thanked his lucky stars that he bought his grooming products from Raymond, two doors down from Uncle Vinnie's Gourmet Italian Restaurant. Even at Raymond's generous salon discount, the shampoo, mousse and hairspray cost a bloody fortune. But in the long run, it was well worth the expense.

"Usually I don't work doubles," he told Micki Mouse.

"Usually you don't work lunch," she said, batting eyelashes that looked like the wispy hairs on a caterpillar.

He shrugged. "I covered Lois Reibach's shift. Tonight was supposed to be my night off. But we're so short-staffed, Al asked me to come in."

"It's like that restaurant in California," she said. "The one OJ's ex-wife ate at before she got herself killed? They were extra busy, too. People are weird."

Surprising him, she rose on her toes, palmed his face, French-kissed him, released his face, took a couple of steps backwards, and blushed for the third time.

The mouse has a tongue, he thought, *and she knows how to use it. In-ter-est-ing.*

He flashed his pearly whites at her then wended his way toward the kitchen. He adjusted his smile to friendly rather than personal as he snaked around tables garnished with red-and-white-checkered tablecloths, glassed-in candles, and small vases filled with seasonal flowers. The salt and pepper shakers were empty wine bottles: Sterling Chardonnay for salt, Monterey Peninsula Black Burgundy for pepper.

Straightening to his full height of six-feet-two-inches, Nico walked through waist-high swinging doors. He entered the kitchen, where he greeted Vincent and Al, both cooking up a storm. Prep cooks were making salads and stuffing dessert plates into a stainless-steel refrigerator. The elderly dishwasher, who couldn't tell the difference between cannoli and cannelloni if his life depended on it, was busy stirring tomato sauce. Nico scowled. He didn't want to tell Vincent and Al how to run their business, but the too-tall, cadaverous dishwasher looked like he should be on a street corner, his arthritic fingers flashing a crudely lettered cardboard sign that read: WILL WORK FOR FOOD. Or maybe he could double for Freddie in one of those Elm Street movies, not that Nico watched those movies. He didn't like horror movies. He didn't like blood-and-guts movies, either. In fact, any kind of violence gave him the shakes. Which was one reason he liked George W. Bush. When Bush was in office, TV reporters and cameramen weren't allowed to show pictures of dead soldiers—not even caskets draped with American flags. It was against the RULES.

As Nico sniffed the enticing aromas of crushed garlic, spicy tomato sauce and warm Italian bread, Vincent and Al barely acknowledged his presence, but later Al would give him a free meal off the menu, a reward for coming in at such short notice. Nico, who had worked at more restaurants than he could count, actually *liked* the food at Uncle Vinnie's Gourmet Italian Restaurant. He heard his stomach growl and realized that Sara Lee's death this afternoon had put a damper on his lunchtime appetite. Now he was ravenous. THE RULES said that servers couldn't eat during a shift, but there was a "scrap plate" in the waiters' station. Filled with guests' leftovers, it was supposedly for the servers who owned pets. Right! Like everyone didn't sneak a bite of succulent Chicken or Veal Parmigiano every now and then. Nico licked his lips as he remembered Micki's succulent tongue. He might forget other things but not tongues.

He grabbed a freshly laundered cranberry-colored apron, tied it around his waist, and stuffed its pockets with two sets of car keys, loose coins, ink pens, an order pad and a corkscrew.

"I am invincible," he sang under his breath, before he remembered that it was a girl's song, sung by Helen somebody or other. He prodded his memory, a trick he'd learned from one of his high school teachers, just before he quit school.

Ready, set, go, ready, set, go—Helen Ready?

His father said he was dumb as two short planks, or maybe it was dumb as two thick planks, but a person didn't have to be a genius if that person knew smart people. He would soon be able to invest in some kind of computer gizmo, invented by a friend of a friend. All he needed was twenty-five thousand dollars. His grandfather had once been offered stock in a new company, but he had to buy a minimum of ten thousand shares at a dollar a share. Gramps had barely weathered the Depression and he didn't have ten grand, so he said no, sorry, can't scrape up the money, maybe next time. The company came out with a camera that developed its own pictures, and Gramps never stopped talking about his lost opportunity. On his deathbed, his last toothless hiss had been, "Ten thousand shares of Polaroid at a dollar a share."

Slithering sideways into the narrow waiters' station, Nico clocked in on the computer and patted Kelly's butt.

Kelly liked to have her butt patted. An older waitress, forty-something, she had cornered him one night in dry storage after their shift, and he had almost killed her by pressing his hand against her face. He was afraid someone would hear her happy moans, which she later insisted were screams. *Liar, liar, pants on fire!* But with his hand over her mouth she couldn't breathe and she fainted and he had never been so scared in his whole life.

She hadn't said one word, thank God, probably afraid she'd get fired too. One of Vincent's strictest RULES was: DON'T MESS AROUND WITH THE STAFF.

Which, to Nico, meant: DON'T GET CAUGHT.

The only other RULE he broke was a stupid RULE. The menu said there would be a twenty-percent gratuity added to tables of eight or more. Vincent insisted servers tell the person paying the bill that the tip had been added. Nico never did that and, more often than not, he'd get double-tipped. Which, in his opinion, was the fault of the guests. Most never looked at their bills. The majority flipped him a credit card. At the end of his shift, he'd pay out the total amount of the food and beverages ordered, tip out the bartender and busboy, and then pocket the rest. So he would add his gratuity to the top line on the credit card slip, leaving the tip space open. Sometimes people said, "Has the tip already been added?" A square shooter, he'd say, "Yes, sir (yes, ma'am), but you can add more if you like." Frequently, they liked.

When he first started working at Uncle Vinnie's Gourmet Italian Restaurant, everybody thought he was gay. He wasn't, and it didn't take his fellow workers long to realize that. The bottom line was he slept with a person, male or female, if that person caught his fancy. Or if there was something in it for him. Lois Reibach was a prime example. He'd taken her out twice. The second time he wined and dined her, especially wined her. She had been under the influence and ripe for the picking and, in her words, Nico "had his way with her." So he had summoned his naughty-boy smile and told her he couldn't help himself; he was so turned on by her bodacious body. Lois made out the weekly schedule. If she liked you, you were in like Flynn, whoever the hell Flynn was, and you'd get the "money shifts." If she didn't—damn, he'd better get his butt on the floor. His station was filling up fast. Wait a sec! Micki Mouse had seated rug-rats at one of his tables. He would have to suck up to her again, teach her NICO'S RULES.

No small children.

No senior citizens.

No foreigners.

No deaf people who spoke with their fingers.

No prom kids—unless, of course, they numbered eight or more.

No black, brown or *yellow* people.

Strolling over to the hostess stand, he draped his arm around Micki Mouse's shoulders and said, "What are you doing after work, pretty M-Lo?"

"Nothing," she said, her irregular teeth pulverizing a wad of green chewing gum. "Why?"

"Why do you think, silly girl? I'd like to take you out. For a drink."

"Me?"

Now she looked like a cow chewing its cud. "No," he said. "Jennifer Lopez. Of course, you."

"I'm not a very good drinker, Nico. I drank champagne once, at my cousin's wedding? But I got sick as a dog and threw up all over the bride and groom and—"

"You threw up on the bride and groom?"

"Yes. No. Yes. The bride and groom on top of the *wedding cake*. I puked champagne. And pigs in a blanket. And Swedish meatballs. Even celery dipped in bleu cheese dressing. And, oh God, carrots. My cousin was so mad, she swore she'd never speak to me again."

"How about we go to my place? No champagne. No wedding cake. Just vodka. You can't get sick on vodka, pretty M-Lo."

"You can't?" Her tongue darted out to lick the spittle at the corner of her lips, and he thought he'd burst. "But you can get *drunk* on vodka, Nico. Yes?"

He couldn't tell if she was serious, putting him on, or just plain stupid. God, she was practically melting at his feet. If she had breasts, they would be straining against her sweat-stained sweater. She wanted to get drunk. She wanted him. He had never come across any woman who wanted him as much as this skinny mouse wanted him, not even Sara Lee.

Micki Mouse was tall for a girl, maybe three or four inches shorter than Nico, and yet she couldn't weigh more than one-fifteen, maybe one-twenty, dripping wet. Three double shots of vodka and she'd pass out cold.

Should she need more, he had more stashed inside the freezer compartment of his fridge.

"If you get drunk," he promised, sincerity oozing from every pore, "I'll take good care of you."

Recalling a line from *The Godfather,* he laughed and pointed toward the kitchen. " 'Leave the gun, take the cannoli,' " he said.

She said, "Huh?"

EIGHT

In her haste, her hands were all thumbs, her fingers slick as butter, but somehow Ellie managed to put on her panties one leg at a time. Then she shrugged her shoulders into a white terry-cloth robe. A voice inside her head kept repeating a Shakespeare quote that she often printed on her diet club's inspirational bulletin board: "They are sick that surfeit with too much, as they that starve with nothing."

Poor Scout must be starving.

As Ellie raced down the staircase, she tied the belt on her robe. Then she entered the family room.

Scout slept on the scrunched-up quilt and—

Jackie Robinson slept in his usual wreath position, curled up against Scout's furry tummy.

Grinning from ear to ear, Ellie tiptoed into the kitchen. Almost immediately, she saw signs of Peter's recent occupancy. Unless a hungry, benevolent burglar had turned off the stove, left an open package of thin-sliced Weight Winners bread and a wooden spoon on the counter, freckled the stovetop with *honey* lasagna sauce, and burgled . . . what?

Aside from her collection of jazz recordings, her new flat-screen TV, her computer, and her first-edition crime fiction novels, the only items of value she owned were paintings by Wiley Jamestone and Garrett Halliday.

She gazed longingly at the coffee pot. It was too late in the evening for caffeine. With a sigh, she filled the teakettle and set it atop the stove.

Peter's note rested against a mug that read: DIETS ARE FOR THOSE WHO ARE THICK AND TIRED OF IT. Inside the mug was an herbal teabag—peppermint. Her handsome lieutenant's thoughtfulness far outweighed his messiness, Ellie mused, as she read the note:

My darling dog-napper and dog-sitter,
I was going to feed your furry guest, but your friend Rachel forgot to include dog food. Dog toys, yes. Dog food, no. Answer: A supermarket. Question: Where does one buy kibble? I'm not sure when I'll be back. Please don't wait up. I might pay my apartment a visit and catch a few Z's. Will you marry me? Love you.

Translation: *You will* NOT *get involved in this waitress murder. And I love you, too,* she thought with a sigh.

A tad chauvinistic, and more than a tad anachronistic, Peter insisted on maintaining his own apartment until she agreed to marry him. But she liked things just the way they were, thank you very much. On her own for the first time in her life, she valued her independence, what her generation had called "more space." Peter's latest marriage bribe had been free health insurance. "If you keep sticking your lovely nose in my cases," he had said, sounding like the narrator of a Nostradamus documentary, "you'll need all the health insurance you can get."

Right now she had to stick her nose in her purse and find Rachel Lester's neatly printed instructions list. She didn't bother checking the box Rachel had filled with toys, food and water bowls, a leash, and Scout's patchwork quilt. If there had been any food, Peter would have found it. After all, he was almost as good a sleuth as Eleanor Bernstein, mature girl detective.

Rachel's list wasn't long or complicated. It included feeding instructions, her cell phone number and her vet's phone number. She used Dr. Ben Cassidy, Jackie Robinson's vet, so Ellie knew that number by heart. However, one of Rachel's directives stood out like a surgically enhanced face.

"There should be more than enough dog food," she had written. "But if you run out, Reigning Cats & Dogs has Scout's special formula on file." She then neatly printed the pet shop's address, located in a small strip mall.

Reigning Cats & Dogs is right next door to Uncle Vinnie's Gourmet Italian Restaurant.

With that thought, Ellie slid Rachel's list underneath a fridge magnet that stated: THE PERILS OF EATING DUCK ARE GREAT, ESPECIALLY FOR THE DUCK.

As she began shoveling her lasagna sauce into a couple of Mason jars, she mapped her agenda for tomorrow. Among other things, she wanted to talk to Theodora Mallard, the waitress who had found Sara Lee. Then she planned to follow Sara Lee's up-to-the-minute agenda—the itinerary, so to speak, that had led to her demise. But right now, this very minute, Ellie's main concern was Scout.

The dog had trailed Jackie Robinson into the kitchen, and Ellie could almost swear Scout looked up at the clock. Could dogs read clocks? Or did they have an internal clock? *Hey, lady* . . . tick . . . *it is way past* . . . tick . . . *my feeding time* . . . tick.

With a lithe leap, Jackie Robinson claimed his usual chair. Scout sat, her rump inches away from the legs of the chair, her tail sweeping the floor. Mouth open, panting, she seemed to say: *Cat would make a great dinner, especially skinned and deep-fried. Or sautéed. Or stir-fried, in what dogs call a walk and people call a wok. If you're squeamish about cooking Cat, a pesky rodent inhabits your backyard. I believe you humans call it Squirrel.*

Ellie looked out the window. Obese raindrops had joined the swirling wind. Her windshield wipers were on their last legs and she did not relish a drive to the supermarket. If Peter had been here, he would have copped a "me man, me battle storm and club fierce kibble" attitude, but she had a feeling Peter planned to avoid her like the plague until he caught Sara Lee's killer.

Ellie debated calling Rachel, but what could Rachel tell her? *Where the damnfool dog food is, that's what!*

"Holy cow, Jackie Robinson, can you say overreacting? A simple phone call to Rachel's husband will solve this particular mystery."

Her most recent Weight Winners members' directory, next to her kitchen phone, included fax numbers and phone numbers.

Pressing the phone's receiver against her ear, she listened to an answering machine. "If you want to speak to Matthew Lester, Rachel Lester, or Scout Finch Lester," Rachel's electronic voice sang out, "please leave a message at the sound of the beep."

Ellie tried to keep her frustration at bay as she left her name, number and a brief message. Then she tried Rachel's cell phone number. No answer.

"We'll have to improvise," she told Scout, whose expression more than hinted that Ellie's tibia might make a tasty bone.

Cat and Squirrel were out of the question, but unless Scout had been brought up kosher, Pig wasn't.

Retrieving Peter's emergency sausages from the fridge, Ellie headed for the microwave.

NINE

Rachel Lester couldn't believe it. Her cell phone was utterly, thoroughly, categorically DEAD!

God's will?

The proximity of the mountain range?

Karma?

I shouldn't have lied. I figured I might go to hell for my Margee whopper, but I didn't figure my cell phone would croak.

The cabin's phone didn't work, either. She had automatically picked up the receiver upon her arrival and there had been a dial tone, but that was before the windstorm, and now it was raining, and she felt miserable.

And, darn it, hungry!

A little voice inside her head whispered *dammit, not darn it,* but she couldn't say the word "dammit" out loud. The nuns had done their jobs well, reinforced by Rachel's zealously devout mom.

To tell the God's honest truth, when Rachel read Stephen King's *Carrie,* she had pictured her mom as Carrie's overly devout mom. Rachel would have bet the farm that in a former life her mother had been a worthy component of the Spanish Inquisition.

Thanks to the Sacred Heart High School sisters and her mom, Rachel did not swear. Instead, when she wanted to cuss, she substituted the names of the seven dwarfs.

"Sleepy, Sneezy, Grumpy," she chanted, marching around

the living room. "I should have stayed home. What made me think an isolated mountain cabin would clear my mind? That's like saying you can win the national spelling bee if you watch *Wheel of Fortune* every day."

Tripping over a small braided rug, admonishing herself to be more careful, Rachel looked down and saw that a folded piece of lined notebook paper had fallen from her purse. Or her pocket. Or maybe, she thought, looking up at the beamed ceiling, from God.

A shopping list?

Yes, ma'am, yes, sir, yes, we have no bananas. That's what it was all right—a G.D. shopping list.

Directly under bananas, topping the list, two words seemed to leap off the paper and hit Rachel square in the eyeballs: SCOUT'S FOOD.

"Doc, Dopey, Bashful and . . . oh, darn, I can never remember the seventh dwarf. Sleepy, Sneezy, Grumpy, Doc, Dopey, Bashful and . . . Vanna White!"

Tears stung Rachel's eyes. She had never used Vanna White, her role model, in a litany of cusses before. It just showed how upset she was, and for no good reason. Logic said that Ellie, planning to feed Scout at five o'clock, would see that the food was missing and drive to Reigning Cats & Dogs, which closed at six. No big deal.

Except it *was* a big deal.

Rachel had undoubtedly interrupted Ellie's evening routine, which was bad enough. Add to that the undisputable fact that she, Rachel Lester, prided herself on her organizational skills. She might not have much else going for her, but she was undeniably meticulous. If truth be told, methodical was her middle name. How could she have forgotten to buy Scout's food?

She hadn't bought the bananas that topped her list, either.

As a matter of fact, she hadn't bought anything on a grocery list that was as long as a "health care for every citizen" speech at a political debate.

Milk. Eggs. Dog biscuits. Cereal—

"Dopey, Sleepy, Grumpy," Rachel swore. Matthew would be livid.

Well, that settled it! She would leave the cabin tonight. Except, it wasn't tonight anymore. According to her watch, it was 12:45 a.m.

Well then, she'd leave tomorrow . . . today . . . shortly after sunrise. She'd tell Matthew her sister was much, much better and—*oh, gosh, how lucky can you get?*—she had been able to book a Red Eye flight.

Yet another fib! No, another lie!

With enough practice, she'd start getting really good at this. Eventually, her nose would grow longer than Pinocchio's and she could audition for the part of a female Cyrano.

Fib or lie notwithstanding, she'd pack the suitcase she had unpacked, dump the burned sauerkraut, heat up the shriveled hot dogs, wash the pots, try to sleep a few hours, and—

Was that the *wind* making such a commotion outside the cabin?

Or was it . . . oh, dear God . . . could it possibly be . . . a bear?

No way! A bear's paw couldn't grasp the doorknob and turn it slowly and—

I didn't lock the door!

First the neglected grocery list, now the unlatched door.

Rachel Methodical Lester was definitely losing what little remained of her mind.

Mesmerized, her heart pounding in her ears, she watched the door open.

A man walked inside, tracking mud. His jeans and sheepskin jacket dripped water. So did his black cowboy hat and the long, thick, sun-kissed hair that fell below his shoulder blades, tamed by three strategically placed rubber bands. His well-trimmed mustache and salt-and-pepper beard glistened with unshed raindrops, and in his hands he held a shotgun. Spying Rachel, he said, "You alone?"

When by some miracle she managed to bob her head up and down, he aimed his gun at the floor, away from his Paul Bunyan feet, and said, "Who the hell are you?"

She just stood there, as if she were Lot's wife.

At the same time, her muddled mind conjured up a theoretical question. Did Lot's wife look back out of curiosity, to see what had happened, or did she harbor an irrefutable longing for her friends and the city she had just left? In short, did she want to return to the old rather than proceed to the new?

Just like Lot's wife, Rachel had left her house behind. And Ellie and Cee-Cee and her so-called book club friends. And her beloved dog.

Up until the windstorm and her burnt sauerkraut and her neglected grocery list, she had honestly meant to make a decision; to resolve whether she wanted to return to the old rather than proceed to the new.

Complicating her decision was the fact that she felt sorry for Lot's wife, and always had, because Rachel knew, without a single doubt, that she would have looked back, too.

The man said, "Cat got your tongue?"

As she burst into tears, Rachel remembered the name of the seventh dwarf: Happy.

TEN

Thursday

Even though she had remained prone for a good eight hours, Ellie awoke exhausted. Her restless slumber had been infested with dreams; images that, this morning, were as substantial as cotton candy.

She had envisioned Sara Lee and Louis Armstrong singing "Hello, Dolly!"—that much was clear in her mind. Sara Lee had been welcomed by Armstrong's angelic choir of jazz musicians and waiters: *So take her wrap, angels . . . find her an empty lap, angels . . . Sara will never go away again.*

Catching last night's late edition of the local news had, in all probability, contributed to Ellie's twitchy sleep and bizarre dreams. The reporter had edited the effusive Al's promotional pitch and substituted an enlarged photo of Sara Lee, contributed by her inconsolable mother.

"Yes, but how did you *feel*, Mrs. Leibowitz, when you heard your daughter had been strangled to death?" the reporter kept asking the distraught woman, and Ellie had wanted to strangle the monkey-faced newscaster.

The family photo had depicted a teenage Sara. She wore a Tigger T-shirt, baggy cargo pants, and a pair of unlaced combat boots. She appeared tough, but in a good way, as if she faced the world with invisible boxing gloves. Her eyes and mouth looked familiar.

Barbra Streisand, Ellie had thought. A young Barbra Streisand, although, to be perfectly honest, Streisand had never looked old, and still didn't.

Speaking of the news, it was time to turn on the TV and catch the early bird news, or as Peter liked to say, "The Worm's update and summary."

First, a quick shower.

Wet auburn strands lashed her shoulders as Ellie toweled herself off. She didn't want to waste time blow-drying her hair, but that didn't stop her mother's voice—the voice that lived inside her head—screeching, "Never leave the house with wet hair, Ellie, or you'll get sick and die."

Craving caffeine, she put on a pair of black jeans and one of her son Mick's touring T-shirts. Since all T-shirts nowadays seemed to advertise something, she'd rather promote Mick's newest rock group, WoolEye, than Old Navy or the Gap. Wool-Eye had scored a modest hit with a song called "Walk on Water," but their second song, "Jade and Jasmine," was rapidly climbing the charts.

With an apology to Scout—and the promise of a long, pre-dinner walk—Ellie let the dog out into the backyard. Jackie Robinson followed. Maybe, together, they could make Squirrel's life hell.

The aroma of fresh-brewed caffeine tantalized Ellie's taste buds as, coffee mug in hand, she turned on the kitchen TV and surfed until she found the early bird newscast.

A more recent Sara Lee photograph filled the screen—a *The Pajama Game* cast photo. Sara Lee's face had been circled by a white grease pencil and, once again, Ellie noted the resemblance to Barbra Streisand.

Holy cow! Before he had lost his chef's hat, hadn't Al said something about Sara Lee sounding more like Streisand than Streisand? And that she'd be auditioning for *Hello, Dolly!*, the John Denver Community Theatre's next musical production?

Ellie snapped her fingers. *The Louis Armstrong dream! That's where it came from!*

But why had her subconscious focused on that particular piece of Al-information? A portent? An ethereal handwriting on the wall?

Should she call Peter? And tell him what? "Honey, yesterday I saw an announcement for the John Denver Community Theatre's *Hello, Dolly!* auditions. Last night I dreamt about Louis Armstrong, and this morning I remembered that Sara Lee was planning to audition. So maybe she was killed by an insecure actress who wanted to snag the lead role of Dolly."

And maybe Eleanor Bernstein, mature girl detective, should add more clues to her arsenal before shooting off her mouth to Lieutenant Peter Miller.

With a sigh, she retrieved Rachel's instruction list from underneath the fridge magnet.

She tapped out Rachel's cell phone number. No answer.

She tried Rachel's home number and got the damnfool answering machine again.

Okay. First stop, Rachel's house.

If I can't get in, or can't find the food, I'll drive to Reigning Cats & Dogs. And if the timing's right, I'll eat a nice, leisurely lunch at Uncle Vinnie's Gourmet Italian Restaurant.

She wanted to talk to the waiter, Nicholas. And Vincent. And Al, whose disingenuous Sara Lee tribute still nagged at the back of her mind.

And, above all, Theodora Mallard, the waitress who had discovered Sara Lee's trashed body.

There was no listing for Theodora Mallard in the telephone directory, not even initials, but surely Vincent and Al kept an up-to-date list of phone numbers so that, when the schedule came out, servers could call each other and trade shifts.

Where would they keep it? In an office, if they had an office. Or—

Wait a sec! She had been inside Uncle Vinnie's kitchen. Once. She and Al's wife and a wonderful woman named Cee-Cee Sinclair had organized a fundraiser for Canine Companions, an organization that trained dogs to help the handicapped.

Wasn't there an employee bulletin board near an employee bathroom?

Yes. Ellie pictured a hand-printed warning, tacked to the cork: GIVEING OUT ENPLOYEES PHONE NUMBERS IS A FIREING OFENCE!!!!!

She remembered the sign so well because of the typos.

So all she had to do was find an excuse to visit the kitchen. She would glance at the bulletin board, memorize Theodora Mallard's phone number, then call and arrange an interview.

Easy as pie, right?

The interview would be easy, too, assuming Theodora's head injury hadn't blighted her memory.

If memory served, Tab's high school girlfriend had always been a wee bit wonky—even without a killer concussion.

ELEVEN

Matthew and Rachel Lester lived on the west side, not far from Manitou Springs, where the homes were old, well landscaped, and well tended—at least from the outside.

Yesterday, Rachel and Scout had met Ellie at the curb, so she had never been inside the Lesters' two-story brick home. Which, today, looked deserted.

Of course it did. Rachel was in Houston and her husband probably worked a nine-to-five job.

Because a house looks *deserted, that doesn't mean it* is *deserted.*

And there's a car in the carport.

Ellie knocked, waited, rang the bell, waited, rang the bell again. About to turn away and return to her curbside Honda, her gaze touched upon the upstairs windows.

Open!

Which, ordinarily, wouldn't have bothered her. "If you don't like the weather, wait a few minutes" fit Colorado like a beloved pair of 1980's stretch pants. Last night's wind and rain had given way to a crisp, autumn, sunshiny day, and yet, even from a distance, she could see that the window curtains were soaking wet. A person might forget to close one window during a windy rainstorm, but not three. Maybe Matthew had not come home last night and Rachel, in a hurry to catch her plane, had left the windows o—

No! Not a chance. Rachel was too grounded, too organized. At diet club meetings she took copious notes and she read every single word on a food label.

Nevertheless, she *had* seemed a tad edgy yesterday afternoon, which Ellie had attributed to pre-flight jitters and her sister Margee's sudden illness.

Rachel had also mentioned calling a cab, which, in all probability, meant her husband had not been home, and when Ellie offered to drive her to the airport, she said no thanks, if the cab didn't show she'd leave her car in short-term parking.

Had the cab arrived on time? Was the car in the carport Rachel's car?

Matthew could have come home and opened the windows, then left again before the storm hit, but something didn't *feel* right.

Woman's intuition? Or too many TV cop shows?

In her head, Ellie heard the soundtrack from *Jaws.*

A latched but unlocked gate led to a fenced backyard. As she walked into the yard, Ellie felt as though she had opened Dorothy's *Wizard of Oz* door, stepped outside, and gone from black and white to Technicolor.

Was there a dead witch under the Lesters' foundation?

How about a dead body *inside* the house?

A pinwheel of color assaulted Ellie's senses. Verdant grass, uncut. Red, gold and orange leaves, unraked. Naked chunks of firewood, stacked neatly, half shielded by a soaking wet, lime-green plastic tarp.

One could easily tell a dog inhabited the tiny yard. It was, in fact, an implicit shrine to SCOUT FINCH LESTER, the name boldly printed across the front of an Emerald City–green doghouse.

There were countless doggie toys and chew bones, an ultramarine water bowl, a bottle-green garden hose, its nozzle resting inside the water bowl, and a flower-decaled kiddy—or in this case, doggie—wading pool, drained of everything but rainwater, a relic from last summer's heat wave.

All the yard needed was a canine version of a swing set. And perhaps a fake fire hydrant.

As she walked toward the back door, Ellie saw that it was ajar. In this neighborhood, one might leave a door unlocked but not ajar. Unless one slammed it shut, then didn't wait around to see if the bolt caught.

Weak bolt notwithstanding, a concerned citizen should investigate.

The *Jaws* music inside her head kicked up a notch.

She walked through a "mud room," neatly organized with coats, shoes, sandals and boots. As she entered a large, bright kitchen, the first thing she smelled was dog. That explained the open windows. Rachel, who spent most of her time at home, probably didn't notice the odor, but her husband might have used her absence to air out the house. And he hadn't shut the windows when the storm hit because . . . ?

Because he left suddenly.

Or had been compelled to leave suddenly.

Okay, her vivid imagination was working overtime, but something still did not feel right.

She spotted a carton of two-percent milk, a Denver Broncos Super Bowl XXXIII coffee mug, empty, and a clean spoon on the kitchen counter. The granite countertop also boasted an open bottle of José Cuervo tequila, an empty shot glass, a box of take-out chicken that smelled somewhat rancid, a spilled can of coffee, and a broken sugar bowl, knocked to the floor by . . . whom?

Matthew? His assailant?

Although she couldn't swear there'd been a scuffle and she didn't see any sign of blood, the open back door and upstairs windows told her that Rachel's husband had been caught by surprise.

Conjecture, a little voice inside her head whispered.

"Right," she said. "There's not enough proof for a probable-cause invasion by one of the CSI or L&O teams, and not even a TV judge would sign off on a search warrant. Of course, one doesn't need a search warrant if one wants to search for dog food, does one?"

There was no dog food in the laundry room, the half bath, the dining room and the family room. No sign of a scuffle, either. Ellie entered a study, neat as the proverbial pin.

Correction: neat as the proverbial pin except for a messy stack of papers spread out across the surface of an open rolltop desk. Unpaid bills? Yes. Next to the scattered invoices and credit card receipts were envelopes and stamps. Peter had taught Ellie how to bank on-line, but it was in character for Rachel to pay her monthly bills the old-fashioned way.

Unless her husband paid the bills.

No. This was definitely Rachel's room. The French provincial writing desk with its decorative sliding cover wouldn't be a "real man's" option, and Rachel had described her husband as "someone who would rather starve to death than eat quiche; someone who listens to a broadcaster quote football stats and thinks it more spiritual, by far, than listening to a church sermon." Rachel had not added "someone who calls his wife the little woman," but Ellie heard it just the same.

She walked toward a wall of floor-to-ceiling bookshelves. The shelves held hundreds of romance paperbacks, alphabetized by author. One shelf sported hardcover mysteries. Those books looked as if they had never been read. Ellie all but salivated at the titles and authors. If Rachel was into crime fiction and hadn't yet read those novels, she had hours, days, weeks of delicious, nonfattening pleasure ahead of her.

Not that Rachel wasn't feasting now, Ellie mused, as her gaze took in a Mary Jo Putney historical romance, bookmarked, that sat on a small, round, doily-infested table. Nudging Putney was a Mary Ellen Dennis historical romance, its bookmark protruding like a stuck-out tongue. Prodding Mary Ellen Dennis was a Marty Blue romantic suspense, also bookmarked.

Ellie adored Marty Blue, whom she had met last spring at a dude ranch. The award-winning author was raunchy but not obscene; rough around the edges but on the level. A straight shoot—

Holy cow! Three bookmarks? Ellie felt her lips crease in a grin. Rachel, the most focused person she knew, read more than one book at a time. A chink in her systematic armor?

Under an ornately framed van Gogh reproduction was a hinged wooden shelf. Ellie imagined she heard Don McLean's "Vincent" as she scrutinized the two silver-framed photographs that dominated the shelf. The first photo showed Scout, wearing a Santa hat, standing in front of a beautifully decorated Christmas tree. The second depicted Rachel and a man, standing in front of the same tree. Rachel looked as if she had pasted a smile on her face. The man, doubtless Matthew, was attractive, assuming one lusted after Richard Gere. Matthew was the same height as his wife, albeit thinner, so a hefty assailant—or Rachel, for that matter—could easily overpower him.

Ellie left the study and hesitated at the stairwell. Then she took a deep breath and began to climb.

She half expected to find a dead body upstairs, but the rooms appeared vacant. No Scout food materialized inside the master bedroom, a full master bath, a second bedroom, or a storage room filled with unopened cartons and what could only be described as garage sale schlock.

Nor was there doggie food inside the closets, which she first scanned with trepidation, then searched thoroughly. Matthew's clothes, rather than Rachel's, smelled of perfume.

Was that another clue? Did Matthew sleep around? Had he been assailed by a jealous husband or lover?

As she approached a fifth room at the end of the hallway, Ellie thought she heard the low hum of conversation behind a tightly closed door. Was Matthew talking on the phone?

"Matthew?" She cleared her throat. "Matthew," she said, upping her voice a couple of octaves, "it's Ellie Bernstein . . . Rachel's friend."

No response.

"Your back door was wide open," she continued, practically shouting.

"Ajar," she amended, grasping the room's doorknob.

"Ordinarily I wouldn't walk upstairs uninvited, but Scout is out of dog food," she said, and instantly realized how pathetic she sounded. Who kept dog food upstairs? "I'm dog-sitting Scout . . . your dog, Scout? And your wife . . . your wife, Rachel . . . didn't pack any food. Any dog food, that is. Just a patchwork quilt and doggie toys. Hello? Matthew? Mr. Lester, are you in there?"

TWELVE

The room—an exercise/sewing room—smelled of sour sweat. If Rachel sewed in here, she would have to stop breathing. Or breathe through her mouth.

A tabletop TV faced a treadmill. A sports channel televised an interview with the Denver Broncos coach, his face both tanned and ruddy as he spouted cliché after cliché. The host of the show wore a tie and a smirk. Ellie often watched the same show while she dusted and vacuumed. Soon the host would interview the smiley Chicago Bears coach, then all the other NFL coaches, and the interviews would replay ad nauseam until next week.

Tempted to turn the TV off, Ellie decided she'd better not touch anything. Except the doorknob. She had already touched the doorknob. And the closet doorknobs. Damn!

Returning to the kitchen, she spied a portable phone. On the counter, next to the phone, were what looked like a thousand business cards, most still shrink-wrapped. Attached to one stack of cards was a yellow copy shop receipt.

Matthew Dillon Lester worked for a real estate firm.

Ellie pocketed a card, found a napkin, carefully picked up the phone's receiver, looked down at another business card, and finger-tapped the firm's number.

The receptionist's voice was colder than a frozen pizza as she stated that Mr. Lester was not at his desk, sorry. He had left yesterday, just before lunch, and never returned. He hadn't even called in for his messages, so it wouldn't do any good to leave a message.

"Perhaps you could check his appointment book," Ellie suggested, "and tell me where he's *supposed* to be."

"No, ma'am, I can't do that, not without a subpoena."

Another *Law & Order* addict, Ellie thought. She identified herself and was in the middle of explaining her Scout dog-food dilemma when the receptionist said, "Ellie Bernstein? Weight Winners?"

"Yes."

"Ohmigosh! My name is Pat Timpanaro." The voice thawed. "This is such a co-inky-dink. I've been planning to join your diet club since last January. It was my New Year's resolution."

Ellie silently counted months on her fingers; in three more months, the receptionist could re-resolute. "Tell you what, Ms. Timpanaro. If you come to Friday night's meeting, I'll waive the registration fee."

After a thoughtful silence, Pat Timpanaro said, "What, exactly, do you need to know?"

"You said Mr. Lester left the office yesterday, around lunchtime. Was he meeting anyone?"

"Wait a sec." Long pause. "Here's his appointment book. That's funny. It was right on top of his desk. Yes, he was meeting somebody. An associate."

"And that associate is . . . ?"

"It doesn't really say who it is, just a fax number and the initials C.J."

Ellie tried to stifle her impatience. "Do you happen to know an associate with the initials C.J.?"

"I suppose he could have meant Charlene Johnson. She's with another realty, and she's the one who suggested, practically insisted, I join Weight Winners."

"Does it say where Mr. Lester and C.J. . . . Charlene Johnson planned to meet?"

"Sort of."

Ellie swallowed a frustrated sigh. "Please define 'sort of.' "

"The appointment book says UVIR." Silence. Then, "I'll bet that stands for the University of Virginia."

No, thought Ellie. *It stands for Uncle Vinnie's Italian Restaurant.*

"Maybe that's why he's not here today," Pat the Receptionist continued. "Mr. Lester goes out of town for seminars, and quite a few are held on college campuses."

"Are there any appointments for today? In Mr. Lester's appointment book, I mean."

"Today? If he's out of town, how could . . . well, h-e-double-hockey-sticks, there are some. The first one says 'S.L. at 8:00 a.m.' Then there's a multiple-listing inspection at 12:30 p.m. and J.D.C.T. at 7:00 p.m. I guess he didn't fly to Virginia after all. I wish Matt . . ." She paused and Ellie could all but hear her blush. "I wish Mr. Lester would spell everything out instead of using initials. It makes it so hard to track him down. I have his private cell phone number, but—"

"Would you give it to me, please?"

"His private number? Oh, I couldn't. That number's for emergencies only."

"If you sign up Friday night, I'll give you a Weight Winners food scale. And a package of Weight Winners breakfast bars."

"Well, I really shouldn't . . ."

After saying goodbye, Ellie tapped out Matthew Dillon Lester's private, emergency-only cell phone number.

A voice-mail voice told her to leave a message.

The voice inside Ellie's head said: *He was supposed to meet S.L. at eight a.m.*

Sara Lee?

No, he's a soap opera fan and he made an appointment to meet Susan Lucci. Of course, Sara Lee.

The initials J.D.C.T. sounded familiar. Jewish something-or-other?

JDCT . . . JDCT . . .

Damn! My mind is blank. Maybe if I don't obsess, it'll come to me.

Should she call Peter?

Wasn't there an apt line in Don McLean's "Vincent"—the song her son Mick called "Starry, Starry Night"? She hummed her way through the chorus until she remembered the words.

" 'Perhaps they'll listen now,' " she murmured, placing the call. Then she amended the line to, "Perhaps he'll listen."

Peter picked up on the first ring, as if he'd already fished his cell phone from the depths of his pocket.

"Honey," she said, "I really hate to bother you, but—"

"Where the hell have you been?"

She blinked. "I've been scouting for Scout's dog food. I drove to Rachel Lester's house and—"

"Where's your cell phone?"

"I didn't take it with me."

"The phone's in your purse. Don't women take their purses everywhere they go?"

Ignoring his chauvinistic remark—for now—she said, "Didn't your Nana ever tell you that women change their purses to match their shoes?"

"What shoes? You wear sneakers."

"Not always." She looked down at her sneakers.

"I've been trying to call you for hours," Peter said.

"Blatantly untrue. I have not been gone for hours. Maybe you called when I was in the shower. Then you waited and called again after I left."

"Where are you now?"

"I told you. Rachel Lester's house."

"You're *inside* the house?"

"No, Peter. I'm standing inside a phone booth. With Superman. It's a tight fit, but it would have been much tighter if I hadn't joined Weight Winners and lost fifty-five and a half pounds."

"This is no time for sarcasm."

"Really! What's a good time? And before you respond, Lieutenant, chill out!"

Silence. Then a deep breath. Then, "You're right. I'm sorry, Norrie. I haven't had more than three hours' sleep."

"Why were you trying to call me?" she said, forgiving him—for now.

"I need your friend Rachel's contact number."

"Why?" Ellie could practically hear him running his hands through his hair. "Okay, what happened to Matthew Lester?"

"What makes you think something happened?"

She told Peter about the soaking wet window curtains, the repetitive TV broadcast, and the messy kitchen. "I wasn't breaking and entering, honey. The door was open. Not just unlocked. Ajar." She paused, caught herself chewing her bottom lip, stopped chewing and said, "It's a homicide, right?"

"Yes. We found Lester's body in the trunk of a car. But we're not releasing any information, Norrie, not until we notify his next of kin."

She gave him Rachel's cell phone number. "I've called it so many times I've got the damn thing memorized. But there's no answer, Peter, and no voice mail. I have a feeling her phone's not working."

"Do you know where she's staying?"

"With her sister Margee, in Houston, but that doesn't help. I don't have a last name and Margee is probably a nickname for Margaret."

"Aw, Norrie, don't cry."

"I'm not crying, I'm sniffling, and that's only because I'm

so . . . frustrated. Poor Rachel. Does Matthew's murder have anything to do with Sara Lee's murder?"

"We don't know."

"C'mon, Lieutenant, what aren't you telling me?"

"I'm telling you we don't know. Matthew Lester was last seen at Uncle Vinnie's Gourmet Italian Restaurant. He ran up a sizable tab, mostly drinks, and according to the credit card receipt, he left a huge gratuity. But Sara Lee didn't serve him. Nicholas did. So her, um, service didn't generate the generous tip. Lester ate lunch with an as-yet-unknown woman and—"

"I'll save you some steps, Peter. The woman he ate lunch with is almost certainly a real estate agent named Charlene Johnson, who also happens to be a member of my diet club."

"How do you know that?"

"I called Matthew Lester's real estate office—his business cards are on the kitchen counter. I bribed the receptionist with a free sign-up membership to Weight Winners and she checked his appointment book and said he ate lunch with a colleague whose initials are C.J. Unless C.J. stands for Catherine Zeta Jones without the Zeta, my guess is real estate agent Charlene Johnson. And while Matthew Lester—who according to his business cards calls himself Matthew *Dillon* Lester—might have been last seen at Uncle Vinnie's Gourmet Italian Restaurant, it looks like he came home sometime afterwards." Ellie's gaze touched upon the box of fried chicken, the open tequila bottle, and the broken sugar bowl. "So if he was killed because he witnessed Sara Lee's murder, he had more than enough time to call the cops before his murder. If he was the murderer, his death could have been some form of retribution. I'm thinking motive here, Peter. Like, revenge. Where was Sara Lee's husband during Matthew Lester's murder? And, for that matter, Sara Lee's murder?"

"Slow down, sweetheart. The husband, who works for a car

dealership, has an ironclad alibi—actually, two ironclad alibis. During Sara Lee's murder, Trenton Zachariah was with a potential customer. A dozen salespeople and mechanics can vouch for him. He took the prospective client for a test drive, either during or after the murder occurred. The client's name was 'Bob' and no one remembers what he looked like—short, tall, fat, thin—just that he had a really big mole on his face. Last night Zachariah locked up his house and mourned at a local sports bar. He got rip-roaring drunk, fed the jukebox some quarters, played Elvis. Then he played Right Said Fred's 'I'm Too Sexy' ad nauseam and stripped down to his underpants. He solicited the cocktail waitress, who thought he was disgusting. A pal took him home and swears Zachariah spent the rest of the night on his knees."

"Praying?" Ellie asked dryly.

"No. Barfing into the crapper. Quote, unquote."

"Who was the pal? What's his name?"

"*Her* name is Angel something. Wait a sec. Here it is. Angel Pitt, double 't'—like Brad. Hey, can you do that Kevin Bacon thing with Brad Pitt?"

She almost snorted. "Brad Pitt was in *Sleepers* with Kevin Bacon."

"I thought Robert Redford was in *Sleepers.*"

"Very good, Peter, but that was *Sneakers.*"

"This case reminds me of your Kevin Bacon game, Norrie. I just wish we could connect the dots as easily as you can connect Kevin Bacon to Brad Pitt."

"Sometimes," she said, "it takes three or four links to connect Kevin Bacon to someone else, but he really is the quintessential six degrees of separation. Eventually," she added, "we'll connect Sara Lee to her killer."

"I wish we were *connecting* right now." It was meant as an innuendo, but it fell flat and she heard the exhaustion in his voice.

"I have to go, Norrie. I'll check in with you later, okay? Love you. Will you marry me?"

"Love you, too, Peter, and not yet." As she hung up the phone, she thought: *Peter confided in me. He gave me crumbs, rather than the whole loaf, but that's an improvement over his usual "don't get involved, sweetheart."*

She was grateful for crumbs, even though crumbs were not allowed on her diet. Once upon a long time ago, she had believed that cookie crumbs and breadcrumbs had no calories.

More recently, at a Weight Winners meeting, shy Rachel had risen from her chair. "If you stand in a dark kitchen," she had said, "and eat ice cream straight from the container by the light of the refrigerator, it shouldn't count as a cheat."

Then she had laughed and everyone joined in the laughter and she looked so happy.

Ellie felt tears sting her eyes. *Poor, poor Rachel.*

THIRTEEN

Rachel Lester couldn't stop smiling. She felt happy. *Happy, happy, happy.*

Seated on top of the kitchen counter, she swayed back and forth to a syncopated rhythm inside her head. As her bare heels nudged the boards under the countertop, she watched Cee-Cee Sinclair's rugged mountain neighbor, Kurt Gordon, prepare Hollandaise sauce for a breakfast dish he called "Eggs Gordon."

Kurt was very attractive with his long, thick hair and the most incredible ice-green eyes. Despite his age, fifty-something, he could have played the hero in one of the romance novels that Rachel was addicted to. A scar slashed through his left eyebrow, adding to his allure. The heroes in her romance novels always seemed to possess some kind of physical imperfection, but their flaws merely boosted their sexiness. For obvious reasons, Rachel preferred facial imperfections to bodily defects.

But instead of *playing* a romance hero, Kurt sequestered himself inside a mountain cabin and wrote romance novels under the pseudonym Lorna Ann Jakes. When he told Rachel that, she honestly thought she'd died and gone to heaven. Except for Marty Blue, Lorna Ann Jakes was her favorite author.

Kurt also played unofficial cabin caretaker, the reason he had grabbed his shotgun to investigate the lights in Cee-Cee's supposedly unoccupied cabin. After all, he told Rachel, it had been well after midnight, lights blazed from every window, and drifters had been known to turn vacant mountain cabins into personal homeless shelters. The shotgun, he said, had not been loaded.

Rachel had always believed that stories of love at first sight were pure fiction, engineered by book publishers, sappy musicians, motion picture moguls, and cosmetics manufacturers.

Not anymore. If she wasn't in love at first sight, she was definitely in lust at first sight. Too bad she was married. Too bad she wasn't widowed yet. Too bad adultery was a sin.

Kurt owned—or as he said, *was owned by*—a "mostly German shepherd" named Ava and two cats, Sinatra and Crusty Boogers.

She had asked where the name Crusty Boogers came from.

"Crusty was lying by the side of the road," Kurt said. "He was around three weeks old and looked more dead than alive. The vet said he had worms, parasites, and flea anemia. He was dehydrated and malnourished and had bacterial and viral infections. In fact, the only thing he didn't have was ear mites. Somewhere north of fifteen hundred dollars, the vet stopped charging me for treatment.

"I fed Crusty eight times a day through an eye dropper. The medications fixed everything except a viral infection he has in his sinus which leads to a bacteriological infection which leads to lots of cat snot, hence his name, Crusty Boogers. Poor guy goes on 'pulse' antibiotic therapy which temporarily clears up the bacteriological infection, but when he goes off the antibiotics I have to pick his sad little nose about five times a day."

Rachel wondered if the hero worship she felt for Kurt showed in her eyes.

With a shake of his head, Kurt had trashed her burned sauerkraut and shriveled hot dogs. Then he had whipped up a dish he called "Quiche Gordon." As she watched, he preheated the oven to 425 degrees and fried some bacon. He then crumbled the bacon into a prepared pie crust. With a wire whisk he beat four eggs, two cups of heavy cream, a teaspoon of salt and a pinch of nutmeg. Lastly, he stirred in a quarter pound of shredded Swiss cheese. He poured that mixture into the crust, baked it for fifteen minutes, and turned the oven to 325 degrees. While the quiche baked for another thirty-five minutes and cooled for ten, Rachel told Kurt an abridged version of her life story. When she had finished, he stuck a knife in the middle of the quiche, held the knife up for her inspection, and said, "Clean."

"Are you saying," she said, still somewhat lost in wobbly remembrances, "that tonight is a clean start? A clean slate?"

"Yup."

"Then I shouldn't eat heavy cream," she had quipped. "I'm on a strict diet."

He put down the knife. "I, for one, prefer shapely women with *real* curves," he had said, his voice downright solemn. "When I see the actresses and models who dictate today's fashions, the first thought that comes to mind is 'she needs feeding.' "

"But you write romances, Kurt, where the women are always slender."

"Underfed," he amended. "Rachel, in the real world very few women look like the women I write about, nor should they. It's like saying Barbie and Ken are anatomically correct."

"Oh my God, are you for real?"

He laughed. "If I'm not, you'd better adopt Ava, Sinatra and Crusty Boogers."

"I'll bet your heroines don't have *this*," she had said, her voice bitter as she held up her deformed hand.

To her surprise, he had gently grasped the proffered claw-hand and kissed her palm.

By the time she'd eaten the Quiche Gordon, her sister Margee's miraculous recovery had been put off for a few days and she had invited Kurt to stay overnight at the cabin. "For protection," she said.

She had meant the stormy weather, or maybe her imaginary bear, but he didn't say "protection from what?" Instead, he left the cabin to fetch Ava, after warning her with a smile that he often called his dog "Ava bin Lauden."

At least, that's what he said he planned to do. Rachel hadn't really expected him to return. But he had, with the dog, his laptop computer, a red wagon full of groceries, and a thick quilt stuffed inside a gecko-patterned quilt cover. The cats were fine alone for a while, he said, as long as they had food and water and a clean litter box.

Cee-Cee's cabin possessed a single, solitary bed. And unless one was a die-hard masochist, the hardwood couch/pew was out of the question. So they'd slept together, but that was all they'd done: sleep. Before she nodded off, physically and mentally exhausted, Kurt had stroked her hair. And with no more pressure than a butterfly's wings, he had traced the contours of her face with the back of his hand. Her tummy had fluttered and she'd wanted more, but she didn't know how to ask for more and he didn't offer more.

Now she surreptitiously scrutinized the robust romance author who stood in Cee-Cee's kitchen. He was bare-chested from the waist up, denim from the waist down. Obviously, he owned a heck of a lot of exercise equipment. Or maybe, she thought, trying to focus on something other than his glorious biceps, he simply chopped a heck of a lot of wood.

"May I read it?" she blurted.

"Read what? The recipe for Eggs Gordon? It's not written down."

"No, no." She gestured toward his laptop. "Your new book."

"I don't mind, but *Dream Angel*—that's what it's called—isn't a full-length book. It's a novella. Do you know what a novella is?"

"A small book?"

"Right. It's for an anthology. I'm one of three contributing authors. My story isn't quite finished. I planned to work on it today."

"Do you mind if I ask where you got your pen name, Lorna Ann Jakes?"

"Not at all. My ex-wife's name is Lorna. When I first started writing I thought our love would last forever, so I used her name. I have a sister, Ann, five years younger than I am."

"And your brother is named Jake, right?"

"No," he replied with a grin. "I don't have a brother. I chose the name Jakes so my books would be situated on bookstore and library shelves next to John Jakes, the bestselling author."

"I have all of John Jakes' books. Is *Dream Angel* a bodice ripper?" Rachel gave a little gasp and clamped her hand over her mouth. "I'm sorry," she said, lowering her hand so that it covered her fearful, thumping heart. Had she rubbed him the wrong way? "I heard somewhere—probably my book club—that romance authors don't like that term. Bodice ripper, I mean. If I rubbed you the wrong way, I sincerely apol—"

"You didn't rub me the wrong way. I'm only offended when the term is used in a derogatory way, more often than not by people who have never read a romance novel." He grinned again. "*Dream Angel* is categorically an historical romance." He glanced at her mystery novels, neatly stacked on top of the carton. "It's also a romantic suspense, which should be right up your alley."

She swallowed her first response, which would have been something about not reading mysteries. "Oh, wait," she said, disappointment slicing through her. "*You* need your laptop to finish writing your book, I mean your novella."

"Eat your breakfast, Rachel. And while you avail yourself of the powder room to do whatever pretty girls like you do, I'll go back to my cabin, check on the cats, and collect my printed manuscript. There might be a few handwritten edits, but it's decipherable, and that way I can work on my laptop while you read the printed copy."

She thought his use of the term "powder room" was adorable. Matthew would have said "can." Or "toilet," only he pronounced it "terlet."

Tears blurred her vision and she turned her face away to hide them. Kurt had called her pretty.

FOURTEEN

With unmitigated delight, Rachel stared at the crisp white pages, marred only by crisp black type.

At first she had felt self-conscious about her reading glasses, but Kurt said she looked like "the pretty people in those ads for eyeglasses." There was that word again. Pretty. However, this time she knew he was just being nice. Her glasses looked more like aviator goggles than pretty-people glasses.

A romantic suspense, Kurt had said. Rachel wondered if that meant that somebody, or more than one somebody, would drop dead. She enjoyed the "suspense" in romantic suspense, enjoyed sitting on the edge of her seat, enjoyed the tension, and yet she hated to read about dead people, especially dead murdered people. She avoided depressing newspaper headlines like the plague, not to mention the nightly news and, above all, TV shows hosted by chitter-chattering gossipmongers who splashed graphic pictures all over the screen and convicted people before they were even arrested.

She herself had never even *considered* killing anything or anybody (*thou shalt not kill*).

Of course, that was before Matthew had been caught "starkers" from the waist down.

With a start, Rachel realized that her abhorrence level, on a scale of one to ten, hovered around five, maybe even lower than five, and she *looked forward* to reading Kurt's story, *the bloodier the better*. At the same time, she hoped he wouldn't ask her for her opinion, or—God forbid—a literary critique.

Although she had washed her hands at the kitchen sink three times—much to Kurt's amusement and, eventually, his mild reprimand—she wished she had packed her white gloves; the gloves she wore to church, despite Matthew's derisive remarks about prissy churchgoers and their prudish wardrobes.

If she wore gloves, she wouldn't accidentally finger-smudge the crisp white paper.

Seated at the kitchen table, a mug of steaming hot herbal tea near—but not too near—her elbow, Rachel very carefully turned to the first page, which started with a date:

Paris, 1850

"The lady's about to fall, Mum," the little girl gasped. Pigtails swaying, her chin tilted like the prow of a miniature ship, as-suming the ship crested a wave.

Without looking at her daughter, Hortense Downing-Cox Kelley said, "That's part of her performance, Charlotte. She pretends she's going to fall. Sometimes it's all right to pretend."

Hortense heaved a deep sigh and slanted an angry glance toward her stepson, Sean. He was the reason she and five-year-old Charlotte were stuffed like sausages into this small compartment, this ridiculous red box, surrounded by other spectators, all of whom were shouting and applauding in French. *He was the reason why, every time she took a breath, she smelled sawdust and horse manure. He was the reason she spent the afternoon at a circus when any sensible woman would be sipping tea in the comfort of her own parlour.*

But then, any sensible *woman wouldn't have married Timothy Kelley.*

Hortense had succumbed to Tim's devilish charms, enhanced by the Irish brogue—and, to be honest, the Irish tongue—that tickled her ears. Twenty-nine years old and plain as a pudding, she had ignored every warning issued by her proper British parents; had even ignored their threat to disinherit her.

Prudently, she hadn't told Tim about her parents' caveat. Which, as it turned out, had been her biggest mistake. When her new husband discovered the truth, he had carted her across the sea to an obscure French relative who smelled of <u>pickles</u> onions and owned a café. Tim had the good grace to wait for the birth of his daughter before setting sail for America, but that had been five years ago and Hortense had not heard from him since. Furthermore, if she had tricked him into marrying her, his own duplicity was far more profound. For he had neglected to tell her that he had buried the first Mrs. Kelley in Ireland, or that the issue from his previous marriage, a twenty-year-old son named Sean, lived above the onion-woman's café.

Sean had been cordial enough during their introduction, but Hortense had been astute enough to read the unspoken words he directed toward his father: Did ye wed yourself an elderly lass with an inheritance, Da?

A pity Hortense had been too busy vomiting in the loo—or whatever the blasted French called it—to hear Tim's response. Carrying a child was a bloody nuisance. Truth be told, Sean had been of more assistance than his father. As Hortense's belly expanded into an unbelievable girth, reminiscent of an elephant, it was Sean who finished her chores, helped her rise from chairs, and fetched the midwife when her labor pains began.

As far as Hortense could ascertain, the only advantage to birthing a child was that one's figure tended to change. Before Charlotte, she had been thin and angular. Now her breasts were globes, her hips bounteous. Even her hair could be considered more mahogany than brown. A pity Tim hadn't stayed long enough to savor his wife's new, enticingly abundant body.

Sean hadn't left with his father, and Hortense knew why. The lad, now twenty-six, had an Irishman's fondness for children. He adored Charlotte, and while one half of Hortense deplored what she considered a lamentable, if not downright disgraceful, weakness in a man, the other half was eternally grateful. In Hortense's opinion, a baby was just as bothersome as a pregnancy. Especially since Charlotte was a sickly child with none of her father's robust qualities.

Nor Sean's, for that matter.

Which was the fly in the bloody ointment, Hortense reminded herself daily. Sean looked too much like Tim. The same thick ebony hair, the same merry green eyes, the same broad shoulders, narrow waist and muscular legs. And if that wasn't enough, her stepson possessed his father's charm. Hortense has seen young ladies pretend to swoon so that Sean could catch them. Not necessarily fille de joie, *either. Well-bred girls swooned!*

If honest, and Hortense was always honest with herself, she had seriously considered the same ploy. However, she feared rejection. Not because she was Tim's wife and older than Sean, but because she knew full well that he wanted to woo an heiress. To that end, Hortense had re-established contact with her parents. It had taken five years, but the Downing-Cox's desire to see their only grandchild had helped a great deal. Finally, Hortense swallowed her pride, begged for mercy, vowed she'd never stray from the fold again, and was anxiously awaiting a reply.

She fibbed, of course. About straying. Despite Sean's many attributes, he possessed one fatal flaw. He could be bought.

"Look, Mum! Look, Sean!"

Charlotte's strident voice pierced Hortense's haze, and she allowed her gaze to follow her daughter's small finger, gesturing toward the building's apogee.

The chit atop the rope was taking dainty, tentative steps, as if she wanted to tease the prudent people who were safely rooted below. She didn't even use a balancing pole or an umbrella. Hortense darted a quick glance toward Sean. His mouth had become unhinged, his attention riveted on the rope. No. His entire focus was on the piece of baggage who had just finished performing a series of dazzling back-flip somersaults.

Hortense's heart sank to the bottom of her shoes. The young girl who now danced across the rope was certainly no heiress, and yet Sean's expression clearly revealed that he didn't give a fig. Hortense's corset felt too tight. The candied apple she'd eaten earlier rose in her throat, whole.

Even while she lost what remained of her breath, her mind raced. She wanted Sean to play the part of her devoted companion. An obstacle to that scheme danced above her head. Surely there was some clever way to get rid of that damn-fool rope walker, that damnable Petit Ange.

Along with the rest of the audience, Sean was clapping and yelling, "C'est magnifique! C'est la plus belle—"

The world whirled and the applause dimmed, and Hortense keeled over.

Rachel hated to stop reading, but she needed to go to the bathroom. Kurt had left the cabin to chop wood since Cee-Cee's stack of fireplace wood needed replenishing.

Upon returning to the kitchen, Rachel made herself a fresh, hot cup of tea and once again settled down with the manuscript pages.

She read about how Sean's first glimpse of the "Small Angel"—whom he now thought of as *his* small angel—had not been during her performance. On the rope, she'd been too high up for anyone to appreciate the perfection of her flashing gray-green eyes and honey-colored hair, and it was this "perfection" that brought him back to the Cirque Nouveau's cellarage.

Rachel especially liked the part where Kurt introduced Angelique.

At home Rachel often read her romance novels aloud to Scout, so she called Ava into the kitchen, told her to lie down, and began to read out loud, savoring every word. "The Cirque changed its bill monthly," she read, "holding over the most popular acts, and regardless of this afternoon's enthusiastic applause, Angelique Aumont feared she might not be held over.

" 'You silly peagoose.' London-born Gartrude Starling, the Cirque's pretty trapeze artist, gave Angelique the budge. 'Even if your rope act weren't spot-on, half the fellows would pay dear for your maidenhead.'

"Since Angelique usually thought in French, it took her a moment to translate Gartrude's remarks. Then, cheeks ablaze, she reached out to caress a dray horse's velvet muzzle.

" 'That cannot be true,' she replied in her heavily accented English.

" 'Wot cannot be true? That they'd pay dear or that you have a maidenhead?'

" 'Do hush, Gartrude, *s'il vous plaît.*'

" 'God-a-mercy, *Petit Ange,* my brother Eadwig wants to marry you.'

" '*Mon Dieu,* I shall never wed a *cirque* performer,' she exclaimed, then smiled to take the sting out of her words.

"As if summoned, Eadwig Starling appeared, and the only English word Angelique could think of was 'dolt.' "

Rachel felt Kurt before she saw him. He had been standing behind her, looking over her shoulder. When she finally sensed his presence, he moved to the side of her chair and gently fingered her chin until she turned her face sideways and looked into his eyes.

"Time for a break," he said.

"Thanks, but I don't need a break." With an effort, she kept her gaze steady on him, even though she wanted nothing more than to return to the manuscript. "You hooked me from the start and I want to see what happens next."

He grinned like a little boy with frogs in his pockets. Then he said, "I need a break and so does Ava, and we'd like your company."

At the sound of her name, the dog raised her head from her front paws and wagged her tail.

"It's a beautiful fall day," Kurt continued, "so I propose we take a walk. I'm really glad you like my story, Rachel, but you shouldn't shut yourself up in the cabin all day, and you can resume reading this afternoon and evening . . . unless you have to go back home."

A question rather than a statement, she said, "No, I don't have to go back, not yet."

"Do you want to check in with your husband? I know you said he doesn't care about—"

"He thinks I'm in Houston. He has no idea I have a key to Cee-Cee's cabin. No one does, except, of course, Cee-Cee, and she's out of town and, anyway, I didn't even tell her I planned to visit . . ."

Rachel swallowed the rest of her response, aware that she sounded bitter and that sullenness did not belong in this wondrous dream. For that's what it was: a dream. It simply could not be happening, not to matronly, overweight, claw-fingered Rachel Lester, the girl most likely to succeed at something not specified.

Please, God, please. Don't wake me up.

As she put on her fake fur jacket, fur-lined boots, and a whimsical hat that looked and felt like rabbit fur, Rachel had another thought.

If Kurt is "Jack the Colorado ripper," he could strangle me in the woods and when I didn't come home, no one would know where to look for me. In a way, it would be like Janet Leigh in Psycho, *only I would be discovered by a hermit or a hunter or a fisherman or a Girl Scout, as soon as I thawed out.*

"Chill out, Ava," Kurt said to his dog, who was wagging her tail like a canine church fan as she frenetically scratched at the cabin's front door.

Fifteen

Once upon a long time ago, Ellie had accidentally overheard her husband Tony bragging to his weekly cluster of poker players.

Friends and family thought that she and Tony were the epitome of a happily-ever-after, till-death-do-us-part married couple: Cinderellie and Prince Charismatic, who was oh so charming. She was what the TV quiz shows called "a stay-at-home Mom" and Tony "brought home the bacon," a stupid euphemism for the euphemism "breadwinner." She devoured the bacon and bread, and to relax from the stress of his job, Tony played poker. On the last Friday of every month, it would be his turn to play host and he'd turn their kitchen table into a poker table, complete with red, white and blue poker chips.

From the very beginning, Ellie had accepted without protest her role as domestic *hausfrau,* but one night, after she had served the gamesters her legendary Nachos Eleanor and been sent away (Tony laughingly called it "exiled"), the cigarette and especially cigar smoke seemed worse than ever, invading the whole house like smog, thick as pea soup. Holding her sensitive nose, figuratively and literally, she had tiptoed into the kitchen to turn on the light fixture's fan and open a couple of windows. Whereupon, she overheard Tony say that he had found several loopholes in the Ten Commandments.

When he saw her, a scowl creased his handsome brow and he held up his hand like a school crossing guard, shushing the other players. He didn't clarify his quip while she was in the room, but she knew what he meant. He meant he couldn't keep it in his pants.

As she entered Matthew Lester's real estate office, Ellie's mouth watered at the thought of Nachos Eleanor, which she had somewhat modified to fit her diet by substituting low-cal sour cream and deleting the chopped black olives. Her nacho recipe required a fifteen-ounce can of chili beans in chili gravy, nine tablespoons of *picante* sauce, a bag of corn tortilla chips, four cups of grated Cheddar cheese, an avocado, one tablespoon of fresh lemon juice, two cups of sour cream, half a small grated onion, three diced scallions, two chopped-up tomatoes, and cider vinegar. After preheating the oven to 400 degrees and mashing the beans with eight tablespoons of picante sauce, she would grease two nine-by-twelve-inch pans and place half the chips in each pan. Then she'd spoon the bean mixture over the chips and sprinkle the grated cheese on top. While the nachos baked for ten minutes—or until the cheese melted and the beans bubbled—she'd peel, pit and mash the avocado, add lemon juice, one cup of sour cream, grated onion, and one tablespoon of picante sauce. Finally, she'd garnish the nacho mixture with the guacamole, the remaining sour cream, the scallions, the chopped tomatoes, a spritz or two of vinegar, and . . . *voilà!*

Tony's friends loved her nachos, along with her celebrated Brown Sugar Smokies and her "Ham-It-Ups"—Black Forest ham roll-ups filled with Cheddar cheese and cream cheese. One poker player, the man who puffed cigars nonstop, had even called after the divorce to ask if she would host a game a month for a percentage—like a Vegas dealer—and he had sounded decidedly tearful when she'd said thanks but no thanks.

Casting off the memory like a too-small coat, Ellie tightened her grip on her purse and shopping bag, and walked toward the receptionist's front desk. After leaving the Lester residence, she had driven home to let Scout and Jackie Robinson inside. Silently chastising herself for not making a brief detour to buy Scout's special food at Reigning Cats & Dogs, she had whisked up an omelet with cheese, leftover sausages and real bacon bits, and served half to Scout and half to her pampered puss. While the animals scarfed down the savory eggs, she had filled a shopping bag with Weight Winners goodies, including the aforementioned breakfast bars.

Then she had washed down a couple of breakfast bars with her leftover breakfast coffee, heated in the microwave.

The hours were going by much too quickly. Every clock seemed to be fast-forwarding, and her carefully thought out agenda was shot to hell, but she wanted to look through Matthew Lester's desk before the police rummaged around inside the drawers and/or confiscated his computer. She knew what she was looking for, or at least she had a vague idea, while they didn't have a clue. And she couldn't clue Peter in. Admittedly, he had given her some much-appreciated information, but he would *not* appreciate her compulsion to persist in her favorite pastime: sleuthing. A search for the missing dog food was one thing. Invading, uninvited, a murder victim's office was an altogether different kettle of halibut.

On the other hand, unless Peter was in an exceedingly nitpicky mood, he'd applaud her resolve to nose around, especially when she informed him that the receptionist, Pat Timpanaro, had been very . . . receptive.

The food bribe was a mere precaution, probably superfluous.

Matthew Lester's office was as uninhabited as a bookstore on Superbowl Sunday, and overheated to the point of suffocation; Ellie would hate to pay their *December* heating bill. As she unzipped her son Mick's outgrown, orange-and-blue Denver Bronco's jacket, she glanced around the room.

Desks that boasted flat-screen monitors and computer keyboards.

One plant that could have doubled for the Audrey-plant in *Little Shop of Horrors.*

Agent-of-the-month wall plaques with photo inserts and names etched on the surface. Even from a distance, Ellie could see that "Matthew Dillon Lester" had been engraved on eight out of ten plaques.

A closed door that she assumed led to a conference room.

A closed door that led to a kid's playroom. No guessing there. Using her brilliant knack for detecting, she had spied the sign above the door that said KID'S PLAYROOM.

Ironically, she had not been inside a real estate office since the day she and Tony had signed the loan papers for their own house. Even though her ex was a real estate broker, he had forbidden her to visit his office, what he called his inner sanctum, insisting that business and pleasure were separate entities. At the time she had not realized what, exactly, comprised Tony's pleasure. After she joined Weight Winners and began to renovate her fragile self-esteem, she discovered that his *pleasures* consisted of college students with generous stipends from wealthy parents. Also, divorced women who wanted to sell their homes or spend their munificent alimony payments on a bigger house, a mansion, a manor. And Tony, tall, dark, handsome, and extravagantly sympathetic, created loopholes galore. Loopholes in the Ten Commandments. Loopholes in his marriage vows. Loopholes in the loopholes.

Then there was the matter of her weight. Tony admitted that he was embarrassed to be seen with her, that her rolls of flab were the target for fat jokes and no one could sense how smart she really was. He sided with her mother, insisting that Ellie's frequent weight gains were due to an abysmal lack of self-control. Almost daily, he'd remind her that gluttony was a sin.

She'd hold back her tears, apologize, promise to do better, swear she'd lose ten, twenty, thirty pounds, and hide cookies, potato chips, onion-studded bialys and custard-filled doughnuts in the laundry room, *her* inner sanctum, a room she knew Tony would never step foot in. "Lose fifty pounds," he'd say, "and you can come to the company picnic. Otherwise, I'm sorry, but you'll have to stay home."

The company picnic wasn't relevant. In fact, it was a bloody nuisance and Ellie would have preferred to hibernate at home. She hated to wear shorts and sleeveless tops, hated even more to wear muumuus, so she'd put on too many clothes and sweat profusely. Every year she'd pick a spot underneath an umbrella or shade tree and sit as motionless as an Auguste Rodin statue, her face frozen in a smile, and she only budged when she needed to refill her paper plate with calorific goodies.

However, she genuinely believed she owed it to Tony to make a wifely appearance, so she'd purge with laxatives, or starve herself until she was falling-down dizzy, or go on some insane rice-and-water diet, and she'd lose enough weight to secure his seal of approval. During those periods, he would treat her with respect and make love to her almost every night (he called it "coital motivation"). He liked to make love in front of John Wayne videos: *The Searchers* or *She Wore a Yellow Ribbon* or *True Grit*. For some reason she couldn't fathom then, but thought she understood now, the kick-ass cowboy turned Tony on.

After the picnic, she would gain all the weight back, and more, until a few weeks before the annual Christmas party, when the process would start all over again.

She often felt as though she rode a carousel horse, its anguished mouth chomping empty air, her anguished mouth chomping empty air. It seemed to her that she'd go to sleep exhausted, her stomach growling a lullaby, and she'd dream about riding up and down, up and down, in repetitive circles, going nowhere, desperately trying to capture the elusive brass ring. Sometimes her fingertips would brush against the ring, but it was always just out of reach. Frustratingly out of reach.

Until she joined Weight Win—

"Oh my gosh, you're the Weight Winners lady!" The receptionist squinted at Ellie. "Oh my gosh, I saw you on TV, the morning show or the noon show, I forget which, the one hosted by that lady who looks like an electric toothbrush." She paused to catch her breath. "What are you doing here?"

As Ellie walked closer, she smelled McDonald's. There was no other smell like McDonald's French fries. Sure enough, scrunched-up McD bags dominated the wastepaper basket. Ellie averted her gaze away from the trash and darted another quick glance around the office. "It's quiet in here," she said.

Understatement, she thought. Not a creature was stirring, except for the receptionist, who had placed her paperback book on the desktop, facedown, next to a bottle of very red nail polish.

Ellie said, "Are you Ms. Timpanaro?"

"Yes, but please call me Pat." She swiveled her chair and made a windshield wiper out of her hand, encompassing the office. "As you can see, all the agents are gone." She swiveled back toward Ellie. "They're all at a multiple listing inspection, and they took off for lunch before the showing. I'm stuck here alone, but there's a handy-dandy McDonald's across the street. That's why I was eating McDonald's." She sounded both guilty and defiant.

Ellie nodded noncommittally. "Are you talking about the multiple listing inspection that was written down in Matthew Lester's appointment book?" she asked, wondering how she could ease into the reason for her visit. "The inspection scheduled for twelve-thirty?"

"Yes, but Matt . . . Mr. Lester isn't there. I know for a friggin' fact—pardon my French—that he isn't there because another agent told me, not because Matt thought for one moment to check in with me." Temper simmering, about to boil over, she leaned forward and waved a bouquet of pink memo slips in Ellie's face like a wilted church fan or a floppy bridge hand. "These are all for *him*. I think that's rude, don't you? I mean, not checking in?"

"Extremely rude. But," Ellie couldn't help adding, "he probably has a good reason."

"Oh, yeah? What reason could he have and what, may I ask, are you doing here? May I assume you don't want to buy a house?"

Uh-oh, Pat's hostility runneth over, and Ellie was now the receptionist's key target. Pat had been caught with her hand inside the cookie jar, or in this case the McDonald's bag, and not just by anybody. By a friggin', pardon her French, diet club leader!

"You were so helpful when I talked to you on the phone earlier," Ellie said, her mind racing. She didn't know how to broach her request without sounding like a snoop. Oh, what the heck, she *was* a snoop. Perhaps honesty was the best strategy. "Pat, I need to search Matthew Lester's desk."

"Why?"

"His wife Rachel is in Houston." *True.* "She left her dog Scout with me, but she forgot to include dog food." *True.* "I haven't been able to get in touch with Mr. Lester." *True, most likely because he's dead.* "So I thought—"

"Rachel buys her food at Reigning Cats & Dogs. I know that for a friggin' fact, pardon my French, because I buy my bagel's food there, too."

"Your bagel's food?"

"My dog's food. He's part beagle, part bassett hound. I call him a bagel. Why do you need to look inside Matt . . . Mr.

Lester's desk?"

"Well, the thing is, Rachel needs to speak to her husband." *Could be true.* "And she hasn't been able to reach him, so she asked me to check his desk at work and see if there were any hints of his whereabouts." *Okay, that's a whopper. Sorry, God.* "Oh, I almost forgot, I brought you some diet club goodies." Ellie placed the shopping bag on the desk.

Pat looked inside the bag. Then she focused on Ellie's face. Then she said, "I suppose it can't hurt. I mean, I'm sure Mr. Lester doesn't have any deep, dark secrets hidden inside his desk. If he did, I'd know. I know everything that goes on here. Everything that goes on inside the conference room, too. You wouldn't believe what goes on inside the conference room."

I bet I would, Ellie thought, *if it's anything like Tony's conference room and has a deadbolt on the door.* "Which desk belongs to Matthew?"

"The last desk on the right, the one closest to the conference room. If you don't mind, I'm going to take a bathroom break. Should anybody walk in, tell them I'll be right back."

"Absolutely," Ellie said over her shoulder as she quick-stepped toward the back of the room.

Sixteen

Matthew Lester's drawers were compartmented with the standard desk-drawer paraphernalia, and disappointingly clue-free. Ellie stared at the computer. Could she get into his E-mail? She took off her jacket, draped it around the back of the desk chair, and lowered her tush to the padded seat. But when she clicked on the E-mail icon, it asked for a password.

Of course it did. What kind of a password would Matthew Lester use? She typed in SCOUT, then SCOUTFINCH. Shoot, that didn't work. She typed RACHEL. That didn't work, either. This was insane. She had never met Matthew Lester and couldn't get into his mind. For all she knew, his password was his birth date or his social security number or the name of his first-grade teacher, and here she sat, wasting time—

Wait a sec! She pictured the Lester's home office, narrowed her focus, and saw the Vincent van Gogh reproduction hanging on the wall.

She typed in VINCENT, then VAN GOGH, then VINCENT VAN GOGH.

Nope.

How about STARRY STARRY NIGHT?

She'd wager her next Weight Winners paycheck he'd chosen that phrase as his password.

In a movie or TV show she'd already be patting herself on the back for being so clev—

STARRY STARRY NIGHT was *not* Matthew Lester's password.

Oh, to heck with it. She'd leave the password deciphering to Peter and his crew.

Matthew's desk calendar and appointment book were a different story. Surely, they contained clues galore. She saw two notations on the calendar. One was a ten-digit number that looked familiar. Of course it did, because it was the fax number for Peter's brother-in-law, attorney Jonah Feldman. What was that all about?

Small world, Ellie thought, beginning to feel like Kevin Bacon's doppelganger.

The other notation read ANGEL PITT CELL, followed by a seven-digit number.

Angel Pitt, as in Brad?

The "pal" of Trent Zachariah?

The woman who escorted Sara Lee's bereaved husband home and watched him puke his guts out on his knees in front of the crapper? *That* Angel Pitt?

Or could there be two women named Angel Pitt, both of whom lived in Colorado Springs?

Don't be an idiot, Ellie!

She'd wager a bazillion dollars, or at the very least a packet of lottery tickets, that Angel Pitt was what Ellie's mother would call "a lady of the night" and Lieutenant Peter Anachronistic Miller would call "a paid escort." Ellie didn't know why Angel's name and number were printed on Matthew's calendar, but the lady's tenuous, and most likely fruitless, link to Trenton Zachariah made her a viable lead.

The only one I have!

Ellie dug her checkbook out of her purse and wrote Angel's cell phone number on the back of a deposit slip. With wry amusement, she saw that the last four digits were her age and

Peter's age, and she wished she had snagged that combination for her own cell phone. She never *could* remember her cell's number, but then she rarely remembered to take the phone with her, and why was she wasting valuable time on personal cell phone minutiae?

Matthew's appointment book was littered with initials. SL showed up occasionally. So did that annoyingly familiar JDCM, the initials she couldn't get a fix on, the initials that teetered in her mind like a car on the very edge of a steep cliff.

Her attempt to establish some sort of Matthew Lester–pattern seemed utterly hopeless. The only thing she knew for sure was that SL was Sara Lee, since one of the entries was followed by the letters DY, and she immediately flashed back to the *Damn Yankees* photo that the local news had plastered across the TV screen—the cast photo where Sara Lee's face had been circled by a white grease pencil.

Just as she was about to give up, a notation leapt off one of the pages and smacked her in the eye: "Breakfast meeting with TAB and NN."

Holy cow, was TAB an acronym?

A person's initials?

An abbreviation?

Or her brother Tab?

"NN" was almost certainly someone's name, but Ellie had a gut feeling—based solely on her Kevin Bacon doppelganger sensation—that TAB meant her brother. There was one easy way to find out.

Pat had returned from her bathroom break and was reading her book. Ellie grabbed her coat and purse and approached the receptionist's desk.

Using her finger as a bookmark, Pat said, "Did you find what you needed?"

Her paperback was a romantic suspense by Marty Blue. "I

know her. Marty Blue," Ellie said.

"Cool," Pat said, and Ellie heard: *Yeah, right, and I have this bridge in Brooklyn for sale.*

"May I use your phone, Pat?"

"Don't you have a cell phone?"

"Yes, but I always forget to stick it inside my purse, and if I change purses—"

"Long distance or local?"

"Local."

"Oh, all right, go ahead, but don't stay on the line too long. Matt . . . Mr. Lester might finally decide to check in and get his friggin' messages, pardon my French."

The chances of that happening, on a scale of one to ten, were around minus three, Ellie thought, trying hard to maintain a dispassionate demeanor. On the other hand, the cops could, and probably would, arrive any moment. "I'll be brief," she said, accepting the receiver from Pat's outstretched hand and finger-tapping her mother's number faster than a Ruby Keeler chorus line.

Tab answered the phone. "If this is a telemarketer," he said, "you can take this call and stick it up your—"

"There's nothing I can sell you that you don't already have," she said quickly, before he hung up.

She heard a faint background racket—rhythmic chanting, a synthesizer and human beatboxing.

"Hi, Sissy," her brother said, even though she had asked him a million times not to call her that.

"How's it going, Tabby?" she replied sweetly, knowing he hated the nickname with a passion.

"Mom isn't home," he said. "She's playing mahjong with her fellow Jerry Springer addicts. Then she has her book club, even though she hasn't read the book, an Oprah classic that's not, by any stretch of the imagination, a bodice ripper."

116

"I need to talk to you, not Mom. Do you happen to know a guy named Matthew Lester?"

"Maybe," Tab said.

Maybe meant yes. In her wonky family, maybe *always* meant yes.

"I thought I'd come over," she said. "Are you planning to be there for a while?"

"I don't know for sure. As we speak, I'm downloading some songs from my computer. A friend showed me how. But I have no idea how long it'll take."

"Legal downloads?"

"What's the difference? Oh, I forgot. You're boinking a cop."

"Boinking?"

"What would you call it?"

Since time was at an essence, she ignored the bait. " 'Every time you download a song,' " she said, quoting from a bumper sticker, " 'a kitten dies.' "

"Really? Shit, you're kidding. *It's a Wonderful Life,* right? The bit about the angel getting his wings. Ha-ha, very funny."

"Depending on traffic, I'll be there in fifteen minutes," Ellie said, and hung up.

She hoped that Tab, intrigued, would stick around. She hoped he wasn't killing too many kittens.

Seventeen

Un-strangled, feeling categorically windblown, sun-kissed, and healthy as the proverbial horse, Rachel Lester uttered a contented sigh, planted her elbows on the table, and palmed her chin with her hands. Once again she sat in the kitchen, her reading glasses shading her eyes, Kurt's manuscript between her elbows.

Ava slept, stretched out in front of the fireplace.

Kurt had taken his red wagon and gone back to his cabin to check on his cats and raid his cupboard for a few more provisions. Rachel drank herbal tea by the gallon but he was a self-confessed caffeine addict, and Cee-Cee's kitchen possessed neither coffee nor coffee machine. Kurt had said he'd also raid his closet for some clean clothes, which delighted Rachel to no end. Because it meant he planned to stay overnight again. She absolutely, positively did not want to commit the sin of adultery, but she knew she wouldn't object if his hands accidentally strayed.

At the thought, she shivered with delight. She felt incredibly pagan, as if she had stepped through Alice's looking glass into a magical world that exhibited no prohibitions and, above all, no biblical tenets.

Cheeks hot, she lowered her gaze to Kurt's manuscript, more than ready to lose herself in the romantic adventures of Sean and Angelique.

She read about how the horrible Hortense visited Angelique

backstage at the Nouveau Cirque, and when Hortense lied and said she was Sean's wife, the heartbroken Angelique made up her mind to travel to New York City, America, and live with her rich auntie. And she took her friend, Gartrude, with her.

Rachel almost cheered aloud. She liked Gartrude.

When Sean learned about Hortense's nasty trick, he followed Angelique to New York City and secured a position with P. T. Barnum. But it was a big city and Sean had no luck finding Angelique.

Meanwhile, Angelique was virtually trapped inside her *Tante* Bernadine's home, for her auntie had arranged a marriage to a despicable, wealthy widower who looked like a *grenouille* . . . a frog. Angelique's only companions were her aunt's seven cats, named for the days of the week, and Gartrude, who had secured a position as a housemaid in *Tante* Bernadine's large household.

With a smile, Rachel called Ava into the kitchen and read aloud the descriptive paragraph that introduced the seven cats: " 'A hungry Tuesday meowed and rubbed against Angelique's drawn-up legs. Thursday was asleep atop Angelique's belly. Friday played with a ball of yarn while Monday chased a billiard ball. None of the cats, including Sunday, Saturday and Wednesday, seemed perturbed by Angelique's shuddering sighs and sobs. She had been weeping steadily for two hours, and the cats, clever creatures, had probably decided she had no tears left. They were on the dot, as Gartrude liked to say. After all, how much salty moisture could a person—even a woman— produce?' "

Ava seemed tremendously attentive. Maybe Kurt read out loud, too. Rachel stood, stretched, and stepped away from the table. As she scratched the dog behind its ears, she remembered that Kurt had said that Ava weighed in at a svelte sixty-five pounds, and that her right ear was perpetually signaling a turn.

Rachel returned to her chair. She continued to peruse Kurt's manuscript, albeit silently. She read about how P. T. Barnum's wife, Charity, threw a dinner party to celebrate the arrival of "the Swedish Nightingale," a world-famous singer by the name of Jenny Lind. Sean and Angelique both received invitations. At which point they were reunited. Their reunion was followed by a very hot love scene, and the star-crossed lovers fell in love all over again.

Rachel kept reading while Kurt bustled about in the kitchen, but she gave a surprised "squee" when she felt something furry brush against her ankles. Looking down, she saw an orange-striped cat.

"That's Crusty Boogers," Kurt said. "I thought I might as well bring the cats and . . ." He stopped mid-sentence and stared at her face.

"What?" she said, then realized that her drowsy eyes and expressive mouth had given her away.

"Are you sure, Rachel? Are you one-hundred-percent sure?"

All she could do was bob her head up and down, just like their very first meeting, his very first question. Was it only yesterday? She felt as though she'd known him forever. And, in a way, she had. Devouring his romances, forming a bond with "Lorna Ann Jakes," and now reading about the brave and beautiful Angelique, Rachel felt she could see into Kurt's heart. And anyway, she reminded herself, she was stuck inside a wondrous dream from which she hoped she'd never, ever wake up.

Kurt practically lifted her from the chair. He placed his arm about her waist and guided her toward the staircase that led to the loft.

Halfway up she felt the first sensual spasm, and she might have fallen had he not tightened his grip.

"If my novella produces this kind of reaction in you," he

teased, "it probably won't need an edit."

"Not . . . just . . . the . . . book," she panted as they reached the top of the stairs.

He looked at her face again, then carefully lowered her to the floor. He took off his AIR FORCE ACADEMY sweatshirt (*when had he put that on?*) and wedged it underneath her head. He unsnapped his jeans at the waistband and unzipped his fly. He didn't wear underpants, and she had a ridiculous, short-lived notion that Haines spokesperson Michael Jordan would not approve.

Kurt straddled her body and leaned forward, and she felt his erection, rock-hard against her belly. Before he had finished tracing her lips with his tongue, she had begun to spiral into uncharted territory.

His wicked, playful tongue explored the inside of her mouth.

He kissed her until she could hardly breathe, then unzipped her jeans and thrust his hand inside her panties.

Her eyes were half shut but she saw him nod.

He wriggled his way down her body, took off her shoes, and began to tug at her jeans and undies.

His hands were warm and she wanted to help him by lifting her legs and butt, but she had already plunged, head first, through the hedonistic looking glass.

EIGHTEEN

Ellie parked her Honda at the curb in front of her mother's house. Tab had said Mom wasn't home, but Ellie had no idea how much time her "interview" with her brother would take and she needed an escape route. If she parked in the driveway, she'd be trapped between Tab's motorcycle and her mom's car—like a mouse in a cat sandwich.

Speaking of cats, her mother's six cats—Danielle Steele, Victoria Gordon, Nora Roberts, Lorna Ann Jakes, Maggie Osborne and Marty Blue—were sprawled on the steps that led to the front stoop. Wending her way through six tails was dicey, and Ellie took a few moments to collect her thoughts and get her bearings.

Erected in the 1950's, her childhood home was enhanced by a Tom Sawyer fence and a well-kept lawn that from a distance looked like the green icing on a St. Patrick's Day cake. The street in front of the house was flat as a pancake but soon dipped into a long, winding hill—great for sledding—that ended in a narrow cul-de-sac, flanked on either side by a nursing home and a nursery school.

Every year, from age eight to eleven, Ellie would don a green skirt, white blouse, and green sash that slanted diagonally across her budding breasts. The sash flaunted embroidered badges, but the crowning touch, so to speak, was her green hat, perched rakishly atop the Irish-setter hair that had been tortured by her mom into Shirley Temple curls. Pulling a Radio Flyer behind her, Ellie would march down the street until she reached the end of the cul-de-sac. There, she'd sell her allotted boxes of Girl Scout cookies to the nursing home and nursery school.

If there were any boxes left over, her dad would sell them to his friends at the bar he frequented, but first her mom would fill a ceramic Winnie the Pooh cookie jar with sandwich cookies. Boxes of chocolate mint cookies would be neatly stacked inside the basement chest freezer. Ellie's goal was to sell more cookies than anyone else in her troop, and she always met her objective. Her second goal was to ignore the sandwich cookies in the cookie jar and stop thinking about the chocolate mint cookies in the freezer, and she never met that objective. Even today, chocolate mint cookies dipped in milk was as good as, if not better than, sex, even though she'd never tell Peter that scrumptious tidbit.

She had no idea if the nursing home and nursery school still existed, but the house her mom and Tab lived in had aged well, even though it was the cheapest model in the development (the most expensive looked like David O. Selznick's Tara). A ranch house, or "rancher," it sported three bedrooms, a guest room, a living room, a dining room, an eat-in kitchen and a basement "rumpus room." The builder, probably a leftover Munchkin from Oz, had constructed very low ceilings and, even as a child, Ellie had been tempted to duck her head every time she walked inside. Except for the kitchen, all rooms were shag carpeted and badly in need of a go-over by the same John Deere riding lawnmower that kept the front and backyards immaculate. Tab had turned one of the bedrooms into a computer room and, almost immediately, her mother had become addicted to E-mail, eBay, and on-line shopping. No wonder Tab had taken advantage of her absence to download his songs.

With delight, Ellie breathed in the perfume from her mother's flowers. Autumn never arrived all at once in Colorado. With an

Denise Dietz

elevation difference of 8,000 to 9,000 feet between mountain-
tops and plains, the shift from summer to fall began on the
tundra in late August and gradually moved down to lower
altitudes. Although she had been born and raised in Colorado
Springs, Mom didn't know squat about the tundra's black
mucky soil and frozen subsoil, or the shift in elevation. As-
sertively planting an elaborate garden that ran alongside the
front of the house, bordered by a row of diminutive hedges, she
simply *willed* her autumn flowers to bloom. And bloom they
did. Up against the house's facade, Russian Sage had already
begun to wear stylish white, creating an exquisite backdrop for
plants with names like Autumn Joy, Desert Sunrise and Lamb's
Ear.

Mom's garden most likely served as the cats' outdoor litter
box, a thought that gave Ellie pause. Her loss of fifty-five and a
half pounds had made her lighter on her feet, but it was still a
choice between tails and turds. Decisively, she walked up the
driveway, skirted Tab's Harley, and carefully tiptoed through the
tulips, which in this case were pink and white ice plants. She
didn't think she had massacred any of her mother's flowers, but
she felt an immense sense of relief when she finally hoisted
herself up onto the front stoop.

Tails waving like furry garden snakes, the cats watched her
trek and ascent.

She had a house key in her purse, but she felt funny about
entering unannounced. Tab hadn't said he was home alone and
she didn't want to interrupt a corporeal romp on the sofa or,
for all she knew, the floor.

Except for Mom, everybody in the family knew that Tab was
gay. No one gave a rat's spit, not even Ellie's extremely wealthy,
eighty-one-year-old paternal grandmother, who had been a
devout and dutiful nun before she renounced her vows of
poverty, chastity and, especially, obedience. Among other things,

124

Grandma Shirley had joined the Peace Corps, won a million-dollar Pillsbury Bake-Off contest, and converted to Judaism. She had outlived, or as she put it "outlasted" two husbands. Along with her thirty-one-year-old Jamaican lover/fiancé, she lived in a spiffy retirement complex in Phoenix. At least she did when she wasn't flying to Israel or Carnival Cruising.

Tab needed a home base. If Mom knew that he was, in her words "a sissy-boy," he'd be out on his ass quicker than Grandma Shirley changed lovers, fiancés, and religions. Ellie had no great love for Tab, who could be meaner than a junkyard dog, but she would never give away the "big family secret."

Her brother had been born in late July. To honor his astrological sign, her mother bought a brass lion's head knocker for the front door. In Ellie's ensuing nightmares, the lion's head would morph into a full-bodied lion and chase her. When she was eight, she read *The Lion, the Witch and the Wardrobe* by C. S. Lewis. She named her favorite dolly, Narnia, and the bad dreams went away. Now, she gave the lion's head a fond pat, knocked loudly, and saw her brother peering at her through the narrow gap produced by the chain-lock's chain.

"You were expecting a terrorist attack?" she asked. "Or were you hoping to keep me out?"

"Don't be a smart-ass," he replied, unlatching the chain and opening the door.

Tab had inherited Mom's genes, except Mom was tall and angular while Tab was tall and slender. His eyes were a rich blue, a color some people referred to as sapphire. His thick hair, more chestnut than red, had an overabundance of blond streaks that, surprisingly, looked natural. She would have to remember to ask him who did his hair.

Entering the house, she instinctively ducked her head. As she took off her jacket, she heard music coming from one of the bedrooms: Nelly Furtado rapping with Timbaland. Peter's niece

Jonina was nuts about Furtado, and Ellie had heard all of Nelly's songs—more than once.

Danielle and Nora, the two Siamese cats, followed Ellie inside.

"Please put Danielle and Nora outside," she told Tab. "They'll yowl and I hate to hear them yowl. I'd put them out myself, but they don't like me and they'll scratch."

"They don't yowl half as loud as Rosemary Rogers," Tab said. "Remember her?"

"Of course. Rosemary gave me headaches, and Mom fed me Hershey bars to cure my headaches."

Making no move to let the cats outside, Tab led the way to the kitchen, and Ellie was immediately transported back to babyhood, childhood and young adulthood.

The kitchen was the focal point of the house, the room where Important Events took place. Forget the living room, for display purposes only, or the rumpus room, for TV and Ping-Pong.

Here in the kitchen, Ellie had opened her acceptance letter to college. Here in the kitchen, she had announced her engagement—"Better plan the wedding quick before Tony changes his mind," her mother had said, only half joking. Here in the kitchen, Ellie had made known her pregnancy—"Better not tell the rest of the world until after the fourth month," her mother had said. "Miscarriages run in our family and you could jinx the fetus." Here in the kitchen, Ellie's excellent report cards had led to celebratory ice cream sundaes with "real whipped cream." Here in the kitchen, her teenage miseries demanded chocolate, and when her classmates nicknamed her Ellie Belly, her mother had mollified—you could almost say fortified—her with fudge.

Banana cream pie when a boy she liked made fun of her . . .

Strawberry shortcake when she "outgrew" her favorite dress . . .

Frozen Three Musketeers when she suffered cramps from her period . . .

All served in the kitchen because God forbid there should be crumbs in any other room. Crumbs liked to hide in shag carpeting, Mom said, and crumbs "attracted cock-a-roaches and ants and all kinds of vermin."

Speaking of vermin, her brother Tab had pulled a can of Coke from the fridge and was popping the top. He didn't offer Ellie anything to drink, and she couldn't get a soda for herself because as soon as she had seated herself in front of the kitchen table, Nora or Danielle—she never could tell them apart—had settled in her lap and was *purring*.

Thirsty, she had a plastic bottle of water in her purse, but she had tossed her purse and jacket on top of the vestibule table and she'd dehydrate before she asked her rat-fink brother to fetch the water bottle.

He seated himself across from her, took a sip of soda from his can, and swirled it around in his mouth as though testing a fine black wine. Then he swallowed and said, "You said on the phone you needed to talk to me about some guy named Matthew something or other. What's he got to do with me?"

"Matthew *Lester*. How do you know him?"

"Hold that thought, Sissy. I've got to download another song."

Ellie wanted to stand up and follow her brother, but Nora or Danielle had joined Nora or Danielle and she now had two cats purring in her lap. She wriggled her tush, hoping to dislodge them, but they just went with the flow and snuggled deeper. Damn!

Impatiently drumming her fingernails on the kitchen table, she glared at the archway that led to the rest of the house and ticked off the minutes in her head. Okay, this was ludicrous. Obviously, Tab was trying to avoid her, and cats or no cats—

"That's Ludicris, my friend's favorite rapper," Tab said. He pointed in the direction of the music, entered the kitchen, and retrieved another can of soda from the refrigerator.

"May I have one of those, please?" Ellie asked, pointing at the can.

"This is the last one," he said ungraciously, seated again.

She said, "How do you know Matthew Lester?"

"Boy oh boy, Sissy, you sure have a one-track mind."

"How do you know him, Tab?"

"Who said I knew him?"

"You did. On the phone you said 'maybe.' Unless you've lost your memory as well as your mind, 'maybe' in our family means yes."

"I haven't lost my mind."

"Right. That's why you're downloading rap songs when you hate rap with a passion."

"I told you, my friend likes rap."

"The friend who taught you how to download songs?"

"Yes."

"Why can't he download his own songs?"

"He can." Tab heaved a deep sigh. "I like him so much, Ellie, and he sings along with the rappers when he listens to them, so I thought if I learned the words to a couple of songs, I'd impress—"

"Tab, you can't carry a tune in a bucket. You're as tone deaf as I am!"

"I know, but you don't have to carry a tune when you sing rap."

She nodded, conceding his point. "Let's cut the bull, okay? You had a meeting with one Matthew Dillon Lester. My guess is that you want out of Mom's house so that you can openly date your rap-loving downloader, whose initials just happen to be N.N. So Matthew Lester, a successful real estate agent, was looking for an apartment or a rental hou—"

"You couldn't be more wrong."

"Then set me straight, please. It's important or I wouldn't ask."

"Just remember, I found him first," her brother said, and for a moment, Ellie thought he meant he'd been the first to kill the real estate agent.

"You found him first," she repeated, at a loss.

"Yes! So I'll reap the rewards, and everybody who ever laughed at me will be sorry because I'll have the last laugh."

"You'll reap the rewards of what?"

"It's a long story."

"Try and make it as short as you can. I'm running late."

"For what?"

"For everything."

"Okay, Sissy, but it's a secret. Matthew Lester knows a man who invented some kind of computer chip." Tab's sapphire eyes glittered like sequins. "You have no idea what the chip can do."

I bet you have no idea either, she thought. "Stop calling me Sissy," she said.

"It's just what the doctor ordered, a perfect, no-risk investment. I can't fail. I mean, *it* can't fail."

"How do you know Matthew Lester?"

"He's the friend of a friend. Not the friend who likes rap music. Another friend."

"Tab, you're making my head spin." She remembered the appointment book. "Okay, where and why did Matthew Lester meet with you?"

"In his office, and the why is because he wanted to make sure we were really, truly committed."

"We?"

"Nico and me."

"Nico and I," she automatically corrected. "Wait a sec. What's Nico's last name?"

"Something Russian, hard to pronounce. I met him the summer I waited tables. We had a . . . relationship. He's bi. Last month I ran into him again at—"

"Uncle Vinnie's Gourmet Italian Restaurant."

"Yes! How'd you know that?"

"Nico is a common nickname for Nicholas," she said, sidestepping Tab's question. "Well, I suppose Nick is even more conventional, but Nico would be more Russian."

"Huh?"

"Never mind, that's not important." Actually, it *was* important, because Ellie had a gut feeling that Nico Something Russian was somehow, in some way, responsible for the death of Sara Lee.

Should she tell Tab about Matthew Lester's untimely demise?

Tonight's news would have the story, she justified. It wouldn't be as big a human-interest story as Sara Lee's murder, and unless he had managed to contact Rachel, Peter would probably do one of his "the name has not been released pending notification of the family" bits, but Tab, with all his faults, was *Ellie's* family, and he deserved to know.

"Tab, I'm sincerely sorry, but Matthew Lester is dead."

"He is not!"

"He is too. Why would I make something like that up?"

"Because Mom likes me best."

"Are you saying I drove all the way out here to lie to you about the death of a man I didn't even know for sure you knew?"

"You knew I knew him. You knew I knew him as soon as I said maybe."

"Tab, listen to me. I'm dog-sitting Matthew Lester's border collie while his wife is out of town. The dog's special-formula food was missing and I went to Lester's house to look for it. The house was wide open and Matthew was missing, too, and Peter called and told me he was dead."

There, she thought. *I relayed the news without giving away any details. Peter would be so proud.*

Peter would be so pissed.

"Peter?" Tab's brow wrinkled.

"Lieutenant Peter Miller."

"Your cop?"

"Stop calling him *my* cop!"

"I thought his name was Paul."

"Mom thinks his name is Paul. I'm really, truly sorry, Tab, but at least you didn't invest any money in Matthew's—"

"Yes, I did." He stood up and began to prowl around the kitchen. Other people paced. Tab prowled. With his streaked hair, he looked like a caged tiger.

She had been about to say "Matthew's *scam*," but she swallowed the four-letter word along with another four-letter word. Instead, she said, "How much did you invest?"

"Five thousand. It was a down payment to show we were seriously committed, Nico and me. The total amount is twenty-five thousand."

"Where the bloody hell would you get twenty-five thousand dollars?"

"From Grandma Shirley. She can't live much longer."

"Grandma Shirley will outlive us all," Ellie said, so angry she wanted to spit. "And anyway, *this* fiancé might be *the* one, and if so, he'll inherit. Where did you get the five thousand?"

"From Mom," Tab said, his lower lip trembling.

"Damn it, Tab, did it ever occur to you that Matthew might be pulling some kind of con?"

"No, he wasn't."

"And you know this because . . . ?"

"I know this *for a fact* because he called the other day and said *not* to invest any more money. He said Nico was cheating. Matt wouldn't have said that if he was trying to con me."

"How was Nico cheating?"

"Matt didn't say and I didn't ask."

Was Sara Lee part of the investment scheme? She worked with Nico. Did she discover that he was cheating, whatever that means? Did he kill her to shut her up? Did he then kill Matthew Lester to shut him up?

Tears were pouring down Tab's face. "Aw, sweetie," Ellie said. "Don't cry."

"You can't possibly understand, Sissy. This investment was my very last chance. It couldn't fail. And I *hate* Nelly Furtado!"

"Stop crying, Tabby. Blow your nose. I hear Mom's car pulling into the driveway. I'm sure you'll figure out what to do, and I'm sorry to be the bearer of bad news, but I really have to go."

She stood up, spilling the cats from her lap. They both yowled cuss words in Siamese, and she willed herself not to walk over to the cabinet where she knew her mother kept a box of Hershey bars.

"Wait, Sis . . . Ellie! Can't your cop . . . can't Paul track down the computer-chip guy by looking through Matt's personal papers or E-mails or something?"

She didn't say maybe, which would have meant yes. "My cop's name is Peter, and I'll ask him," she said, watching her brother prowl again. "Hey, Tab, not to change the subject or anything, but who does your hair?"

"My hair?" He stopped mid-stride and patted his head. "A stylist named Raymond, only I call him Raoul."

"But Raoul is French for *Ralph,* not Raymond."

"So what? He doesn't care as long as I put a humongous tip on my credit card."

"Mom's credit card," she snapped, but Tab wasn't listening.

"Raoul is a bit of a dickhead," he continued, "and much too effete for *my* taste, but when it comes to hair, he's an artist. His salon is in the same strip mall as Uncle Vinnie's Gourmet Italian Restaurant, a video store, and the Merry-Go-Round consignment shop. Why?"

"You're looking good, Tabby," she said, paraphrasing the lyrics from "Hello, Dolly!" Ever since her Sara Lee/Louis Armstrong dream, the song had persistently invaded the right hemisphere of her brain.

She left her brother standing in the kitchen, still patting his head. She wondered if he even knew he was doing it. Maybe the repetitive motion helped him think, although she knew he'd weasel his way out of this jam, just as he had weaseled his way out of every other jam. If nothing else, Tab was as resilient as a dribbled basketball.

NINETEEN

She met her mother on the way out. "Hi, Mom. Bye, Mom."

"Hold your horses, Ellie. Where do you think you're going, and what are you doing here?"

I'm selling Girl Scout cookies, she thought sarcastically . . . and childishly.

She had a feeling *I just happened to be in the neighborhood* wouldn't fly, either.

"I stopped by to see Tab," she said.

"Why?"

"A friend taught him how to download music from the computer," she improvised, digging inside her purse for her bottle of water, "so I thought I'd ask him to make me a CD of Nelly Furtado's 'Promiscuous.' For Jonina."

"Paul's niece?"

"*Peter's* niece, yes." Damn! Mom blocked the doorway, and there was no way to get out without physically pushing her aside.

"She's a nice girl, that Joanna."

"Jonina."

"What kind of a name is Jonina? You must have misunderstood."

"Mom, I spent ten days on a dude ranch with Jonina. How could I misunderstand?"

"Now a name like Oprah, that's very unusual, but I swear to God it's from the Bible. I looked it up and it means deer."

"I think it means fawn, Mom."

"Fawn, deer, what's the difference? Speaking of Oprah, there was a new red-hat lady at my book club today—we're reading one of Oprah's picks—and when I told her how old I was she didn't believe me. You should have seen the look on her face. I thought she'd faint dead away."

It was Ellie's cue line. "You don't look a day over fifty, Mom," she said. *Which means you gave birth to me when you were nine.*

"Clean living, Ellie, that's what it is. I have never smoked, except for a couple of puffs of a Kent filtered cigarette, behind the high school with Ronny Sourdellia. He double-dared me, so I took two puffs and coughed up a lung. I've never touched a drop of hard liquor, either, except . . ." She paused, blushing.

Except for the night you got rip-roaring drunk and conceived me. Daddy told me all about it.

"Except for the half glass of champagne I drank at my wedding. But champagne is wine, not hard liquor, so it doesn't count."

Ellie heard but didn't hear her mom's champagne comment.

However, she had heard her mom's cigarette commentary loud and clear.

Cigarette butts, she mused. *If Sara Lee was taking a smoke break, there'd be cigarette butts in an alley ashtray or on the ground.*

Could the cops DNA the butts? Of course they could. Unless a smoker used a Holly Golightly cigarette holder, it was virtually impossible to smoke without getting some spit on the butt. But what would DNA prove? If Nico Something Russian was the killer, and if he smoked, there'd be no way to tell when his butt landed near Sara Lee. But what if Nico Something Russian wasn't the murderer? What if—

"You're not listening, Ellie."

"Sure I am, Mom." She nodded toward the back of the house and began to palm her ears, then remembered the water bottle and dropped her hands. "It's just that Tab's rap song is a bit overwhelming."

"Tab has this friend and she likes that awful music. Tab plays it so loud you can hardly hear yourself think. But do I complain? No. It's a mother's duty to make her children happy, and anyway it's about time Tab found himself a steady girlfriend. Why, only this morning I was e-mailing your grandmother Shirley and telling her about Tab's new girl—"

"Sorry to interrupt you, Mom, but I've got to go."

"Potty?"

"No. Home."

"Why don't you stay a little while, Ellie? Yesterday I baked a rhubarb pie with that new diet sugar they advertise on TV. You're not the only one who watches her figure." She patted down her lanky body, clothed in an orange wool dress, accessorized by a ghastly necklace whose center stone looked as if it would ward off a pack of demons. As she patted, her bracelets, one for each cat, clinked noisily. "So I'll put up a pot of decaf, we'll have pie and coffee, and I'll show you some of the things I bought on eBay for almost nothing."

"I wish I could, Mom, but I have to stop at a pet shop on my way home and I'm running late."

"A pet shop?"

"Yes. I need to buy some dog food."

"You mean cat food."

"No. I mean dog food."

"You have a dog?"

"Not really. I'm dog-sitting for a friend. You should have seen Jackie Robinson. At first he just stared—"

"Oh my God!" She sneezed. "How dare you come into my house with dog hair all over your face and clothes? You know I'm allergic."

Ellie listened to her mother sneeze three more times. "I don't think I have dog hair on my face, Mom. For one thing, I never kissed—"

"Get out! And don't come here again until you've showered and washed your clothes and . . . and disinfected your house!"

Ellie bit back several retorts, including "Tab can't pay you the five thousand dollars he owes you!" Opening the front door, she stepped outside. Nora and Danielle slithered out behind her.

The two beige and brown cats joined Maggie, Victoria, Lorna Ann and Marty Blue on the stoop steps. Ellie stomped across the stoop and down the steps like a West Pointer on parade. Miraculously, she didn't step on any tails.

She walked up the path, swung open the fence gate, swung the gate closed, and slid behind her Honda's steering wheel.

She needed to shrug off her mother and brother.

She needed to ease her racing heartbeat.

She needed to slow her pulse rate down to something that was more akin to a fifteen-minute gym workout than a footrace with a locomotive.

Then, calmly and rationally, she needed to figure out what she had learned from Tab and do a "save" in her head.

Unfortunately, she had learned very little.

Tab had been involved in some sort of investment deal, or investment scam. Another investor was Nico Something Russian, who waited tables at Uncle Vinnie's Gourmet Italian Restaurant. A third investor was the recently deceased Matthew Dillon Lester.

Or had Matthew merely been the middleman?

And if he had, what did that have to do with Sara Lee?

There was an excellent possibility, more a probability, that both Nico and Matthew had enjoyed brief, or not-so-brief, affairs with Sara Lee. Which could, or could not, be tied to her murder.

But the most important part of the discussion with her brother was that he had been told, by Matthew, to stop investing more money because Nico was "cheating." If Nico knew about that stipulation, it gave him the perfect motive for killing Matthew.

On the other hand, if Matthew had been eighty-sixed while Nico was working the dinner shift at Uncle Vinnie's, Nico had an ironclad alibi. He couldn't have visited Matthew's home unless he had been—what was the word Tab had used during his waiter days, the one that always reminded Ellie of *Star Trek*?

Oh, yeah, "phased," short for "phased out." Nico couldn't have killed Matthew unless he had been *phased* early. Or Matthew had been killed much later. Come to think of it, Peter had never actually given her a time of death.

Of course, the waiting tables alibi wouldn't fly if Nico had killed Sara Lee during or immediately following their lunch shift. Were there *two* murderers lurking? That seemed excessive.

Damn, damn, damn! Ellie had meant to ask Tab about Angel Pitt. Peter had said Angel Pitt spent the evening, or night, with Trent Zachariah, but what did her cell phone number on Matthew's calendar imply? It seemed far too coincidental that Angel Pitt would hook up with both Trent and Matthew, even if she *was* a "lady of the night." Perhaps she was a high-priced call girl who had saved enough money to invest in the miraculous computer chip. Perhaps she had nothing whatsoever to do with the chip and merely wanted to buy some investment property.

Speaking of which, Matthew's demise could have zilch to do with an investment scam or with Sara Lee's strangling. Considering the Matthew Dillon Lester agent-of-the-month plaques on the real estate office wall, his murder could very well have been committed—or commissioned—by a zealous, jealous real estate broker.

Ellie felt sorry for Rachel, and she'd be available if the poor woman needed a shoulder to cry on, but she didn't want to focus on Matthew's murder. Peter could unravel that tangled web.

All she wanted to do was find out why everybody didn't like Sara Lee.

TWENTY

Rachel wanted to get back to Kurt's manuscript, so she was more relieved than disappointed when he said he had to drive to Colorado Springs "on business" and wouldn't be back until after dark. While there, he would replenish their food supplies. Did she want him to shop for anything special? Fresh-baked bread, her favorite wine, chocolate-covered cherries?

She shuddered at the word cherries, and felt her hand curl. Thrusting her hand behind her back, she straightened her fingers one by one, then kept her hand rigid, praying it wouldn't curl again, even though she knew her prayers were a waste of time. She was an adulterous. She had sinned on the floor, sinned on the comfy feather mattress, and even worse, she wasn't the least bit repentant. To be perfectly honest, she fully intended to repeat yesterday's performance, assuming Kurt wanted an encore. He had been a tender, responsive lover, crooning endearments, even teaching her how to intensify her own pleasure and his, but she had no idea what he really thought.

Any groceries he bought would be fine, she said. However, she wanted to pay her share of the grocery bill. He said they would "settle up" when she left the cabin for good, since he wanted to pay her the standard "reader's fee" for *Dream Angel*. With a grin, he said that Ava would "guard her" while he was gone.

Then he sat on the couch-pew to tug on his cowboy boots. Leaning sideways, he picked up a few of the books she'd placed

140

on top of Margee's carton. He began to flip through them, looking at the covers, but stopped short to lean over again and, this time, peer more closely at the carton's address label. "You didn't tell me your last name was Lester," he finally said, his voice accusatory.

"You didn't ask," she replied. "When I told you my name was Rachel, you never—"

"Are you the wife of Matthew Lester?"

"Yes. Why do you look so upset, so . . . angry? Kurt, are you mad at me?"

"Of course not."

"Yes, you are. How do you know Matthew?" When he didn't respond right away, she blinked back a few unbidden tears and said, "Please tell me."

"Don't cry, Rachel. My reaction just now has nothing to do with you and everything to do with my ex-wife."

"Your ex-wife," she repeated.

"Before she was my ex, Lorna decided we should buy a couple of acres in Black Forest or Woodland Park. Her strategy was to find a house for sale—with everything she wanted, including a sauna—or we'd build our own. That's how she met your husband."

"Oh, no."

"Oh, yes. She fell madly in love with him. I take it he looks like Richard Gere."

Rachel nodded.

"Lorna always had a thing for Richard Gere."

"Kurt, I'm so sorry."

"Why? It's not your fault. Some people don't honor their vows . . ." He shrugged. "To make a long story short, Lorna asked for a divorce. We had no kids and she didn't want Ava and the cats, so the divorce didn't take very long. She was convinced Lester would marry her, but it turned out he was just

141

stringing her along. She tried to commit suicide—"

"Oh my God!"

"Since then, she's had counseling and rebuilt her life, but it was touch and go for a while."

"Do you hate her, Kurt?"

"I'd be lying if I said no. But I hate your husband even more." He stood and stretched. "Rachel, let me ask you a question. Do you think the ends justify the means?"

She pictured a mean-spirited nun rapping knuckles with a ruler so that her students would learn respect and religion. "No, not always." She pictured Jonah Feldman in his office, talking about her lawsuit. "Yes, sometimes."

"A definite maybe," Kurt said with a tender smile.

"Let me ask *you* a question, Kurt. Do you always honor your vows?"

"Yes," he replied with no hesitation at all. Gently grasping her by the shoulders, he stared into her eyes. "My father believed one's word was the measure of a man, so I was brought up to *always*, without exception, honor my commitments."

He sealed his declaration with a kiss. Then he put on his jacket and cowboy hat, grabbed a pair of black leather gloves, and opened the door. "Stay, Ava," he said to the dog, standing attentively at the doorway and looking hopeful.

Rachel shoved the story about Kurt's ex-wife and Matthew to the back of her mind. Instead, she poured herself a steaming-hot cup of tea, settled herself at the kitchen table, and returned to Kurt's manuscript.

She read how *Tante* Bernadine had placed a notice about Angelique's pending marriage on the society page of the newspaper. Sean, thinking Angelique was irrevocably lost to him, assembled performers and traveled throughout the country with his own circus. Angelique escaped from her aunt's house and, upon learning that Sean had left New York City, decided to follow his trail. Thanks to Charity Barnum, Angelique joined Jenny Lind's entourage, but Angelique often wondered if she wouldn't have been better off setting out on her own. Jenny was spiritual and devout, but she hated thanking people, disliked staying at a table after she'd finished eating, was wracked with headaches and rheumatism, and plugged up her ears with wool stoppers at night to "shut out the noise of the world." Angelique knew that as the tour progressed, Jenny was growing increasingly distrustful of Monsieur Barnum.

Then Angelique learned that *Tante* Bernadine had been murdered in her billiards room and the only eye witnesses were her seven cats. No matter how hard she tried, Angelique couldn't mourn her aunt's death, but when she read in the newspaper that she was a prime suspect and the police were searching high and low for her, she knew it was even more imperative that she find Sean and join his circus. As a circus performer, she could fade into the background.

Sean was her lifeline. He could protect her. If not, God help her.

Rachel looked up at the ceiling. Kurt was her lifeline. He could protect her. If not, God help her.

TWENTY-ONE

As Ellie drove west, away from her mom's house, she saw low-hanging clouds, so low that the tops of the mountains looked like a Willie Wonka industrial assembly line doughnut machine. Every mountaintop pierced a hole in a cloud, and the only thing the scene needed was Lucy and Ethel, to stand on the assembly line and scoop up the cloud doughnuts when the wind's velocity intensified. Granted, the candy factory chocolates on the classic *I Love Lucy* show were much smaller, but—

Ellie wished she had a camera.

Ellie wished she had decent windshield wipers!

Because a thunderstorm was on its way and the perforated doughnut clouds would soon transform themselves into gigantic showerheads, plumbed with no drains and only one tap handle: COLD.

She desperately needed to pick up some dog food for Scout, and she supposed she could stop at a gas station along the way to buy new windshield wipers at a vastly inflated price, but her other option was to head straight home and outrace what was sure to be a *very loud* gully-washer.

Jackie Robinson wasn't fond of thunder. As a Colorado cat he had to deal with it, but what about Scout? In new surroundings, without her beloved human—essentially, without any human at all—would the dog freak out?

One of Ellie's diet club members, Ingrid Beaumont, owned a dog named Hitchcock, part Great Dane, part Labrador retriever, and, according to Ingrid, "as big as Marmaduke." At a Weight Winners meeting, Ingrid told a funny story about how Hitchcock was so scared of thunder, he'd eat anything he could wrap his jaws around until the storm blew over. On a particularly stormy night, when the thunder sounded like the clash of nearby cymbals, Hitchcock ate a partially defrosted pork roast, a key to Ingrid's rolltop desk, and before she could stop him, the TV remote. At least he had *tried* to eat the remote, but only managed to swallow a couple of triple-A batteries.

Scout was a medium-size dog, smaller than the celebrated Lassie.

With that thought, Ellie realized she had already made up her mind. She would drive home. If the storm clouds had not dispersed by the time Reigning Cats & Dogs closed for the day, she'd stick some frozen hamburger meat in the microwave to thaw, add a raw egg, a few squirts of teriyaki sauce, a few shakes of garlic powder, and a small amount of hand-crushed saltine crackers, to absorb the egg. Then she'd cook up some hamburgers. In fact, she'd call her improvised recipe "Scout Burgers."

The ride home from her mother's house ordinarily took twenty-five minutes, fifteen if she used the interstate. An hour later, Ellie parked in her driveway. As she untensed her hands, legs and shoulders, she uttered a sigh of relief. Traffic had been horrendous, and raindrops had pelted her car like colorless M&Ms shot from a BB gun. At every red light and stop sign, she had retrieved the towel she kept under her seat and swished it across the windshield above her dashboard. At one stop sign, the driver in the car behind her had blared his horn so incessantly, she had been tempted to get out of her car, walk over to his car, and say, "You honked?" And the first thing on her to-do list was the purchase of new windshield wipers—before she even made another futile attempt to solve Sara Lee's murder.

At least the rain had slowed to a drizzle, but the sky looked untrustworthy.

She collected her mail and a new *Big Mouth Shopper* from her mailbox, unlocked the front door, stepped inside, and made her way to the kitchen.

Jackie Robinson, a black wreath on top of his customary chair, gave her his patented shark-yawn, but Scout went berserk. Tail wagged dog as she emitted little whimpers of joy. She tried to find a patch of bare skin to lick, easier when Ellie hunkered down and said, "Sorry I was gone so long, pup. I'll make it up to you with a nice long walk, especially since I seem to have missed my morning jog."

The kitchen retained a lingering trace of yesterday's lasagna sauce. Ellie's stomach growled and she realized that, except for the two Weight Winners breakfast bars, she had skipped breakfast and lunch.

Prioritize, she told herself. *Bathroom, quick snack, walk Scout, call Angel Pitt and set up an appointment, defrost hamburger meat.*

While Angel Pitt might not have anything to do with the recent murders, Ellie wanted to double-check Trent Zachariah's nighttime alibi. She couldn't shake the feeling that Angel Pitt possessed the kind of informal information that would add another piece—even a small, irregularly cut piece—to the jigsaw puzzle that documented Sara Lee's strangulation.

She wanted to get in touch with Rachel, too, but figured she'd touch base with Peter first. She didn't want to be the one to tell Rachel about her husband, especially over the phone, and if that made Ellie Bernstein a gutless wonder, too damn bad.

As she headed toward what her ex-husband called the "downstairs comfort station," she stopped briefly to glance around the living room. Scout's quilt had been lugged across the polished-wood floor, brought to a standstill by an impervious Oriental area rug, but the dog hadn't touched her toys.

Instead, to amuse herself during Ellie's absence, she had found an old leather glove, probably under the couch, and chewed off the fingers. The thumb was still intact.

Perhaps Scout was bored with her old toys. After all, *children* got bored with their old toys.

Ellie paid a quick visit to the bathroom and uttered another sigh of relief. Humming "Hello, Dolly!" she scrubbed her hands and ran a washcloth over her face, paying special attention to the cheek and chin Scout had earnestly licked. Then she opened the front hall closet, in search of new toys.

The hockey stick and baseball bat leaning against the wall at the back of the closet behind sweaters, jackets and her good coat, looked practically new. Much to Tony's disgust, Mick preferred music to sports and would rather spend all his free time playing his guitar and banjo. When Mick was fifteen, Tony had suggested, sarcastically, that he take up ballet. But when Mick calmly said that "learning how to dance like Baryshnikov" might be fun, Tony shut up for good. He'd much rather brag about a son who belonged to a rock group than a son who had joined a ballet troupe. He was deathly afraid Mick would inherit the same family genes that "made Tab gay," and Ellie never *could* convince him that one's sexual penchants weren't inherited. Or contagious.

Critically, she eyed the baseball bat and hockey stick. If Scout chewed too vigorously, the wood might splinter and lodge in her throat like a chicken bone.

The basketball on the top shelf, wedged between an old-fashioned typewriter and a slew of boxed Trivia, Scrabble, Clue and Monopoly games, had distinct possibilities—if she let some of its air out. How on earth did one let the air out of a basketball? A beach ball, easily done, but she couldn't find, much less extricate, the air-hose thingy on the basketball, and she knew she'd break at least three fingernails trying . . . ah, a cylinder filled with fuzzy yellow tennis balls that looked chewable and were too big to lodge in a dog's throat.

She placed a tennis ball in front of Scout, who eyed it as if it were a strange bird, a headless canary minus feathers and feet. Scout sniffed the ball, nudged it with her nose, picked it up in her mouth, cocked her head, and looked at Ellie as if to say, *what do I do now?*

Then, opening her mouth, Scout dropped the ball on the floor and looked at Jackie Robinson, and Ellie could have sworn her cat gave the dog a "dude, you're so dumb" glare.

With the grace of a panther, Jackie Robinson leapt from the couch, pranced over to the ball, and swatted it with one paw.

Ears raised, Scout watched the ball roll a few feet away.

Jackie Robinson swatted it again.

This time Scout gave chase, picked the ball up in her mouth, and deposited it in front of the cat's front paws.

Tempted to watch the ballgame for as long as it lasted, which, Ellie guessed, wouldn't be very long, she tried to remember where she'd last seen her cell phone—the kitchen counter, her good purse, or the fireplace mantel.

Her ring tone eliminated all guesswork—the bookcase!

For her ring tone, Ellie had requested a diet theme. None existed, so she modified her request to food songs. That gave her choices galore. Trying to decide between "Maximum Consumption" by The Kinks and "Peter Percival Patterson's Pet Pig Porky" by The Monkees, in the end, she had chosen The Kingston Trio's "Goober Peas."

"Good girl," Peter said, after she had pressed the TALK button. "You remembered to put your cell phone in your purse. Where are you?"

"At home."

"Good girl," he repeated after a moment of silence. "I'm glad you're safe at home. The teachers went on strike yesterday, which means classes aren't in session, and parents are frantically driving their kids to impromptu babysitters, movie matinees and the mall. There are fender-benders all over the place, thanks to the damn downpour, and your windshield wipers are shot. Please get some new ones ASAP."

"Don't tell me what to do, Peter. As it so happens, I plan to buy new windshield wipers the very next time I go out."

"I'm not telling you what to do, Norrie."

"Good boy," she said sarcastically, and immediately realized she had acquired some leftover causticity from her Tab visit. Changing her tune, she said, "Where are *you*, honey?"

"I just left Trenton Zachariah's house and I'm working my way back to the precinct, but I stopped on the way to pick up a sandwich and coffee."

Scratch a home-cooked dinner together, she thought. "I could have sworn you said Trent Zachariah had an ironclad alibi."

"I did. He does. I'm just tying up loose ends."

"So . . . what loose ends did Trent tie up for you?"

"None. It was a tad difficult to get any information out of him, especially since he's habitually stoical and this afternoon he was half drunk."

"How can you be half drunk? That's like saying someone is half pregnant."

"Point taken. Zachariah was well on his way to comatose. Either he misses his wife's cooking or he's discovered that she had no life insurance. Vincent and Al offer both health and life for their restaurant employees, and Zachariah was positive she had a policy because she *told* him she did."

"Well, there's your motive."

"Sure, if Zachariah hadn't provided us with an ironclad alibi."

"Did you check out the life insurance thing anyway? I mean, Sara Lee could have made someone else the beneficiary, someone who doesn't have an ironclad alibi."

"Of course we did. Turns out the restaurant's policies were expensive, even though Vincent and Al paid half, so she said thanks but no thanks. She was so damn young, Norrie. She probably thought she'd live forever, even though nobody lives . . ." He stopped mid-sentence, perhaps remembering his young fiancée, an undercover cop who had died in the line of duty.

Ellie quickly, and she hoped tactfully, changed the subject. "You said you were on your way to the precinct, Peter. What's at the precinct?"

"Charlene Johnson."

"Oh my God, did *she* kill Matthew Lester?"

"There's no evidence that suggests she had anything to do with his murder, but she was the last person to see him alive, so she agreed to come in for question—"

"Charlene wasn't the last person to see Matthew Lester alive, unless she killed him. If she didn't kill him, the person who killed him was the last person to see Matthew Lester alive."

"My God, Norrie, you sound just like your brother."

"What a horrible thing to say . . ." She paused. "Okay, Peter, how'd you know I saw Tab?"

"You're not the only person who can decipher appointment books and E-mail."

"Holy cow! You got into Matthew's E-mail? I couldn't figure out his password. What was it?"

"Gunsmoke."

"Of course. Matthew Dillon Lester. Matt Dillon, the sheriff . . . or was he the marshal? . . . on *Gunsmoke*. How'd you think of it?"

"I didn't. Jonina did. She's the genius of the family, especially when it comes to computers."

"Your niece is much too young for *Gunsmoke*."

"Very true, unless one is crazy about horses and watches old

Westerns on cable channels."

Ellie smiled. "How is she?"

"Fine. She said to say hi. She called to tell me that she won't be coming down from Denver for a while because she snagged the lead in her high school musical and rehearsals have, in her words, commenced to start."

"That's redundant but typical Jonina-speak. What's the musical?"

"*My Fair Lady,* played on Broadway by Julie . . . um . . ."

"Andrews."

"Andrews, right. And in the movie by Katharine Hepburn."

"Audrey Hepburn."

"I knew that. I was testing you."

"Sure you were. My God, Peter, it's amazing how losing twenty pounds can jumpstart one's self-confidence. I'm so proud of Jonina, and I plan to use her as inspiration for my teen diet club members."

"Jonina wants you to Kevin Bacon Julie and *Audrey,* and last but not least, she wants me to tell you that she uses Dove soap and shampoo because she likes the girls in their ads and she won't buy any other stuff because all the models who use or pretend to use products other than Dove look like anorexic toothpicks. Quote, unquote." Ellie heard the smile in his voice, just before he said, "I've got to go, sweetheart. Damn, my coffee's ice cold! I have no idea what time I'll finish up my paperwork, so I'll probably catch a catnap at my apartment again. I'm really sorry but I'll make it up to you."

"There's nothing to be sorry about, Peter."

He yawned. "Did Tab tell you anything important?"

"Not really. He was downloading songs for his new boyfriend, and he invested in some kind of computer chip that is either the best thing since sliced bread or a total scam. He once waited tables with Nicholas, known to his fellow servers as Nico, the waiter you told me about, who works at Uncle Vinnie's Gourmet Italian Restaurant. Nico also invested in the mind-blowing computer chip. The recently deceased Matthew Lester was supposedly another investor, or the one who put the deal together. Matthew told Tab that Nico was cheating, whatever that means, and Tab hates Nelly Furtado."

"That's basically what he told me, minus the Nelly Furtado morsel. For the record, I think she's drop-dead gorgeous."

"I hope that's a platonic drop-dead gorgeous. Nelly's old enough to be your daughter."

"Low blow, Norrie. What are your plans for tomorrow?"

"I have a Weight Winners meeting at nine a.m." *After which, I'll pick up Scout's dog food and eat lunch at Uncle Vinnie's, where I hope I can grill Nico and get a contact number for Theodora Mallard, the waitress who found Sara Lee's trashed body.*

"Talk to you tomorrow, then." He yawned again. "Love you, Norrie. Will you marry me?"

"Not yet, Peter, and I love you, too."

As she carried her cell phone into the kitchen and placed it on the counter, she wondered how he'd react if he asked her to marry him and she said maybe, which in her dysfunctional family meant yes.

TWENTY-TWO

Jackie Robinson lay on the couch, on his back like a turtle, his furry head thrust forward as he tongue-washed his belly. Ellie envisioned a kitty aerobics class with Jackie Robinson as its group leader.

She glanced fondly at Scout, asleep on her quilt, with a yellow tennis ball between her black paws.

Admittedly, Ellie knew nothing about dogs, but she did know that Scout needed to be walked, and she hoped her phone call to Angel Pitt wouldn't take very long.

What other items were on her mental priority list? Oh, yeah, food.

A pot of leftover chicken and veggie soup, legal Weight Winners fare, sat on the refrigerator's middle shelf. Ellie retrieved the pot and placed it on top of her stove's front burner.

Then she picked up her cell phone, hit TALK, and tapped in the number for Angel's cell phone.

A voice said, " 'I'm no angel but I've spread my wings.' "

"Holy cow, Mae West!" Ellie said, delighted. She had once worked in a library and memorized more offbeat quotes than she could use in a lifetime. " 'I saw the angel in the marble and carved until I set him free,' " she said.

"Michelangelo. Who *is* this?"

"Ellie Bernstein—"

"I don't know you."

Ellie heard a click and a dial tone. She looked at the phone

Denise Dietz

as if it had betrayed her then redialed.

"Friends are kisses blown to us by angels," the same voice said in greeting.

"That's one I don't know." Ellie heard loud noises in the background and a male voice shouted, "Hey, Angel, it's your turn."

"Hold your water, bud," she shouted back. Then, "That quote is my own extract from a poem I wrote. You can use it any time, with accreditation of course."

"Thanks. Is this Angel Pitt?" *Stupid question. Who else could it be?*

"No, it's the tooth fairy." Angel's sarcasm traveled easily through the phone wires. Apparently, she thought Ellie's question a stupid question, too. "Who's this again?"

"Tinkerbelle," Ellie snapped. To her surprise, her mockery spawned a distinct chuckle. "If you have a few minutes," she continued, encouraged, "I'd like to talk to you . . . in person."

"About what?"

"Trenton Zachariah."

"Are you a reporter?"

"No. I'm a diet club leader."

"Where'd you get my phone number?"

"From a calendar."

"Sorry, but you're not making any sense."

"I know. I'm hungry . . . make that ravenous . . . and I've got a dog that needs to go outside very badly and I apologize for bothering you. I'll call again another time."

"Tell you what, Tinkerbelle. I'm playing pool in a bar called Olive or Twist." She gave Ellie the address. "Now, walk your dog!"

"How long will you be there?"

"Until I leave," she said, and Ellie heard a click.

Okay, now what?

Food!

She sniffed but didn't smell soup.

Well, no wonder. She had forgotten to turn the stove on. Damn!

At least that solved another crisis. She wanted to get her butt over to Olive or Twist as soon as she could. She didn't have time to fiddle around with burgers, human or doggie, so she'd pour the homemade soup into Scout's bowl. She only hoped that Scout was a vegetarian as well as a carnivore.

First and foremost, the dog's potty walk.

Ellie placed her thumb and first finger between her teeth and whistled.

As Scout bounded into the kitchen, Ellie's gaze lit upon something she saw every day but hadn't really noticed until now—a cat door, neatly inserted into the kitchen door, leading to the backyard.

Jackie Robinson was a large cat, although a goodly portion of his bulk was fur. On the other hand, quite a bit of Scout's weight was fur. Or, as her mother would say, "hair."

Ellie eyed the cat door, then Scout, then the cat door. It would be a tight squeeze but doable.

Rachel's kitchen didn't have a doggie door. Could Ellie teach Scout a new trick?

She slid her fingers between the dog's neck and collar, led Scout to the cat door, thrust her shaggy head outside, and gently pushed at her backside until she went all the way through. Opening the main door and walking into the yard, Ellie showed Scout how to go back into the kitchen.

It only took a couple of tries before Scout twigged.

"What a smart dog . . . aren't you the clever pup," Ellie crooned, as she poured the chicken and veggie soup from pot to bowl.

Scout lapped up the broth and chowed down the few chicken

bits, but ignored the vegetables, except for the cooked carrots. Then she wriggled her way through the cat door again.

Ellie quickly changed into a pair of black jeans and the Tinkerbelle sweater Grandma Shirley had bought at Disneyland—a birthday gift for Ellie when she turned thirteen. "If you really, truly believe," Grandma Shirley had said, "you can do *anything*. You can even fly without wings. All it takes is desire and imagination . . . and a few flying lessons wouldn't hurt." She had thoughtfully and kindly given Ellie an adult size large, which fit her back then and fit her even better now.

Ellie admired Tinkerbelle in the mirror. Then, perched on the edge of her bed, she double-knotted the laces on her sneakers.

Although she hated snobs, and emphatically did *not* want to behave like one, the Olive or Twist was located in a far less affluent neighborhood than she ordinarily frequented, so Ellie decided to leave her purse at home. She thrust some money and her driver's license into her jeans pocket, zipped up her Broncos jacket and grabbed her car keys. Humming "Hello, Dolly!" she sped toward the front door.

She was off to see, not the wizard, but a "lady of the night" who wrote poetry, quoted Mae West, and right off the bat recognized a Michelangelo quote.

Ellie stopped humming as she felt her mouth stretch in what Peter called her pumpkin grin. Even though snooping was a serious business, if taken seriously, which of course she did, she had a feeling she might have some fun tonight.

Speaking of Peter, should she leave a note for him, just in case he changed his mind and came home?

No! She was in a hurry and, anyway, she didn't have to report her every move to Peter. He might be a trifle chauvinistic but he wasn't unreasonable.

Except when you're playing Ellie Bernstein, mature girl detective, and putting yourself in danger, said a little voice inside her head.

When she did that, Peter could be unreasonably unreasonable.

But, she justified, she'd only be gone a couple of hours, or as long as it took to ask a few simple questions. She'd be inside a bar-slash-pool hall, surrounded by other people, also known as witnesses, and if Angel Pitt looked and sounded like Jason's mommy in *Friday the 13th,* or was delicately digging out the dirt from underneath her fingernails with a switchblade, Ellie would say she had to go to the restroom and, in Peter-speak, skedaddle out of there.

For some reason she couldn't fathom, she was unable to dismiss the notion that Angel was a call girl, even though she had very little to base that supposition on. An evening with Trent in his underpants and a mention on Matthew's calendar did not a call girl make, not even on a TV detective show where suppositions just about always paid off. Of course, TV shows had *writers* to connect the coincidental dots.

Even though sleuthing was her compulsion, what Peter called her addiction, and even though it was the one part inspiration rather than two parts perspiration that turned her on, right now, this very minute, she wished she had a writer-in-residence, a rational scribe named, oh, say Agatha or Sir Arthur Conan, who'd connect her cerebral dots into a workable script.

On her way to the Olive or Twist, she stopped at a gas station and bought some vastly overpriced windshield wipers.

TWENTY-THREE

Nicholas Vladimir Nureyev called in sick. It was the first time he had ever called in sick. Waiters didn't get sick pay and guests didn't leave tips for waiters who weren't there to serve them.

One of the most important RULES at Uncle Vinnie's Gourmet Italian Restaurant was COVER YOUR SHIFT, but Al said not to worry about it. He said that something must be "going around" because the hostess Michelle, that tall, thin girl everyone called Micki, was a no-show. Not only that, but she hadn't called in, which was a firing offense, except they were so short-staffed, he would just write her up. *As a warning,* Al said in a voice that made Nico want to hide in the corner and cover his ears with his hands. Then Al said if he couldn't get Nico's shift covered at the last minute, he'd work it himself.

Nico wished Al hadn't said "at the last minute." That was nasty, not that Nico gave a rat's ass. He couldn't have worked tonight's shift if his life depended on it. His eyes were bloodshot, his legs felt like Jell-O, and his throat was raw from puking. Even the mousse in his hair had let him down.

He'd probably caught whatever was "going around" from Micki Mouse—a flu bug or a stomach virus or mad cow disease.

He winced when he pictured her sprawled across his king-size bed, her black uniform pants down around her ankles, her eyes shut, her wicked tongue tucked away inside her slack, drooling mouth.

She had wanted him, he had been right about that, but for

158

the life of him, he couldn't remember if they had done it or—

Oh, God! Nico groaned. He had to throw up again, but there was nothing left in his stomach.

Al had said to lie down and get some rest, so Nico lay on the couch with a couple of overstuffed pillows under his head. He turned on the TV and surfed to a cable channel that televised reruns of quiz shows and reality shows. Kelly or Lois, or maybe Sara Lee, had said that a "reality rerun" was an oxymoron, and then she and the others had laughed their fool heads off. But Nico didn't know what oxymoron meant, so he didn't get the friggin' joke.

Wasn't an ox one of those cow-like animals with horns and a snotty nose? Moron meant stupid. As a kid he had been called moron more than once, so there was no guesswork there. But why would Kelly—or Lois or Sara Lee—call a reality TV show a stupid ox?

There was nothing else on TV that interested him, so he watched some rerun about some unmarried guy picking some girl he had never met before to be his wife. The guy had a lot of girls to choose from and they were all blondes, except for one girl, and they all had the same hairdo, long but not too long, and they all had big boobs or wore push-up bras; Nico prided himself on being able to tell the difference. The unmarried guy, who looked like he used the same mousse Nico used, cried like a friggin' baby about how hard it was to choose only one girl and how he didn't want to hurt anybody's feelings.

It wouldn't have been hard for Nico to choose. He'd have picked the dark-haired girl, who didn't wear a push-up bra. But he would have insisted she streak her hair, and he wouldn't have taken no for an answer. Blonde-streaked hair was such a turn-on.

Then, to his horror, the TV screen changed to a blood-and-guts movie, and the really scary thing was that Nico didn't remember pressing the button on the clicker to change the channel.

He hated violence, had always hated violence, so he squeezed his eyes shut, and when he opened them again, the guy who wanted a wife was standing in front of a table and holding a red rose. Behind him, on top of the table, were more red roses, but then the red roses, for no reason, began to *bleed,* so Nico picked up the clicker and tried to find the Disney Channel.

Damn, he couldn't remember the number of the Disney Channel, and he had hundreds of channels and the friggin' blood-and-guts movie was back on his friggin' screen.

With a shaky hand, Nico turned off the TV and reached beneath a couch cushion for one of his comic books. He hid his comic books under the bed and under couch cushions, just in case friends visited his apartment. His comic books were all about Spiderman and Captain Marvel and Sonic the Hedgehog, and he didn't want his friends to make fun of him. He had placed a copy of *The Godfather* on the small table next to his couch, and he liked to tell people it was his favorite book, even if he'd never read it. He had seen the movie on TV, though, and the first time he saw it he'd been surprised and sickened by the scene with the horse's head in the director's bed—*all that blood*—and he'd puked his guts out. But now he was ready when that scene came up and he closed his eyes. He closed his eyes when they shot Sonny, too.

After watching the movie the first time, he'd written a book report on *The Godfather,* pretending he had read the book, and his teacher gave him a B. It was the only B he'd ever gotten in school. He wanted to frame the book report with the big red B, but he dropped it on the way home from school and when he retraced his steps, he couldn't find it.

He had learned some of the lines from the movie, like "Leave the gun, take the cannoli" and "I'll make him an offer he can't refuse." He especially liked it when Marlon Brando said "I'm drinking more," and Al Pachinko—was that his name?—said, "It's good for you, Pop."

Nico had given his father some Chianti and said "It's good for you, Pop," only he had doctored his father's wine first, and later that night his father died, and suddenly there was no more *thick as two short planks* bullshit!

He had said it to Micki, too. He had said, "Drink some more wine, pretty M-Lo. It's good for you," and she had said "Huh?" So he changed it to "Drink some more vodka, it's good for you." Talk about thick as two short planks!

Nico had never made believe he was school-smart, but he liked to think of himself as street-smart, and he double-damn well knew what *that* meant.

It meant he drove a car good.

Twenty-Four

After a delicious dinner of Thai takeout, Rachel leaned back in her chair and said, "My mother always insisted that if a man strayed, it was his wife's fault, that she had done something to make him unhappy, or hadn't tried hard enough to make him happy, which I guess is the same thing. So when Matthew strayed, I figured I hadn't satisfied him." She felt her cheeks bake. "You know . . . in bed."

"I have no complaints," Kurt said with a grin. "Did your father stray?"

"Oh, I doubt it. I don't think my parents were into sex, except for breeding purposes, but my father was a very religious man. He'd never bend much less break his marriage vows. My mother was extremely religious, too. And yet she had one so-called vice. Movie magazines. We were dreadfully poor, but she'd save a penny here, a nickel there, and buy the latest *Photoplay* or *Movie Mirror* or *Look*. Oh, and *Screen Stories;* that was the magazine she liked best. She copied hairstyles and she sewed dresses—out of scrap material—that looked exactly like the gowns her favorite stars wore, and she thought movie stars who got divorced were horrible. The only time I ever heard her use foul language was when she lay dying and she ranted on and on about Eddie Fisher dumping Debbie Reynolds for Elizabeth Taylor. My mother adored Debbie Reynolds."

"Your mother cussed out Eddie Fisher on her deathbed?"

Rachel nodded. "Sandra Dee got a mention, too."

"Because she divorced Bobby Darrin?"

"No. Because she starred in the Tammy sequels. My mother thought Sandra Dee stole the part from Debbie Reynolds, the original Tammy, the one and only Tammy, the 'just think, that same moon that's shinin' down on me, is shinin' down on Pete's tomatoes' Tammy."

" 'The ole hooty-owl hooty hoos to the dove' Tammy?"

"Yes! Oh my gosh! How—"

"Good ole Tammy, I remember her well. I dated her in college. She majored in ornithology, minored in botany."

"Oh, you!" Rachel giggled, then realized she couldn't remember the last time she had giggled.

"Tell me more about your mother, Rachel. I find her fascinating."

"You do? To me, she was scary. When I was a teenager, she cited Spencer Tracy as the perfect paradigm of a real man. He was in love with Katharine Hepburn but wouldn't leave his wife for her because he was a good Catholic."

"Does that mean you wouldn't leave your husband for me?"

"Do you *want* me to leave my husband for you?"

"I'd like you to consider it."

She thought *okay* but blurted, "Why?"

"What do you mean, why? You're pretty, you're funny, you're smart, and you like my books."

"I don't like your books, Kurt."

"You don't?"

"No," she said with a grin. "I love your books."

"And," he added, "I feel responsible for you."

"Responsible?"

"Absolutely." He paused. "Didn't you ask me to *protect* you when we first met?"

He said it lightly, but Rachel had a feeling he'd meant something else. What else *could* he mean? He had gone to

Colorado Springs today on business. What kind of business? The kind of business that was none of her business?

"Tell you what," he said, walking toward the kitchen. "You deserve a reward for sticking with my book all day, so I'm going to make you a very special dessert."

Again, the blithe tone. Well, two could play that game. "Something Gordon?" she asked, making sure her voice sounded happy-go-lucky.

"You bet."

"Can I help?"

"No, thanks. I want it to be a surprise." He opened a drawer underneath the silverware drawer and pulled out a red rubber ball. "This belongs to Sydney, Cee-Cee's Australian shepherd," he said. "You've been cooped up in the cabin all day, so why don't you go outside with Ava and play drool all over the ball? Seriously, Ava loves to chase balls, and you can watch the sunset at the same time. Up here in the mountains, sunsets are stunningly spectacular."

He tossed her the ball. She caught it with her good hand. "Okay, Kurt," she said. "I could probably use some fresh air."

But before she breathed fresh air or watched a stunning sunset, she wanted to call Ellie and check up on Scout, and maybe find out if there was anything . . . unusual . . . happening in Colorado Springs. For the first time since she'd met Kurt, she felt completely isolated.

She picked up her cell phone.

No dial tone.

The cabin's phone was dead, too.

TWENTY-FIVE

Peter had once told Ellie that she had five and a half senses. Sight, hearing, taste, touch, smell, and more smell.

Unfortunately, she was the recipient of a super-sensitive nose. Strong perfumes made her eyes water, hairspray made her sinuses clog up, scented soaps and laundry detergents were a smidgen away from cloying, and she could always tell if milk had soured before she even opened the refrigerator door. While her sense of smell was above average, she had read somewhere that the average human being was able to recognize approximately 10,000 different smells.

And tonight they had all congregated at the Olive or Twist.

Mesmerized, Ellie looked around. The room that housed the bar was small—*compared to what?* Compared to her usual haunt, The Dew Drop Inn. The only time its owner, Charley Aaronson, had broken fire laws was when he'd thrown a "Mash Bash" during the televised *M*A*S*H* finale.

The Olive or Twist was doubtless breaking fire laws left and right, filled to the rafters with local patrons—most of whom were greeted by name—and karaoke enthusiasts. Several amateur singers and their supporters were crammed—four, five, even six bodies deep—into wooden booths with thinly padded, faux-leather seats. The PA system was silent, the video screens were blank, and the karaoke host—one SANDI PONTIUS, according to a huge sign—wasn't due for another two hours, but it appeared that the vocalists followed a "first come, first sing" honor system and woe to the singer who broke that code. In this neighborhood, a slashed vocal cord would probably be the least of his or her problems. The sign also boasted KAMIKAZE KARAOKE, whatever that meant.

Hair colors ranged from brown to iridescent green. Ages ranged from very young to very old. Clothing varied from miniskirts to coveralls and muddy work boots. Ellie had shrugged off her jacket and slung it over her arm, but even in her funky Tinkerbelle sweater, she didn't feel the least bit self-conscious—until people started bumping into her and/or rudely shoving her out of the way.

A man with a mullet hairdo said, "Are you lost?" and she realized she hadn't moved left, right or forward since she'd entered the bar, most likely because she had no idea what Angel Pitt looked like.

Wings, she thought incoherently. *An angel has wings.*

Then she remembered that the human Angel had said she was playing pool.

"Where's the pool hall?" she asked the man with the mullet hairdo.

He stared at her as if *she* had sprouted wings, then pointed to a doorway that didn't have a door.

With any luck, Ellie thought, the majority of pool playing participants would be men, which would make her search for a woman a lot easier. And in a pinch, she could always tie a scarf over her eyes and play Blindman's Bluff.

Except she didn't have a scarf, so she simply strolled into a room that wasn't, by any stretch of the imagination, a hall. There were a few pool tables, a dozen or so men, two women, and 5,000 rather than 10,000 different smells.

The many odors ranged from stale beer belches and what her mother euphemistically referred to as passed gas, to hair gel, fragrant underarm deodorant, mouthwash, greasy hamburgers,

French fries, onions, jalapenos, and tortilla chips. Ellie could probably name the other four-thousand-eighty-nine smells, except she needed to focus on a woman she had never seen before.

As she remembered, with relief, that bars in Colorado were required by law to serve food, her stomach rumbled so loudly she was afraid everybody would stop what they were doing and look at her.

But the men, like cocks at a birdfeeder, were all crowded around a pool table in the farthest corner, and the two women were approximately twenty feet away from the men. One of the women was asexually skinny. She sat on a metal, three-legged stool and yawned without covering her mouth. She didn't look like an angel. An angel would cover her mouth.

A second woman, a girl really, slumped against the wall. She was very pretty but either vastly overweight or vastly pregnant. Overweight, Ellie guessed. As if to draw attention away from her body, the girl had pierced her eyebrow, one nostril, and her lower lip, all embellished with hoop earrings. She had long blonde hair, half curled, half straight, as if she had waged a campaign against the humidity and lost the battle but not the war. Somehow, she'd squeezed herself into a short white denim skirt, and she wore a scoop neck T-shirt that said I'M PROUD TO BE AN AMERICAN IDOL. The word IDOL had been hand-printed with a black felt-tip pen. "When we gonna leave, Jerry?" she whined loudly.

A voice from the mob of men said, "Shut up, Janice. I got money on this shot."

Strike two, thought Ellie. The girl's name was Janice, and anyway, the voice on the phone had not sounded like a foghorn.

Janice finished the beer in her mug and belched twice. Her face contorted as she turned her head toward the pool table. "Jerry," she said in her loud, hoarse voice. "I don't feel good."

The woman who had yawned with her mouth open slid off her stool and walked over to the belching girl. "Come on, honey," she said. "Let's go to the little girl's room. I'll hold your hair for you."

Ellie was about to follow the two women when she heard cheers and groans, and one of the men shouted, "Angel, you're an angel! You just won me fifty bucks."

The swarm of men parted like the Red Sea and a tall woman strutted away from the pool table. She held a cue stick, and as Ellie watched, she blew on its chalked end as if blowing on the barrel of a smoking gun. She said, "Collect my winnings for me, Jerry," and walked straight toward Ellie. "You must be Tinker-belle," she said, "even though you look much younger on the phone."

Ellie felt her jaw drop before she remembered Grandma Shirley's gift sweater. "I know we haven't officially met, Ms. Pitt, but how, may I ask, can I look much younger on the phone?"

"Well, if you're going to be persnickety about it, you *sound* much younger."

Angel Pitt's ash-blonde and red-streaked hair was butterfly clipped in an untidy ponytail. She wore formfitting jeans and a black T-shirt with white press-on letters that stated: PHILOSO-PHY WILL CLIP AN ANGEL'S WINGS. The letters enhanced her phenomenal Kristin Chenoweth–breasts.

Angel looked *very* familiar. Ellie was certain she'd seen the young woman before, but, just like Matthew Lester's JDCT appointment book notation, recognition teetered on the perimeter of her memory. "John Keats," she said.

"What?" Angel glanced down at her breasts. "Oh, my shirt. Yeah, good ole Keats. Hey, I didn't mean to dump on you with my snarky age remark. It came out wrong. Actually, I'd say you're very well preserved."

"So are you," Ellie replied, guesstimating Angel's age as somewhere between twenty-six and twenty-seven.

"Touché, Tinkerbelle. By the way, what's your real name? You told me but I can't remember."

"Ellie."

"I like Tinkerbelle better. Let's get out of here."

"Sure. Where do you want to go?"

"The bar. I'm dry as a mummy. You ever heard that expression, dry as a mummy?"

"Not since the fourth millennium. Nowadays, it's dry as a bone. I don't think we'll find an empty table in the bar."

"Oh, we'll find a table, don't worry."

"What about the noise?"

"Trust me, after a few minutes it becomes white noise." She led the way to a small table with a piece of folded cardboard on its surface.

"How'd you get them to reserve a table for you?" Ellie asked, reading the cardboard.

"I'm what's known as a recurrent regular. I wouldn't miss karaoke night unless I was on my deathbed, and I tip the wait staff very well. You might even say exorbitantly."

"Do you sing?"

"Yes. You're awfully nosy."

"I prefer the word curious. May I ask what else you do? For a living, I mean."

"You can ask whatever you want, Tinkerbelle, as long as you pay for my drinks."

"Okay," Ellie said, wondering if she'd stuffed enough money into her jeans pocket. She had hoped to order a hamburger or nachos but she hadn't brought a credit card and she didn't want to run short of cash.

As if she had voiced her thoughts out loud, a cocktail waitress placed a bar napkin, a double shot glass, a slice of lime, and a salt shaker in front of Angel. "José Cuervo," the cocktail waitress said. She pointed to the bar. "Jon put the bottle in the freezer this afternoon, knowing you'd be here tonight."

"Thanks, Cher," Angel said. She then sang a few bars of "I've got you, Babe," sounding just like the real Cher.

Ellie stared at the cocktail waitress. "Cher?" she said. "Cher Wilcox?"

"That's my name, don't wear it out. Who're you? Oh my gosh, it's Eleanor Rigby from the Opinion Institute of Nutrition Control!"

How the heck had Cher remembered that? Upon first meeting the woman, Ellie had conjured up the acronym up on the spot, misspelling the word OINK. Cher Wilcox was from Ellie's distant past, if one considered eleven months ago distant. While trying to solve the diet club murders, Ellie had pretended to take a product survey. Cloaked in her pseudonym, she had been searching for men who wore knit stocking caps and Old Spice. "How are you, Cher?"

"Not getting any," she replied with a laugh.

"I need another drink," Angel said. "Could we have less conversation and more service?"

"Sorry, Angel. What'll you have, Miss Rigby?"

"Her name is Tinkerbelle," Angel said.

Ellie said, "I'll have tequila, too, I guess, but please make mine a single shot."

"And I'll have another double." Angel held up her empty glass.

Ellie's gaze went from the glass to Angel's face. She didn't look like a call girl. And at her height, she'd tower above most of her clients. Wouldn't that be a wee bit intimidating, or did men prefer loftier call girls? Ellie's perception of a hooker was Julia Roberts in *Pretty Woman,* and while Julia hadn't exactly *towered* over Richard Gere—

"A teacher," Angel said to Ellie.

"Excuse me?"

"You asked what I did for a living. I'm a teacher, high school English. Now, let me ask you a question. Fair is fair. You said you saw my name and phone number on a calendar. That's not as bad as a restroom wall, but I never, *ever* give out my number to anyone I don't know, so I was wondering—"

"The calendar was a desk calendar. It belonged to Matthew Lester," Ellie interrupted, trying to regain her equilibrium. Angel's schoolteacher bombshell had thrown her for a loop, and wasn't equilibrium sense number six? Sure it was. Sight, smell, taste, touch, hearing and balance.

Angel said, "Who the hell is Matthew Lester?"

"A real estate agent."

"How did he get my name and number?"

"I don't have a clue."

"What's *his* damn number? I'll call and ask him."

"That would be a tad difficult. He's . . . out of touch."

"Out of the country, huh?"

Ellie nodded. *Way out,* she thought. *Way, way out of the country.*

Cher returned and carefully transferred the single and double shot glasses from her tray to the table. Ellie's tequila came with a paper-thin slice of lime and a second salt shaker. Cher hadn't taken very long, but bless her for taking as long as she had. If Angel kept downing double shots double-quick, Ellie would have to write an IOU and leave her car for collateral. "If you don't mind, Cher, I'll pay now, rather than run a tab."

"I don't mind, but these drinks ain't on your tab. The guys over there bought 'em." Cher pointed to a couple of men seated at the bar, who grinned and waved. "And Angel's first drink is always on the house. My boss says she brings in more business than a full-page newspaper ad."

"Well, I can certainly understand why. I was too late to catch her whole pool game, but from the sound of the crowd she made one heck of a phenomenal shot."

"Yeah, some come to watch her play pool . . . right, Angel? . . . but most people come to hear her sing. There's no one as popular as our Angel, except maybe a waitress from that Italian restaurant, Uncle Jimmy's I think it's called. Her name is Farah, or Tara, or Sarah, and she likes to sing 'I Will Always Love You' from that bodyguard movie. Some people say she's a ringer, that she sang professionally with a backup group, but it don't matter. Our Angel can top her with the Leonardo DiCaprio Titanic song."

"She's not a ringer," Angel muttered, then downed her drink with a practiced flick of the wrist.

Ellie wanted to ask how Angel knew that, but held her tongue. Her gut feeling told her it was too early to ask Sara Lee questions.

As Cher headed toward the bar, Angel said, "Is your name really Eleanor Rigby? Were you named for the Beatles' song?"

"No and no. Rigby was an alias . . . it's a long story. Is Angel your real name?"

"It is now. I changed it legally. I was christened Los Angeles."

"You're kidding, right?"

She shook her head, her mahogany, gold and red-streaked ponytail flicking from side to side. "My brother and sisters and I were all named for the cities in which we were born. I have an older sister named Cheyenne and twin sisters, Kenner and Metairie. They lucked out. My baby sister's name is Boca Raton."

"I bet she'll want to change it, like you did yours."

"No, she likes it." Angel gave Ellie an Elvis-lipped smile. "But you didn't come here to talk about names." The smile faded. "Why *did* you come here?"

"Would you believe me if I said I wanted to watch kamikaze karaoke?"

When Angel didn't respond, Ellie decided to use the same strategy she'd used in Matthew Lester's real estate office: tell the truth.

"I thought you were involved with Matthew Lester, who might have been perpetrating some sort of major fraud," she explained. "However, it's obvious you don't even know him, so I guess my second question would be . . ." She paused as she remembered that Peter had said Angel was Trent Zachariah's pal, but opted to ask her question anyway. "What, exactly, is your relationship to Trenton Zachariah?"

For a moment, Angel looked baffled. Then she said, "Trent is my brother."

Twenty-Six

Earlier, Ellie had noted the resemblance—or at the very least, she had thought Angel looked familiar—but now it hit her like an icy snowball in the face. Pictures of Trent Zachariah had flooded the *Denver Post* when he had been traded to the Denver Broncos, when he'd performed for the Broncos, and, especially, when he had been dropped from the team for unnecessary roughness. Only yesterday, after Sara Lee's murder, he had been asked how he felt by the monkey-faced reporter, and a close-up of his face had filled Ellie's flat screen TV.

Ellie habitually memorized team stats. When he played for the Broncos, Trenton Zachariah was six-four and weighed two-hundred-and-thirty pounds. Angel was four, perhaps five inches shorter than her brother, and weighed a hundred pounds less, but mentally blot out the crimson and blonde streaks, and her hair was the same rich brown. And while she wasn't a mirror image, her eyes and mouth were near-as-dammit-identical.

"But your last name is Pitt," Ellie blurted, thinking that was one of the dumber things she'd ever said. As if to prove it, Angel gave her the same "dude, you're so dumb" look Jackie Robinson had bestowed on Scout.

"Zachariah is my maiden name," Angel said. "I divorced my sleazeball of a husband three and a half years ago but decided to keep his name. When my students ask if I'm related to Brad Pitt, I tell them yes. I say if they behave in class, get a passing grade on their exams, and turn their work in on time, my cousin

Brad will pay them a visit at the end of the term. The students go nuts. Brad is the quintessential 'women want to sleep with him, men want to be him' prototype, or maybe a better word would be paragon. That even held true after he left the immensely popular Jennifer for Angelina. Go figure."

"What happens when Brad doesn't show up?"

"Nothing. I ask the kids to keep it a secret from next term's class and they always do."

Ellie wondered if she could get away with saying she was related to Carl Bernstein, but who under the age of forty remembered Watergate?

Cher appeared with a couple more drinks and, again, pointed to the guys at the bar, who, again, smiled and waved. Ellie now had two full shots in front of her. No way would she drink on an empty stomach and then drive home.

Angel nodded toward the bar-guys and said, "They're kind of cute," and Ellie realized that the high school English teacher—Trent Zachariah's *sister*—was finally getting a buzz from her double shots. Because even if you squinted, even if you were blind as a bat, the bar-guys weren't cute. Just terribly young. One looked barely older than his shoe size.

It was time for Ellie to ask about Sara Lee, but before she could, Angel said, "Why'd you ask me about my brother?"

"I bet he was born in Trenton, New Jersey," Ellie said, sidestepping the question.

"No, he was born in Trenton, Transylvania," Angel said sarcastically. "What has Trent got to do with the real estate guy who wrote my phone number on his calendar?"

"I don't know. I was hoping you could tell me. Has your brother ever mentioned anything about investing twenty-five thousand dollars in a miraculous computer chip?"

Ignoring the salt shaker, Angel raised her shot glass to her mouth. Her hand wobbled as she gulped down the tequila, placed the glass on the table, and sucked the pulp from her slice of lime.

"Yes," she finally replied. "Trent said I could double my investment in less than three months. I said I didn't have that kind of money lying around and he said all I needed, for now, was five thousand. He said he'd put up the other twenty when the time came, and we'd split the profits fifty-fifty. I knew he didn't have twenty thou in the bank, so I asked him where he planned to get it, and he said not to worry, that he'd get it. He sells used cars and sometimes he lucks out and they give him a bonus check, so I figured that's where he'd get it. I'm chicken-shit when it comes to gambling, except, of course, when I play pool." She gave Ellie a smile that didn't reach her eyes. "So I said I'd think about it and he said a man would be contacting me. Oh, hell, the real estate guy."

As Ellie nodded, she thought, *Sara Lee's nonexistent life insurance policy! That's why Trent told his sister not to worry about the twenty thousand. Sales bonus, my foot! And while Trent might have an ironclad alibi for Sara Lee's murder, that didn't mean he hadn't hired a hit man. Or a hit woman.*

Angel said, "You gonna drink that?"

Before Ellie could respond, Angel downed the two untouched tequila shots, this time with her usual flick of her wrist. Correction: two flicks. No wobbles.

"Love this stuff," she said then grimaced. "Trent loves it too much . . . José Cuervo, just like me."

Before Ellie could stop herself, she said, "And tonight you're drowning your sorrow, right?"

"Sorrow? What kind of sorrow?"

"The death of your sister-in-law, Sara Lee."

The bar's lighting was dim, but Ellie had no trouble recognizing the expression that transformed Angel's face from beautiful to ugly.

Pure, unadulterated hate!

"Good riddance to bad rubbish," Angel said.

"I take it you didn't like Sara Lee."

It wasn't a question, and if it had been a question, it was a rhetorical question, but Angel said, "Sara Lee made my SOB ex-husband look like a saint."

"My God, what did she do?"

"She screwed around with every man who looked at her cross-eyed. I knew that for a fact because she'd come to this bar to sing, and the guys would flock around her like a fish to a worm."

Mixing our metaphors, are we? Aloud, Ellie said, "Did you tell your brother about the flock of guys?" *Which would give him yet another motive for killing his wife.*

"Oh, I couldn't tell Trent. He'd be so hurt, and Sara Lee knew I'd never say anything, damn her soul! Trent would phone her at work. *She* thought he was jealous and that he called all the time to check up on her, but the truth is, he called because he was so damn scared she'd leave him. He was afraid he might call the restaurant one night or one afternoon, and her boss would say she'd taken off for New York or Hollywood or Nashville. Trent would come over to my place when Sara worked nights, and he'd say, 'She's gonna leave me, Angel,' and he'd cry like a baby. That's why he drank so much. His drinking problem and his broken heart . . . all Sara Lee's fault . . . and I'm glad she's dead! Do you hear me? Glad, glad, glad!"

After that outburst, Ellie felt emboldened enough to ask, "Where were you yesterday between two and three o'clock?"

Angel's eyes turned squinty and her mouth curled in an Elvis sneer. "I was at school. From eight to three I was at my school. And now you can take your prying, officious, *nosy* self out of my sight. I don't know why you've developed an avid, and I suspect unhealthy, interest in my brother, or for that matter Sara Lee,

177

but I liked you better when you were Tinkerbelle."

Ellie decided not to argue, or even try to explain. She had learned more than she'd come for, and if Angel wasn't delicately picking the dirt out from underneath her fingernails with a switchblade, she looked as if she wanted to.

Suddenly bone-weary, Ellie stood up, slung her jacket over her arms, withdrew some crumpled bills from her jeans pocket, and left Cher a ten-dollar tip, hoping it was "exorbitant" enough. Then she walked away from the table, turned and walked back. "You've had a lot to drink, Angel," she said. "You're not planning to drive home, are you?"

"That's none of your damn business!"

"It *is* my business. Friends don't let friends—"

"We're *not* friends! But don't worry, I have at least a dozen buds who'll drive me home. And I can always ask *them*." She blew a couple of kisses at the two munificent bar-guys, who elbow-nudged each other, smiled like animated puppies, and made identical come-hither gestures with their paws.

The white noise inside the Olive or Twist morphed into real noise when Ellie walked through the doorway and hit the cracked sidewalk. Cars splashed through puddles, horns beeped like an accelerated *Roadrunner* cartoon, someone practiced his or her drums in front of an open, two-story window, and from far away, she heard the rhythmic wail of an ambulance.

Her tired mind began rehashing the day and evening.

If she wanted to solve Sara Lee's murder, she now had four bona fide suspects.

Nico Something Russian, who had "cheated" at God-knows-what and pissed off Matthew Lester.

Matthew Lester, who might be a wee bit difficult to question, unless Ellie kidnapped that kid who saw dead people.

Trent Zachariah, who could very well have hired a hit man or hit woman.

And, at the head of the class, Angel Pitt, who hated Sara Lee with a passion; a passion fueled by her love for her brother.

Ellie didn't believe for one moment that Trent had wept over the possibility of losing his wife to Hollywood, Nashville or New York City. Oh, he might have conjured up a few fake tears to dupe his naïve sister, but based on his football history, if Sara Lee tried to leave him, he'd get both mad *and* even.

Unlocking her Honda, Ellie slid behind the steering wheel and started to salivate when she thought about ordering a double hamburger, large fries and a frozen shake at one of the fast-food emporiums that dotted the area. She had only driven a few blocks when she saw the pinafore. On top of the pinafore, a freckled face and bright red pigtails beckoned.

While waiting at the take-out window for her Mandarin chicken salad, a new thought invaded Ellie's exhausted mind.

Earlier, during his phone call, hadn't Peter said that the schoolteachers went on strike yesterday?

But Angel Pitt had said she was at school yesterday, during Sara Lee's murder.

So that meant that Brad Pitt's "cousin" had lied through her pretty teeth and her alibi had just gone up in smoke.

Fake alibi notwithstanding, Ellie wished she had stuck around the Olive or Twist long enough to hear Angel sing the "Leonardo DiCaprio Titanic song."

TWENTY-SEVEN

Friday

Ellie awakened early to find the sky as gray as smoke. But the sun hadn't come up yet. When it did, if it did, it would burn away the fog.

She dragged her tired, stiff body out of bed and took a nice long jog, Scout racing by her side. She wished she could take Scout off the leash but didn't dare. The way her luck was running recently, Scout, like Lassie, would "come home," only Scout would come home to the Lester residence. Luckily, Rachel's leash extended like a tape measure—or perhaps a fishing line would be a better analogy—so that Ellie could reel Scout back in whenever the dog roamed too far afield.

As she leaned against an aspen to catch her breath and check her pulse rate, Ellie watched Scout investigate every tree and shrub in her limited vicinity, then squat and leave liquid Post-it Notes for other dogs. With a smile, Ellie wondered how many smells a dog recognized. In all probability, more than 10,000.

Which brought her back to the Olive or Twist and her conversation with Angel Pitt.

Ellie liked and admired the pool-hustling singer. Or at least she had until Angel revealed her unguarded hatred for her dead sister-in-law. But honestly, could Angel Pitt—a karaoke star who sang Celine Dion's haunting, melodic, not to mention sappy "My Heart Will Go On"—murder someone in cold blood? No matter how much she loved her brother, no matter how much she believed, or wanted to believe, in his angst-ridden lies, she wouldn't sneak up behind Sara Lee and kill the young waitress with a Daffy Duck necktie.

Or would she?

Angel was tall enough to reach a small person standing on a crate, and she had a moderately reasonable motive, but it would be like shooting somebody in the back, and unless Ellie was *way* off the mark, Angel didn't seem the type to shoot anybody in the back. Not even ducks at a carnival booth.

Ellie flashed back to the image of Angel blowing on the end of her cue stick. But that was no "smoking gun." Sara Lee hadn't been shot. She'd been strangled, for Pete's sake.

Speaking of Pete, should she call Peter and tell him about Angel's fake alibi?

But then she'd have to tell him about the Olive or Twist. He'd insist she stop snooping, and she had a lot of snooping—make that *sleuthing*—on her agenda for today, following her Weight Winners meeting.

By the time she returned home from her jog, the fog had lifted, her endorphin rush had kicked in, and she felt less stiff, more awake, and ready to face her busy day. She showered and dressed in what her mother called "Sunday clothes;" good clothes; church clothes; in this case, diet-club-leader clothes.

The Weight Winners organization insisted lecturers set a good example by wearing spiffy outfits. Although she preferred jeans and baggy sweatshirts, Ellie totally agreed with the concept. As a member attending weekly meetings, she had scrutinized and evaluated her own leader's outfits, from shoes to jewelry. And woe to the lecturer who bulged.

With satisfaction, Ellie saw that she did *not* bulge, not even around the waist, where, if she didn't watch herself carefully, she had a tendency to develop love handles.

She had decided to wear last night's Tinkerbelle sweater,

tucked into her tailored black, size eleven-twelve slacks. All she need do was add her spiffy, albeit ancient, black blazer, a string of black pearls, and her favorite pair of soft leather, charcoal-gray, low-heeled boots, another birthday gift from Grandma Shirley.

Next, breakfast. Ellie poached a couple of eggs and gave one to Scout. She ate the other egg with a multigrain bagel, after downing four ounces of orange juice and two heavenly cups of coffee. Then she set Jackie Robinson's daily allotment of cat food on the kitchen counter where Scout couldn't reach it. The hand-printed letters on the cat's bowl read: I'M ON A SEAFOOD DIET. I SEE FOOD AND I EAT IT.

As she sipped another half cup of coffee, Ellie turned on the TV, hoping to get an update on the murders. Instead, every channel had live coverage of the strike, with teachers holding their signs aloft and marching up and down in front of their various schools. No one mentioned when the strike had begun, and Ellie didn't have time to stick around.

On her way to the meeting, she filled her Honda with gas and made a brief stop at the supermarket, where she picked up two pounds of shrink-wrapped fat. The butchers there all knew her and, long ago, they had stopped questioning her weird requests.

She left her car in the Good Shepherd church's parking lot. Then she walked into the church, stepped inside a classroom, and greeted her assistant Wanda, hugely pregnant with—according to Wanda—"a fullback or one of those giant pumpkins that always wins a blue ribbon at the county fair and makes the front page of the tabloids."

"When are you taking maternity leave?" Ellie asked, as she noted with pleasure that the classroom was standing room only. Due to the teachers strike, several mothers had brought their kids along, but there was no rule against children, and Ellie was just happy that the moms hadn't used the strike as an excuse to skip the meeting. If one missed a meeting, it was so hard to come back again.

"Maternity leave?" Wanda snorted. "Surely you jest. I plan to have my baby right here, and if I go into labor during a Friday morning meeting, so much the better." With a grin, she gestured toward a woman standing by one of the windows. "That's my gynecologist. So far she's lost twenty-three pounds."

Ellie grinned back. Then, because it was September and autumn and not too early to start thinking about the holidays, she found a piece of chalk, faced her "inspirational blackboard," and printed:

PEOPLE FRET ABOUT WHAT THEY EAT BETWEEN CHRISTMAS AND THE NEW YEAR WHEN THEY SHOULD BE WORRIED ABOUT WHAT THEY EAT BETWEEN THE NEW YEAR AND CHRISTMAS.

She began her lecture by passing around the fat sample she had picked up at the supermarket. "Those of you who have dropped two pounds, this is what you've lost," she said, and listened to the intakes of breath. People never realized how heavy two pounds of pure fat could be.

Then Ellie abandoned the lecture she had prepared and focused on the visiting kids, at least the ones who were old enough to understand and retain her words. She spoke about the hazards they'd have to maneuver in order to stay both healthy and active. "Never give in to the temptation to snack on a pizza because 'everyone else is eating pizza,' " she said, "and most of all, don't eat food when you're sad. Eating cookies and candy doesn't really make you happy."

"It makes *me* happy," said a roly-poly child of ten or eleven.

"Hush, Madison," her mother chastised.

"No, that's okay." Ellie smiled. "What else makes you happy, Madison?"

"I don't know. Yes, I do. Reading."

"Well, the next time you're sad, read a book. Or reread a book you really like. Do you know what I call that? I call it a comfort read. And if you're hungry while reading, eat an apple. How many of you have dogs? Please raise your hands." She looked around the room and grinned at Wanda's gynecologist, who had raised two hands. "The next time you feel sad, take your dog, or dogs, for a nice long walk. And if you don't have a dog—"

"Walk your cat," Madison said, and everybody laughed.

"Walk your parrot."

"Walk your gerbil."

"Walk your hamster."

"Walk your snake."

Snake? "I was going to say walk yourself," Ellie called out, but no one was listening.

Walking suggestions were flying left and right, and now included lions and tigers and bears. Oh, my, the kids were growing rowdy, but in a good way, and even the adults were smiling or laughing. Still, Ellie felt it might be time to put a lid on the discussion.

In fact, checking her watch, she was astonished to see that the meeting had gone into overtime.

She left Wanda and a second assistant to shut everything down, but before she could reach the front door, Madison's mother, Helen, intercepted her in the hallway.

"That was brilliant," Helen said, her eyes sparkly with moisture. "The reading suggestion, I mean. Madison and some of the other kids have decided to form a book club, and they're even talking about pooling their books and starting a kid library." Tears streamed down Helen's face. "To be perfectly honest, Ellie, Madison has no friends. She's always been an odd duck and very, very shy." Helen smiled through her tears. "And just now she didn't want to leave the meeting. She was too busy writing down E-mail addresses and giving out hers. Monday, if the teachers are still on strike, the kids are all getting together at our house. If not, they'll meet at our house after school. I'll bake some chocolate-chip cookies and . . ." She paused, her face red.

"There are legal recipes for cookies," Ellie said. "All you have to do is Google Weight Winners. You'll find cookbooks galore for sale, but you'll also find blogs that have the same, or nearly the same recipes. For free."

"I bet Madison can find a cookie recipe she'd like to sample, and a dozen other legal recipes as well. Then, together, we'll make a shopping list and . . . oh, I can't thank you enough, Ellie."

"You're more than welcome. Before you leave, Helen, let me ask you a quick question. Do you know when the striking teachers walked out?"

"They talked about going out on Monday, but negotiations broke down for good on Tuesday, so they began their strike on Wednesday, the day before yesterday. By the way, I'm one-hundred percent in favor of the teachers. They're not asking for more money, you know, even though their salaries are shameful. They just want smaller classes and a few measly benefits. And now, if you'll excuse me, I have to drive Madison to the library. She insisted."

Ordinarily, the teachers strike would have headlined the news, Ellie thought, waving goodbye to Madison, her mom, and numerous other members. Except, nowadays the "news" favored stories about missing persons—as long as they were beautiful—and murder victims.

Especially if the murder victim just happens to be the wife of an infamous football player.

Dollars to doughnuts, news kingpin Larry King would book Trenton Zachariah, assuming the bereft widower was sober enough to make a guest appearance.

Despite her abhorrence of, and repugnance for, gossipy shows, Ellie knew that if Trent appeared on King's program, she'd watch the sly, sordid interview. Because even diffused by TV cameras, she might be able to gauge the ex–football player's sincerity. And there was always a slim chance that Angel could be right about the depth of her brother's anguish and the intensity of his love for Sara Lee.

Meanwhile, Ellie Bernstein, mature girl detective, had dog food to buy and the staff of Uncle Vinnie's Gourmet Italian Restaurant to grill. And if she didn't run out of time, which was becoming a precious commodity, she'd interrogate the whole damned strip mall.

Twenty-Eight

Uncle Vinnie's Gourmet Italian Restaurant served homemade, seasoned croutons on their salads, and, just like cake crumbs, croutons were a no-no.

With that thought, Ellie turned her Honda's steering wheel to the right and exited the highway. Then she drove a few feet, made a sharp left turn, and began looking for an empty parking slot in the strip mall's jam-packed parking lot.

Her car radio was stuck on Barry Manilow, who sang "My Eyes Adored You." Ellie wanted to sing along but knew she'd massacre the tune, and she was afraid Barry might emerge from the radio like a genie from a bottle and cut her throat, not that she'd blame him.

There were only two vacant parking slots, both stenciled SMALL CAR. One was taken up by a humongous double-cab pickup truck, what her son Mick used to call a pick-me-up truck. Despite cruising cars and SUVs, the other slot remained empty, and Ellie immediately saw why. On the driver's side, a pothole as big as Sicily had, with yesterday's rain, become a puddle that looked as deep as the Bermuda Triangle. On the passenger side, the pick-me-up truck hogged the white line, and unless one was shaped like Olive Oyl, sliding out from one's car and making one's way to the curb was virtually impossible.

Maybe she could take a deep breath and jump over the puddle, Ellie thought. No way! She looked down at her expensive, soft-leather boots. Absolutely no way!

Damn! There were no other empty parking slots. It was the start of lunchtime and, she presumed, Uncle Vinnie's Gourmet Italian Restaurant was doing a steadfast business.

Wait a sec. She reached under her seat, pulled out a couple of sugarless gum wrappers and the same towel she had used yesterday; the towel she employed to wipe the inside of her front window when the cold and humidity clashed. Which was fairly often. She loved her car, but the defroster liked to hibernate in the wintertime, and it responded irritably and slowly when roused.

Ellie aimed her car's hood at the curb and pulled into the slot. She took off her boots and socks, rolled her pant legs up past her knees, and placed the towel around her shoulders like a prayer shawl. Then she thrust her socks inside her boots. She anchored the boots with her armpits, secured her purse with her chin, and like a tightrope walker, she slowly, carefully, navigated her way to the curb.

When she arrived, she heard applause. A family of five, an elderly woman leaning on a walker, and a group of black and white teenage boys, most with skateboards, had watched her performance. The boys all wore jeans that barely hugged their hips and butts, revealing the top third of their underpants. "Cool," said one, admiringly. He and another boy formed a chair with their arms so that she could sit and dry her legs and feet and put her socks and boots back on. *Cool,* she thought.

Upright again, she thanked the boys and watched them skateboard down the sidewalk, wondering why their pants didn't fall down. She had landed in front of The Merry-Go-Round consignment store. A pair of adult rubber boots in the window caught her eye. A small sign said they were "On Special" for twenty dollars. The same sign said they were a size seven, her shoe size. If the pick-me-up truck hadn't moved by the time she was ready to leave the strip mall, she'd spring for the boots. A wire mesh mannequin, whose face had been constructed out of a second-hand tennis racquet, "stood" suspended above the boots.

The rubber boots were bright red and Ms. Racquet Face wore a shiny yellow slicker, but an authentic carousel horse dominated the window display. Upon first seeing the horse a few months ago, Ellie had fallen in love with it and named it Gigi, but to buy it she'd have to mortgage her house.

She took a few steps toward the pet shop at the other end of the strip mall, retraced her steps, then turned and entered the consignment store. There were no customers, not even browsers.

"May I help you, ma'am," asked a dark-haired woman who looked like a grown-up Lucy from the *Peanuts* comic strip.

"I'd like to try on those red boots in the window, please."

"Of course. Quite a few people have asked about those boots since the rainstorm yesterday, but they object to the price, which is ridiculous. Brand-new boots like that pair would cost at least fifty dollars in any reputable shoe store, more in a department store." She sighed. "But when you run a consignment shop, people always try to Jew you down."

"Please don't use that expression!" Ellie contemplated turning on her heels and leaving immediately, if not sooner.

"Oh, I'm sorry," the woman said. "I didn't know you were Jewish."

I'm not. I'm Catholic. "Whether I'm Jewish or not isn't the point," Ellie said. "The expression is offensive and—"

"I didn't mean anything by it. It's just an expression. Look, I'll take five dollars off the boots."

"That's not necessary. Just think twice before you say something like that again."

"Yes, ma'am." The woman pulled the boots from the window. "She was Jewish too, you know."

189

"Who?"

"That waitress who was killed. The one who waited tables at Uncle Vinnie's Gourmet Italian Restaurant."

"You knew her?"

"Not really. I just thought it was funny that a Jew waitress worked in an Italian restaurant. In my opinion, she should have waited tables in a Jewish restaurant."

No way would Ellie spend one cent of her hard-earned or inherited money at this shop. But as long as she was here, she had a few questions on the tip of her tongue. "I've always wanted to own a consignment store," she said. "I think it would be fun to sort through vintage clothes and authentic antiques. But my friend says there's too much paperwork, especially if you hire people to work for you. You'd have to fill out all those tax forms and . . . may I ask how many people work for you?"

"Two girls work for me. I own another consignment store in Manitou Falls and ordinarily I'm not here from Monday to Friday, but this locale has been extra busy since the teachers strike. My girls are on their lunch breaks right now."

She handed the boots to Ellie. They felt cold. Ellie said, "Do either of your girls smoke?"

"Oh my goodness, no! I wouldn't hire a smoker. She'd smell. Her clothes would smell, too. The whole shop would smell. I wouldn't *consign* any clothes owned by a smoker, either, not even a smoker who quit smoking." Agitated, she waved her hands, as if Ellie had blown cigarette smoke in her face.

No smokers almost certainly meant that no one would have witnessed Sara Lee's smoke break, Ellie thought. Aloud she said, "I've decided I don't want these boots after all."

Upon exiting the consignment store, Ellie waved goodbye to Gigi the carousel horse, then entered the video mart.

The girl behind the counter said that none of the people who worked there smoked, and that the alley behind the video mart was off limits, ever since one of the employees, long gone now, had covertly sold used videos in the alley. Somewhat wistfully, she said that before he'd been caught he'd "made a fortune." She said she knew Sara Lee, but only as a waitress.

Before leaving the store, Ellie decided to peruse the children's section. There, she found *Lassie Come Home, The Incredible Journey,* and *Cat Tracks,* narrated by Johnny Depp. She wondered if Scout had a preference. She had a feeling dogs— and cats, for that matter—didn't give a rat's spit which movies their humans deigned to show, but she paid the rental charge for all three.

Next to the video mart, a sports equipment store was locked up tight, its display windows empty except for a full-size, six-foot-three, cardboard cutout of ex-quarterback John Elway— eternally posed to throw a pass—who leaned forlornly against the plate glass window's narrow side wall.

Had there been too much competition from the larger malls? A FOR LEASE sign on the door told the story. Maybe she could buy the cardboard figure and give it to Mick, who was a Broncos fanatic. Ellie smiled. No way! She'd display the cutout herself, give John Elway a place of honor in her small, sunny study, where maybe he wouldn't look so . . . forsaken.

She had planned to eat lunch before she checked out the strip mall's shops, but she thought *what the heck,* and tugged at a heavy wooden door and walked into the beauty salon. If the smell of food more often than not made her stomach rumble, the smell of the beauty products, especially the mousse and hairspray, gave her an instant headache.

The salon's receptionist was on the phone and the computer at the same time. Ellie pretended to study the price list on the wall next to the desk, until the receptionist hung up. Her hair color was similar to Angel Pitt's, except the receptionist had added slapdash orange streaks, as if she had decided at the last minute to mix the red and ash-blonde together.

Ellie said she was thinking of streaking her hair strawberry blonde. Her brother had had his hair colored here and it looked great and he highly recommended his stylist—*whose name she couldn't remember! Roy? Rick? Richard? Damn!*

Suddenly, it came to her. "I think my brother said his name was Raoul."

"We don't have anyone here by that name, ma'am."

"Well, I could be wrong about the name, but I'm positive this is where my brother had his hair done." Taking her cue from the consignment shop, Ellie sniffed and said, "I smell cigarette smoke."

"Do you?" The receptionist closed a humongous appointment book and started fiddling with her pen, clicking it like a *Jeopardy!* contestant who knew the question to the answer. "I guess I'm used to the smells in here," she said. "Can't tell one from the other. I'm very sorry, ma'am."

"Oh, that's okay. It wasn't a criticism. I'm a smoker."

Which was a lie but had a modicum of truth to it. She had attended a Catholic high school where several girls, more than half her class, smoked in the schoolyard or sneaked their smokes inside the girls' bathroom. Rebelling against her mother and hoping to lose weight, or at least modulate her metabolism, Ellie had smoked, too. Eventually, she quit. Not because it was a death sentence, but because she didn't like the taste of cigarettes, nor did she like the way her mouth felt the next morning.

Relieved, the receptionist said, "Some of our stylists smoke. That's probably why you smelled—"

"I think I'd rather have a smoker do my hair because . . ." *Because why?* "Because we'd have something in common. And he or she wouldn't complain about the cigarette smell on my clothes."

"Great." The receptionist opened her humongous appointment book. "Of course we don't allow smoking inside the salon, but you can go out back, in the alley behind the salon, while your color is processing. Everybody does. Everybody who smokes, that is."

"Are any of the stylists who smoke here today? I'd like to speak to them. About my hair. Because . . ." *Because why?* "Because I'm very nervous . . . practically shaking in my boots. You see, I've never had my hair colored before."

"Really?" She looked at Ellie as if she'd never seen an Irish setter before. "Jeeze Louise, I'd give *anything* for your color. Of course, it would look fab streaked," she added quickly. "There's only one smoker here today, Anne-Marie. In fact, she's headed for the alley right now."

Ellie said thanks and took off for the back of the salon. She opened a green door and stepped into the alley.

"I know karate," said a girl with very black, Cleopatra hair.

"So do I," Ellie said. "My boyfriend taught me."

"Oh, sorry. You startled me. After what happened to Sara Lee, you can't be too careful. Sara Lee was the waitress who—"

"Yes, I heard about that. Did you know her?"

"We weren't friends or anything, but we'd smile and wave at each other during our smoke breaks, and I saw her in *The Pajama Game* . . . the community theatre show? She was very talented. I always meant to invite her out for a drink, after our shifts. Now it's too late."

"Did you see her on Wednesday, the day she was killed?"

"Yeah. Me and Raymond and Bruce were all taking a smoke break. But we went inside before she was . . . you know."

"Strangled. Was she alone?"

"Hey, are you a reporter?" Anne-Marie's eyes narrowed, or perhaps the smoke from her cigarette had constricted them.

Ellie shook her head. "I never met Sara Lee, but I know her

sister-in-law. She's afraid the police are focusing on her brother, so I thought I'd help her out by asking a few questions. She's a teacher and can't leave the picket line." Ellie almost choked on her last nine words. "Was Sara Lee outside alone?"

"Yeah. Well, she was alone after Vincent yelled at her. I forgot about that when the cops questioned me."

"Do you know why Vincent yelled at her?"

Anne-Marie shook her head. "I couldn't hear him, but you could tell he was mad. I'm into body language, big-time, along with yoga, and he made a fist."

"Vincent hit Sara Lee?"

"Nah. From what I could see, she laughed at him and he said something else and then he went back inside the restaurant. The kitchen, I guess."

"Then what?"

"Then nothing. Sara Lee climbed up onto a crate and I went back inside the salon. We all did. Bruce and Raymond and me. I wish we hadn't. Maybe if we'd stayed outside and smoked some more, she wouldn't of been killed. But a friend of mine says it wouldn't of mattered, that she'd have been killed some other time. I've got to believe that." Anne-Marie flipped her long, straight, Cleopatra pageboy, sucked her cigarette filter, discovered she wasn't drawing any smoke, tossed the filter toward some scraggly weeds, and looked at her wristwatch. "Sorry," she said, "but I can't talk to you anymore. My next client is due any minute. If you find out who killed Sara Lee, give the bastard a few karaoke chops for me. By the way, I love your hair. What color do you use?"

"It's my natural color."

"Right. And I've got some swampland in Florida for sale. See ya."

Not if I see you first, Ellie thought childishly. Her hair *was* natural, and she could prove it!

TWENTY-NINE

Ellie walked back through the salon. The receptionist was busy with some paying clients. In any case, Ellie had decided that she'd be insane to streak her hair. She liked it fine just the way it was, thank you very much.

Outside again, her stomach rumbled as her gaze touched upon Uncle Vinnie's green-and-white-striped awning.

First, Scout's food.

Reigning Cats & Dogs' window display included a chess set with dogs as queens, kings, rooks, knights, bishops—thirty-two pieces in an assortment of the most popular breeds. To Ellie, the exhibit conjured up an Ogden Nash proverb: "Happiness is having a scratch for every itch."

Inside, the shop was more a boutique than a pet supply outlet.

A human boutique, to be exact.

A boutique for *wealthy* humans.

As Ellie unzipped her jacket, her gaze took in a couple of clothing racks, and she wanted one of everything, in particular an appliquéd and embroidered blazer. The appliquéd cats were so cute, so colorful, and she could wear the blazer over a skirt or slacks. She desperately needed something new to wear to her Weight Winners meetings and—

The blazer was on sale, only . . . $99.95.

Holy cow!

Why had she come here? Oh, yes, Scout.

In the corner of the shop, almost as an afterthought, were

small decorative barrels filled with doggie biscuits. Shaped like hearts, diamonds, clubs and spades, their labels boasted ingredients like "wheat flour" and "cultured whey."

She saw a large, gingerbread-flavored, all-natural biscuit that actually looked like a dog biscuit. Manufactured by Old Mother Hubbard, the sticky-tag read PEACE. *What the heck,* Ellie thought. *Why not? I believe in peace, and the biscuit costs a heck of a lot less than the appliquéd-cat blazer.*

Speaking of cats, she snatched up a rubber mouse flavored with nothing.

The woman behind the counter said she owned the shop, her name was Cindy Silberblatt, and she was more than happy to pull "Scout Finch Lester's" index card. She disappeared into a back room and soon returned with a kibble-filled brown paper bag, as if Ellie had purchased a contraband copy of *Playdog.* The plain brown paper bag was, in fact, the boutique's only basic, unadorned item.

Ellie heard a snuffled *woof.* She looked toward a rack of doggie raincoats and saw a shaggy white puppy with a black tail. At least she thought it was a puppy. It could have been a small adult dog.

She told herself to look away, pay for her items, and leave the store.

Might as well tell herself to sit in the corner and *not* think about a white bear. Or to stop eating. Or to stop sleuthing.

"Oh, how cute," she said, walking over to the rack of rain gear. "What kind of a dog is he?"

"She," Cindy Silberblatt said, joining Ellie. "She's a Jack Russell, mostly, with a smidgen of something soft. We're not sure what. My daughter says she's part Jack Russell, part teddy bear."

"She doesn't look very old," Ellie said with a smile.

"The vet figures two and a half months."

"The vet? Is she sick?"

"No, but she's a stray, so we wanted the vet to check her out. And she needed her puppy shots."

"She looks like a Muppet," Ellie said, watching the puppy gnaw a pet toy—one of the same toys that Scout had disregarded. "What's her name?"

"She doesn't have one. She was haunting the alley behind the Italian restaurant. The servers were feeding her scraps, but the owner objected rather vehemently to her hanging around his Dumpster, so we took her in. But we can't keep her, so we've decided whoever adopts her will name her. Right now we're calling her Jane Doe."

"Oh. You mean she doesn't belong to anybody?"

"Not yet."

"I would think any pet lover who came into your shop would walk out with her. She's so cute."

"Yes, she's a stunner, but she doesn't have a pedigree."

"And that's a problem because . . . ?"

"Look around. For the most part, our customers have pedigrees a mile long. So do their dogs. Rachel Lester is the exception, not the rule." Cindy scrutinized Ellie's whimsical Tinkerbelle sweater, just before she said, "Please tell me you're in the market for a dog."

"No. Not a chance. I have a cat."

" 'Jane' is young enough to get along with cats."

"But my cat is too old to get along with . . ." Ellie swallowed her next word, which would have been "dogs," as she pictured Jackie Robinson asleep against Scout's tummy. "The thing is . . . you see . . . I've never owned a dog."

"Really? You can say any idiotic thing to a dog and the dog will give you a look that says, 'My God, you're right! I never would've thought of that!' I'm paraphrasing Dave Barry."

I've read that quote, Ellie thought. *Barry said "foolish" rather than "idiotic," otherwise you're spot-on.* "A friend shares my house," she said. "Not always, but sometimes." She felt her cheeks bake. "Let me ask him how he feels about adopting Muppet. If he says okay, I'll think about it. Why are you laughing?"

"Because you've already named the dog. Tell you what. I won't give *Muppet* away until I hear from you."

"No, no, give her away! May I change the subject and ask you a question?"

"Sure."

"Before, you kept saying 'we,' as in 'we took her to the vet.' Did the we refer to your daughter or your employees? And if you meant your employees, do any of them smoke?"

"My daughter is seven and very smart," Cindy said, "but I meant my staff. Unless one is a closet smoker, they are not, nor have they ever been, nicotine addicts. Why do you ask?"

"I'm a friend of the sister-in-law of the waitress who was killed a couple of days ago. She waited tables at Uncle Vinnie's Gourmet Italian Restaurant, her name was Sara Lee, and—"

"You want to know if any of my employees saw her in the alley."

"Yes."

"Well, you're in luck. I did." Cindy hunkered down and scratched behind the puppy's ears. "This sweet little girl isn't one-hundred-percent housebroken yet, though she's learning very quickly, so I take her into the alley as often as I can. On Wednesday I saw Sara Lee walk outside from the restaurant's kitchen. She didn't meet up with anyone, if that's what you were wondering. She was all by herself."

"Did you see Vincent, the restaurant's owner and chef?"

"No, but I wasn't in the alley very long. The puppy piddled and I took her back inside."

"Did you happen to see any other smokers?"

"No. Yes. One. But she was way down at the other end of the alley. She works in the consignment store."

"What? Are you sure?"

"Absolutely. I've bought a few items of clothing from her. Why?"

"The owner of the consignment store said she'd never hire anyone who smoked."

"When you check a person's references, if you even bother to check references, 'does she smoke' is rarely one of your questions. And for all we know, the poor girl quit smoking and then started again."

I could go back to the consignment store, thought Ellie, *but I don't want to get the girl in trouble, and anyway, Peter most likely interrogated everybody without exception. Except I bet he doesn't know that Vincent was pissed off at Sara Lee—pissed off enough to raise his fist.*

She paid for her pet items and sneaked one last peek at "Muppet," who wagged her black tail like a furry windshield wiper. As Ellie exited the shop, she put her three videos into the food-biscuit-mouse sack. Then she walked back to the sports shop, pulled out her checkbook, killed another deposit slip, and jotted down the phone number on the FOR LEASE sign. Purchasing the cardboard cutout made much more sense than adopting a dog. After all, John Elway didn't need to be walked or fed.

Speaking of fed . . . Ellie took a few steps toward Uncle Vinnie's Gourmet Italian Restaurant.

A light breeze had invaded the strip mall. The smell of homemade tomato sauce wafted toward her nose. Her sense of smell revved into fifth gear and she told her stomach to shut up.

THIRTY

Ellie pulled open the door to Uncle Vinnie's Gourmet Italian Restaurant. Holding her purse and her Reigning Cats & Dogs bag with one hand, she stood behind a PLEASE WAIT TO BE SEATED sign.

The hostess was very tall, very thin, very pale. From the expression on her face, she suffered from a migraine or a hangover, and she kept patting her head as if she'd just discovered she'd been cast in a Tim Burton movie.

"My friend told me about a waiter, Nicholas," Ellie said to the pale-faced hostess. "I think he's called Nico, and I'd like his section, please."

"I'm sorry, ma'am, but Nico doesn't work the lunch shift."

"That's funny. I'm sure my friend said Nico worked the lunch shift two days ago."

"Yes, but he cov . . . covered for . . . for another ser . . . server."

"Are you feeling all right?"

"Yes. No. Oh, God."

The hostess pressed her hands against her mouth and ran toward the back of the restaurant. Ellie followed, opened the ladies' room door, guided the girl inside a stall, and helped her kneel.

The girl heaved once, quickly, as if it were an encore, then staggered over to the sink, splashed cold water on her face, and patted it dry with paper towels. "He swore it wouldn't make me sick," she said, "but he lied. I missed work yesterday and was almost late today. And for the first time in my whole life, I got *written up.*" Her eyes filled with the biggest tears Ellie had ever seen.

"Who swore what wouldn't make you sick?"

"Nico. He's a waiter here."

"Yes," Ellie said softly. "I know."

"He said vodka wouldn't make me sick."

"He took you out drinking?"

"He *invited* me. To share some vodka. With him. At his apartment. Wednesday night. I was flattered. Most people can't see the passion that lurks beneath my outer surface."

Was I ever that young? Ellie wondered. *I was never that thin.*

"Nico can sense passion," the hostess continued. "He reminds me of Don what's his face. That guy in *Man of La Mancha.*"

"Don Quixote," Ellie said. "Played by Peter O'Toole, who was in *Kinkade's Home for Christmas* with Marcia Gay Harden, who was in *Rails & Ties* with Kevin Bacon."

"Huh?"

Ellie felt her face redden. "Nothing important. Go on."

"Nico carried me to the car so I wouldn't get my shoes wet. Isn't that romantic?"

"Yes. Very."

"He carried me into his apartment and he gave me some vodka. I thought he wanted to . . . you know . . . but he kept giving me more and more to drink, and the funny thing is he kept asking me how I felt. He seemed annoyed when I said I felt okay. Finally, I got up the nerve to make the first move. I took my clothes off. Well, not all of them, and not all the way off. I pulled my pants down and my undies, too. Ordinarily, I wouldn't do that on a first date, but by then I felt numb, you know, like a zombie? I didn't even care that I was naked, except I was so woozy I couldn't get my slacks and undies over my shoes. I have big feet. Nico said how do you feel and when I said not too good, he smiled and said to drink more vodka because it would make me feel better, only it didn't. Would you believe I felt worse? I told him I felt dizzy. He said 'poor M-Lo' and put me to bed and I guess I passed out. He left the apartment. When I woke up, he was sleeping next to me and—"

"Wait a sec. If you passed out, how could you hear him leave?"

"I didn't hear him leave. But he must have because the next morning his shoes were wet. And muddy."

"That's understandable. Wednesday night it rained cats and dogs. In fact, it poured."

"Yes, ma'am, but his waiter shoes were almost dry. His *sneakers* were wet and muddy. After he woke up, he kissed my forehead and talked about how many times we had . . . you know, done it. But we didn't do it. Wouldn't you know if you did it?"

Absolutely, Ellie thought with a blush.

"So anyways, I went home and started to get ready for work. But I felt crummy. Dizzy again and sick to my stomach. I slept a little and threw up a lot, but I felt so nauseous I didn't remember to call the restaurant and tell them I couldn't come in. That's why Al wrote me up."

"You poor thing," Ellie commiserated. "I was wondering if you worked two days ago, during the lunch shift," she added, dropping the word *subtle* from her mental vocabulary.

"Yes, ma'am, I did. Oh, God, I've got to get back on the floor or I'll get written up again and lose my job. Thanks so much for listening." Her acne-scarred cheeks turned crimson. "I swear I don't know what got into me. I never, ever blab to strangers. Except once, after my sister's wedding, when I took the bus home because nobody would ride with me in a car. I told this old black lady about the wedding, but she was asleep so I don't think it counts."

"That's okay. Strangers often blab to *me*. And if you tell me your name, we won't be strangers."

"Micki . . . M-i-c-k-i."

M-o-u-s-e, Ellie sang silently.

"I'll put you in Lois Reibach's section," Micki said. "Not counting Nico, she gets the most repeat customers. Oh, God, I mean *guests.* Sara Lee . . . the waitress who got killed in the alley and trashed in the Dumpster? . . . she had more request tables than any other server."

Everybody liked Sara Lee, Ellie thought. She remembered the photo of Sara as a feisty teenager, clothed in a Tigger shirt and combat boots, and her heart ached for what might have been.

"Nico always has a black tongue," Micki continued, "because he licks his pen before he writes down an order. I think that's cute, don't you? Nico is so macho, and then he opens his mouth and his tongue is all inky. Nico makes lots of money. He and Sara Lee would have contests to see who ended up with the most money at the end of a shift. Nico won every time. Last week Sara Lee pretended to punch him out when his tips were double her tips. She accidentally gave him a bloody nose, but he just laughed. Want to know what he did then? Bloody nose and all, he kissed her. *On the mouth.*"

Before Micki turned away and scurried toward the restroom exit, her eyes flared with . . . anger? Resentment? Jealousy?

Every emotion except grief, thought Ellie.

THIRTY-ONE

By the time Ellie finished her Cobb salad, the lunch rush had died down.

Clutching two pots of coffee, one in each hand, Micki stood tableside, her gaze straying toward the croutons that seemed to march across Ellie's side plate like toasted soldiers.

"Everything was delicious," Ellie said with complete sincerity. "Do you think I could go into the kitchen and thank Vincent personally?" *And check the employee bulletin board for Theodora's phone number?*

"Vincent isn't scheduled to cook today, ma'am. Al's the chef on duty."

"Then I'd like to go into the kitchen and thank Al, please."

"Al is kind of busy right now, cooking for that eight-top in the corner? I'll be happy to tell him what you said, but if you want to talk to Chef Vincent, he should be here in ten, maybe fifteen minutes. Theodora, the waitress who found Sara Lee, hurt her head and decided to quit waiting tables. She picked up the envelope with her tips but she wants her paycheck, and both Al and Vincent have to sign the paychecks, so Vincent said he'd drive over—"

"Theodora Mallard is here, at the restaurant?"

"Yes, ma'am."

"Could I talk to her? She, uh, used to date my brother and I haven't seen her in years."

"I don't see why you can't. It's not like she's busy on the

floor or anything. Wait right here, don't move, and I'll get her for you. I'll also get the theatre brochure Lois said you wanted."

Theodora Mallard wore a white blouse under a blue-checkered pinafore. Above her platinum braids she sported a turban of bandages. She looked as if Dorothy had clicked her way back to Kansas, aged thirty-plus years, moved to Colorado Springs, bleached her hair, and converted to Hinduism.

"I remember you," she said, sinking onto a chair opposite Ellie. "Tab's sister, right?"

"Right."

"You've lost a ton of weight."

"Not quite that much."

"Micki, the hostess, said you wanted to talk to me."

Ellie nodded. "If you don't mind, I'd like to ask you a few questions about Sara Lee."

"Why?"

The sister-in-law excuse was wearing thin and Theodora Mallard seemed a tad hostile, so Ellie said, "I'm a private investigator, and Sara Lee's mother, Mrs. . . . Leibowitz . . . hired me to—"

"That's bull! Mrs. Leibowitz doesn't have a pot to piss in. She can't afford a P.I."

"Okay, Theodora, I'll tell you the truth but it's a secret. I'm a writer, and I plan to write a true-crime novel. After the killer's been caught, of course. But it's never too late to start. I like to start at the very beginning, a very good place to start . . ." Ellie snapped her mouth shut. In a few more seconds she'd start singing *doe a deer, a female deer.*

"Hey, wow, cool," Theodora said. "Will you mention me in your book?"

"Absolutely."

"Please use my nickname, Tad. Most people know me as Tad, not Theodora." She patted her swami's headdress. To Ellie, it looked like an habitual gesture to make sure that every strand of hair—or in this case, every strand of bandage—was in place. "Oh, shoot," Theodora said with a pout. "I don't think you need me to answer your questions. I told the cops everything I could remember."

"Yes, I'm sure you did, but I wonder if they asked you what you saw *before* you found the body."

"You're kidding, right? I saw the Dumpster. The puke-green, putrid, icky Dumpster! Then I saw Sara Lee. Her eyes were open and—"

"I mean *before* you looked inside the Dumpster. You were in the alley and all the shops use the same alley. This is very important, so please take a moment to think. Did you see anyone walking down the alley toward the restaurant? Or walking down the alley toward one of the stores?"

"No."

"How about someone who ducked into a store through the back door?"

"No. Just Anne-Marie, Bruce and Raymond. He likes it pronounced Ray-moan, but no one ever says it that way. They were on a smoke break."

Whoa, wait, didn't Ann-Marie say they went back inside the salon before Sara Lee was killed? "Theodora, I spoke to Anne-Marie and she said that she and Bruce and Raymond went back inside the salon before Sara Lee was killed."

"Well, heck, they probably did. But they smoke like chimneys, so my guess is that they were taking another smoke break."

"Did Bruce and Raymond know Sara Lee?"

"Of course. They eat lunch here all the time."

"Did Raymond or Bruce . . . or Anne Marie, for that matter . . . have any kind of grudge against Sara Lee?"

"Heck, no. Everybody liked Sara Lee."

Everybody except Trenton Zachariah, Angel Pitt, and unless I'm way off base, Micki the hostess. "Theodora, this is very, very important. Did Sara Lee ever serve anyone who looked . . . malicious?"

Theodora's eyebrows merged and she patted her headdress again. "Did Sara Lee ever serve anyone who looked delicious?"

With an effort, Ellie kept her hands unclenched and her face in deadpan mode. "No, *malicious,* as in sinister," she said. "Creepy."

"Oh, creepy. No. Not unless you count the man with the small scar and the really big mole on his face. He wore a black cowboy hat, but he took it off to eat. I think leaving your hat on to eat, even in a restaurant, is very rude, don't you? Sara Lee talked to the man with the mole for a long time. She looked sad, then mad, and she bought him dessert. We all wondered about that because Sara Lee never gave anyone *anything* for free."

"Was the man with the mole inside the restaurant when Sara Lee took her smoke break, before she was killed?"

"No."

"Who was? Inside, I mean."

"The cops asked me that, Ellie, and I told them a teensy fib. I said I didn't remember. I think customers . . . I mean *guests* . . . should be entitled to their privacy, don't you? Waitresses are like psychiatrists and psychiatrists are doctors and doctors don't have to give out any information, not without a subpoena or something."

"I totally understand, Theodora, but a crime writer has to get every single detail straight, otherwise a publisher won't buy the book."

"Yeah. That makes sense. Okay, let me think. There were eight tourists from Canada. I remember because Nico could add the gratuity. He was really happy about that. Most tourists don't tip worth sh—"

"And?"

"And a couple of bar regulars. They always drink shots. Sex on the Beach. Don't you think that's a funny name for a drink?"

"Yes. Very funny. Who else?"

"Two of Sara Lee's tables. A three-top, more tourists I think because they spoke funny, you know, like a movie with subtitles? And a lady . . . oh, darn, I never *can* remember her name, but she comes in twice a week, alone, and she reads books. We call her 'the book lady.' She sits at a four-top rather than a one-top, or even a two-top. It doesn't matter if the restaurant is crowded, either, which I think is *extremely* rude. What's worse, she doesn't even read *real* books. She reads the stuff we used to have to read in school, you know, William Shakespeare and Charles Dick—"

"Theodora!"

"Sorry. What was the question again?"

"Who was inside the restaurant when Sara Lee took her smoke break?"

"Oh. Right. Gosh, there wasn't anybody else, except Mr. Lester and—"

"Matthew Lester? He was still here?" Staring at Theodora's face, Ellie hoped the ex-waitress didn't try to bluff at poker. "Do you know if Matthew Lester and Sara Lee were . . ." *How to put it delicately? There was no way to put it delicately.* "Do you know if they were sleeping together?"

"Yeah."

"Yeah, you know? Or yeah, they were?"

"Yeah, they were. Everybody knew. Everybody at Uncle Vinnie's, that is. But we all liked Sara Lee so much, we kept her little secret."

"Someone told me . . . I was under the impression . . . wasn't Sara Lee, um, messing around with Nicholas?"

"Nico? They got it on a couple of times but it wasn't serious.

Nico messes around with *everyone*. Sara Lee had a *thing* for Mr. Lester. She was crazy-nuts about him. Uh-oh, there's Vincent, my boss, I mean my *ex* boss. Gotta go, Ellie. Please say hi to Tab for me and be sure to let me know when the book comes out."

"The book? What book? Oh, *that* book. You bet."

"From now on I'll be waiting tables at The Olive Garden," Theodora called over her shoulder. "Ask for me if you eat there and I'll give you free breadsticks."

Ellie nodded. She counted out the money for her lunch then added a five-dollar tip. She no longer needed an excuse to visit the kitchen and memorize Theodora's phone number, and she had no desire to face off with the surly Vincent. Anyway, she couldn't picture herself saying, "I'm writing a true-crime book, so I need to know why you quarreled with Sara Lee and raised your fist." If Vincent was the killer, he'd drag Ellie Bernstein, mature girl detective, by her un-streaked, naturally red hair, out the kitchen door and into the alley, where he'd trash her in the puke-green, putrid, icky Dumpster.

How would she ever explain *that* to Peter?

Should she visit the beauty salon again, ask Anne-Marie what she had seen the *second* time she went outside for her smoke break?

Or perhaps the best game plan would be to drive home, walk Scout, and try to figure out a game plan.

As she collected her Reigning Cats & Dogs bag and her purse, Ellie looked down at the *Hello, Dolly!* audition brochure that the hostess Micki had left on the table. It included a theatre logo, an address, a phone number, a descriptive cast list, and, of course, an audition time. Tryouts started at seven p—

Holy cow! JDCT!

JDCT wasn't Jewish something-or-other. The initials JDCT stood for John Denver Community Theatre. And according to his appointment book, Matthew Lester had penned a seven p.m. appointment for tonight, the night of the *Hello, Dolly!* auditions.

Although she could be dead wrong, Ellie didn't think Matthew Lester was the sort to take part in a community theatre production. Did the notation refer to a rendezvous with Sara Lee? Sure it did.

Deciphering JDCT must have honed her wits because Ellie suddenly pictured the cartons inside Matthew and Rachel Lester's upstairs storage room. Several boxes had been mailed to Rachel, and their return address labels had clearly stated: Houston, Texas.

Ellie couldn't recall the house numbers or zip code on the return labels, her memory wasn't *that* good, but she remembered the name of the street. Mainly because it sounded, somewhat, like the name of one of her favorite film stars, Jacqueline Bisset.

And that brought to mind something Rachel had once said.

Rachel had said that her sister Margee worked at Murder By The Book, an "awesome" mystery bookstore on Bissonnet Street.

THIRTY-TWO

As Ellie took Scout for a potty walk up and down neighboring streets, her mind raced.

She now felt an intense compulsion to call Rachel.

Yesterday she could justify *not* calling because Rachel's cell phone wasn't working. But today, this afternoon, she could get the phone number for Murder By The Book from their Web site or from an information operator. She could then call the bookstore and, when she explained the situation, they'd give her a home phone number for Margee. If Margee answered her phone, she could direct Ellie to Rachel. Even better, Margee could tell her sister about Matthew. If Rachel picked up the phone—

Then I'll play it by ear. Since she was outside, well away from her computer and telephone, Ellie decided to shelve her game plan, at least for the moment. Instead, she tried to focus on what she had learned at the strip mall.

She already knew, or at least suspected, that Sara Lee and Matthew Lester were having an affair, but she hadn't known that Sara Lee was "crazy-nuts" about Matthew. What if the motive for her murder was a simple cliché. What if she had said, "If you don't leave your wife, I'm going to tell her about us."

Except, there was one major problem with that premise. Sara Lee would have to leave her husband, and Ellie didn't think Trent Zachariah would take the news lightly.

Neither would Angel Pitt.

211

But if Trent hadn't hired a contract killer, he had an ironclad alibi—while Angel did not.

Vincent's threatening gesture at Sara Lee might be important or might not be important, but Ellie didn't believe the smoke-breakers from the beauty salon and the one smoker from the consignment store had anything to do with Sara Lee's murder. Too bad they hadn't seen a stranger lurking.

Speaking of strangers, Theodora had said that Sara Lee looked "sad" then "mad" while talking to a man with a big mole on his face. Was *that* an important clue or was Ellie Bernstein, mature girl detective, grasping at straws?

How about the hostess, Micki? Could she be a viable suspect? She didn't seem to be a team player. In other words, unless Ellie was sadly mistaken, Micki wasn't one of the "everybody liked Sara Lee" contingency. Micki was what some people might call "vertically challenged," but that hardly mattered in the big picture. Trent was six-four. Vincent was at least that tall. Angel Pitt was "basketball tall."

Was Nico tall? Rats! Ellie had never thought to ask Theodora. Or Micki. And what was all that nonsense about taking Micki home and getting her drunk enough to pass out? Was she supposed to be Nico's alibi? For what? And why were his sneakers muddy?

Hell, there could be a dozen explanations for muddy sneakers. Nico could have left his apartment in the dead of night to buy a pack of cigarettes. Or more vodka. Maybe he wanted to buy drugs. Maybe he wanted to play in the mud. Maybe he planned to kidnap and kill Matthew Lester.

If the same person had killed Matthew and Sara Lee, what would be Nico's motive for Sara Lee's murder? Has she discovered he was "cheating"?

Cheating at what?

A large, chocolate-colored dog crossed the street and

wandered toward Scout. Ellie tightened her grip on Scout's leash. The dogs sniffed each other.

"Let's say Sara Lee and Matthew were having a torrid affair and Nico was consumed by a jealous rage," Ellie said to Scout and the chocolate-colored dog, both of whom were bonding by sniffing each other's butts. "What if Nico had felt more than a casual interest in Sara Lee? What if he was obsessed by her?"

Except, a jealous lover was such a cliché.

Which brought Ellie back to Matthew Lester. Why had Matthew ended up as dead as a spawning salmon? What was the connection?

There was no connection.

Yes, there was.

Matthew was connected to Sara Lee by their affair, but he was also connected to Nico—and Angel—by the miraculous, neater-than-sliced-bread computer chip. And Audrey Hepburn was in *Always* with John Goodman, who was in *Death Sentence* with Kevin Bacon. Which didn't have anything to do with anything, except Jonina had asked Peter to ask Ellie how Kevin Bacon was connected to Audrey Hepburn. And, at the very least, the Kevin Bacon Six Degrees of Separation Game was something Ellie could chew over in her mind, assimilate, digest, and ultimately come up with an answer, dammit!

The dogs had finished sniffing butts, touching noses, wagging tails, and trying to out-piss one another. As Ellie turned toward home, she idly wondered how Lassie was connected to Kevin Bacon. Probably through Elizabeth Taylor.

"I'm sorry to cut your walk short, kiddo," Ellie told Scout, "but I need to track down your human."

Perhaps, she thought, a connection between Sara Lee and the killer could be found at tonight's *Hello, Dolly!* auditions. Dollars to doughnuts Peter would consider the auditions a waste of time, even if she told him about the entry in Matthew's appointment book. Peter would say that with Rachel out of town, her husband had simply scheduled a Sara Lee–tryst, and Peter was probably spot-on.

Still, it couldn't hurt to attend the auditions.

And it couldn't hurt to call Boulder and speak to her son Mick's fiancée, Sandra, who had once been an active member of the John Denver Community Theatre.

First, Rachel. The phone call to Houston could not, and should not, be put off any longer.

With any luck, Peter would have already gotten through to Rachel and she'd be winging her way back to Colorado Springs—for her husband's funeral.

On the other hand, if Peter had not gotten through and Ellie managed to get through, Rachel would, at the very least, have her sister close by—for comfort.

Except, according to Rachel, her sister was practically at death's door.

Ellie tightened her hold on Scout's lead and maneuvered around the cars that dotted her street. Once again, the pothole people were doing their tar thing on the main thoroughfare. Cursing the traffic, Ellie entered her house, shrugged off her jacket, and gave her pets their gifts from Reigning Cats & Dogs. Then she turned on her computer. She clicked herself into the bookstore's Web site, reached for a scratch pad, and wrote down the telephone number for Murder By The Book.

Before she could change her mind, she strode toward the kitchen phone, but stopped mid-step as her mind conjured up the perfect solution to her Rachel dilemma.

If Margee is too sick to be of comfort, I'll buy a plane ticket and fly to Houston.

She now knew two things. Walking the dog was a great way to think things through, even if the things thought through didn't quite mesh, and offering to help Rachel in her time of need was the best game plan of all.

Correction: she knew three things. Lassie was in *The Magic of Lassie* with Mike Mazurki. Mike Mazurki was in *Amazon Woman on the Moon* with Kelly Preston. Kelly Preston was in *Death Sentence* with Kevin Bacon.

THIRTY-THREE

Rachel Lester sighed and said, "I'm glad it wasn't the cats."

She lazed at the kitchen table, having just read the last two chapters of *Dream Angel*. Tomorrow, Kurt promised, she could read his "special dedication."

He had worked at his laptop computer all day, finishing up his novella. Now he was putting the finishing touches on a dinner concoction he called "Pot Luck Gordon." Which smelled heavenly, Rachel thought with a smile.

"I guess I'm not very good at solving mysteries," she continued. "You played fair with your clues, Kurt, but up until the last chapter I thought it was Gartrude and the seven cats who killed Angelique's auntie. I never guessed it was a hit man."

"Assassin," he said.

"Excuse me?"

"Hit man was a term coined in 1968. Usually a hit man works for a crime syndicate. Way back then, contract killers were called assassins."

"Okay, *assassin*." She smiled. "I suppose you have to do a lot of research to get everything right, huh?"

"Some," he said brusquely. "Rachel, I need to drive back to the Springs this Sunday. If you want to ride with me, we can return your car at a rental agency not far from my cabin. I know it's been idyllic up here in the mountains, but it's time to think about going home. And while you won't be facing the music, you'll be facing your demons, so I just want you to remember that I'm on your side and in your corner."

It wasn't an ultimatum, but it did require a decision she wasn't sure she wanted to make yet. Stunned at the suddenness of his proposition, all she could think of to say was, "Why do you have to go back to Colorado Springs?"

"Business."

"What kind of business?" A few days ago, she wouldn't have been brash enough to ask that question, especially since it was really none of *her* business.

"Bank business," he said, stirring the beef stew, which had been on low simmer in the Crock-pot since early this morning.

"I thought all the banks were closed on Sundays."

He took a long time answering, too busy adding spices to the beef, carrots and green beans. Instead of the ordinary potatoes you'd expect in a beef stew, Kurt had cooked up some perogies, the "luck" in his pot luck. Perogies, he explained, were dough rounds filled with everything from potato, bacon and cheese, to potato, cheese and sauerkraut. He had inherited his Polish grandmother's favorite perogie recipes.

"My accountant isn't closed, Rachel," he finally said. "We go over my investments, I sign a few checks, and then we watch the Broncos play football . . . while we drink beer. I don't drink and drive, so I'll stay overnight and come back on Monday."

Her gaze drifted toward the living room window, as if she could see her rental car parked under a tree. She had left her own car at the airport. Maybe all along she had planned not to go back, reckoning Scout would have a good, proper home with Ellie. Maybe Rachel Lester, the girl most likely to succeed at *something*, had left her car in the airport parking lot because that way, if anybody searched for her, they'd think she flew off in a plane. Of course, all they'd have to do was check out the airlines' rosters or the car rental agencies. But by the time they did that, she'd have moved to Greece, like Shirley Valentine, or if that was a hassle, she'd have stayed in Colorado with a new name. An alias wouldn't be too difficult to establish. In the romance novels she read, the heroines were always changing their identities and—

What a dreamer! What a naïve Pollyanna Pangloss!

Because Rachel Lester, the girl most likely to succeed at *nothing,* was such a scaredy-cat, she had been ready to leave Cee-Cee's cabin and return home the very same day she arrived. If it hadn't been for Kurt—

All of a sudden, she wondered why Kurt's business explanation made her feel so jittery, why a calm terror—and wasn't *that* an oxymoron?—had coursed through her body. His reply had made perfect sense, and yet his tone seemed to have a false ring to it, as if Quasimodo's bell had been fissured.

Baloney! Her imagination was working overtime.

For as long as she could remember, the taste of fear had tainted her breath and her morning mouthwash had been low self-esteem. She had tried adding self-confidence, rather than excess calories, to her home-cooked meals, and she had joined Ellie Bernstein's diet club with the fervent hope that less weight equaled more self-respect, but everything she tried, everything she accomplished, only seemed to lead to more self-abuse. She knew Matthew was responsible for that. She had thought he held the key to her emotions but, happily, it appeared that her heart's dead bolt could be opened by a universal key by the name of Kurt Gordon.

She had come here to Cee-Cee's cabin to make the most important decision of her life, a decision about the rest of her life, and now that the rest of her life had begun, she couldn't seem to make a decision. One could even say she couldn't make a decision to save her life.

Forget delusions, forget decisions, Rachel admonished silently. Right now, this very minute, what she really needed was a change of subject. "Kurt," she said, "do you earn lots of money?"

Oh, dear. She hadn't meant to say that, but she had been thinking about it ever since their first walk together, ever since he'd shown her his cabin. They hadn't gone inside but, unlike Cee-Cee's cabin, Kurt's A-frame looked as if it had been built by an architect. A high-priced architect. Parked near the house— you really couldn't call it a cabin—was a riding lawnmower and a snow blower. And a brand-new Jeep, or at least the latest model, with, she presumed, all the bells and whistles.

"I earn enough to maintain a comfortable lifestyle," he said as he put the lid on the Crock-pot, "but my ex-wife gobbles up a goodly portion of my income. My divorce lawyer wasn't the swiftest horse in the race. To be honest, I must assume some of the responsibility, but I'm not trained in the law and—" he smiled at Rachel "—I've never researched it."

"What went wrong?"

"My divorce lawyer and I never thought about my books. Lorna, it turns out, gets fifty percent of my profits, including royalties, for any and all books I wrote before and during our divorce. That's a huge chunk of my earnings, so I supplement my income with day jobs."

"I thought you wrote during the day."

He smiled. "That's just an expression, Rachel."

"What do you do? For your day jobs, I mean."

"This and that . . ." He paused. "Does my income matter? Will what I earn help you make a go-or-stay-with-Matthew-Lester decision?"

She shook her head so vigorously, her pageboy flipped from side to side. "I've never wanted to be rich, Kurt. All I need is a roof over my head, enough food to eat, and my dog Scout." She remembered her lawsuit. Should she mention it? If successful, the payoff might very well be her ticket to Independence, and she didn't mean Missouri. She had no idea why, but for now she'd rather keep her lawsuit a secret and, once again, she decided to change the subject. "You said you planned to watch the Broncos on a TV at your accountant's house. Do you watch a lot of TV?"

"No. The reception isn't very good up here in the mountains, unless you spring for a satellite dish, and I've never sprung." He grinned. "I do, however, like movies, so I've hooked up a CD player to my big-screen TV. Does my watching TV matter? Will it help you make a go-or-stay decision?"

"No." She laughed.

"Do you watch a lot of TV, Rachel?"

"Gosh, no. I much prefer to read a good book, and I avoid the news like the plague."

"I get *Newsweek* and *Time, Sports Illustrated* and *People,* and I have access to *The Washington Post* and *The New York Times* on the Internet. I also read political blogs. Does your decision to go or stay hinge on my political opinions?"

Again she shook her head. "One last question, Kurt. Do you know your Bible?"

"As well as the next guy, I suppose."

"Have you ever heard of Lot?"

"Sure. Sodom and Gomorrah. I never quite understood why God burned Gomorrah. Or the significance of the salt. Why do you ask?"

"If you had been Lot and God had told you not to look back, what would you have done?"

"That's an interesting question, Rachel. Okay . . . here's my answer. I don't like being told what to do. On the other hand, I hate looking back and I try to avoid it if at all possible."

"That's an interesting answer, Kurt, except you haven't really answered my question."

"Is my answer important? Will *that* help you decide whether to go home or stay here?"

"Yes."

He raised an eyebrow, the one without the scar. Then he said, "I'd have looked back."

THIRTY-FOUR

Scout gleefully chewed the gingerbread-flavored biscuit.

Jackie Robinson sniffed at the new mouse, gave Ellie a you've-got-to-be-kidding-have-you-ever-tasted-rubber look, and began to stalk Scout's wagging tail.

Ellie picked up her phone, took a deep breath, and tapped out Murder By The Book's number. It was seven o'clock, Texas time. Perhaps the store had closed for the day and she could leave her message on an answering machine.

The man who answered the phone identified himself as David . . . and Ellie stalled.

No way would the store give out an employee's personal telephone number. For all David knew, Ellie could be a "prying, officious, nosy" reporter. Angel's prying-officious-nosy remark had stung, but she hadn't been wrong, at least not from her perspective.

I should have asked Peter to call the bookstore, Ellie thought, just before she said, "My name is Ellie Bernstein. You have an employee named Margee. I know she isn't there right now, at the bookstore, but I need to get in touch with her sister Rachel. It's extremely important, a matter of life and—"

"Margee's here today. She's doing inventory."

"She is? But I thought she was ill, practically at death's door."

"Margee? I don't know where you got that idea. Margee's so healthy she'd make a vampire think twice about immortality. Hold on and I'll fetch her for you."

"Wait! I really need to speak to her sister, Rachel. Rachel Lester."

"Is that the sister Margee sends books to?"

Ellie pictured the cartons in the Lesters' spare room. "Yes."

"She's not here."

"Is she at Margee's house? A hotel? Do you have a contact number for her?"

"I mean she's not here in Houston. Margee even said something about inviting her sister to visit sometime next month. Hold on a minute."

Gobsmacked, Ellie held on for dear life. If she held on any tighter, her fingers would create deep grooves in the phone's exterior.

"I've just been told Margee's gone for the day," David said. "If you give me your phone number, I'll have her call you back."

Ellie gave David the information, disconnected, and stared at the phone.

If Margee wasn't sick and Rachel wasn't in Houston, where the heck was she?

Had she murdered Sara Lee?

And her philandering husband?

Then flown the coop?

No. Rachel couldn't kill a fly.

Neither could Norman Bates.

Maybe Rachel had hired a hit man. Then she skedaddled, taking off for . . . where?

Some place where she could establish an alibi. But if that were true, why hadn't she flown to Houston and used her sister Margee as an alibi?

In any case, shy Rachel would never hire an assassin. Unless she could dial 1-800-GUN-FOR-HIRE, she wouldn't even know where to start. It actually made more sense for methodical Rachel to pretend to leave town and then do the dirty deed herself.

Ellie took another deep breath and tapped out Peter's cell phone number. She really had no choice. He had to know about Rachel. Using his credentials, he could track down Margee through David, and find out if *she* knew anything about her sister's whereabouts.

Speaking of sisters, it might be prudent to let Peter know about Angel's fake alibi. Correction: It was *imperative* to let him know. She should have called him first thing this morning.

Even Peter's hello sounded exhausted. Ellie told him about remembering the name of the bookstore where Margee worked, and her phone call to the store, and her conversation with David.

Peter wrote down the information.

Then Ellie told him about meeting Angel at the Olive or Twist.

"That was a waste of time," he said, his voice colder than a Starbuck's mocha Frappuchino. "We questioned Angel Pitt and verified Trent Zachariah's alibi."

"But you didn't verify Angel's alibi, honey, and she hated Sara Lee with a passion. Angel said she was at her school. But Sara Lee was killed on Wednesday, during the teachers strike, so, obviously, Angel lied through her pretty teeth." When there was no response, Ellie said, "Peter, are you still there?"

"I'm here. I'm just counting to ten . . . very slowly. Ellie, what makes you think we didn't check out Angel Pitt's alibi?"

Uh-oh, Peter had called her Ellie rather than Norrie. He was beyond pissed off.

"I'm sorry," she said. "Of course you checked. So you already know Angel lied."

"She didn't lie."

"But the teachers walked out on Tuesday and Angel said she was—"

"At her school. Yes, I know. But she didn't say she was *in* her school, did she?"

"Yes. No. Oh my God, she was one of the strikers walking the picket line in front of her school!"

"Correct. She was *at* her school, just like she said she was."

"That seems a rather convenient alibi," Ellie said, reluctant to relinquish her Angel-killed-Sara-Lee hypothesis.

"It might be convenient, but it's also true. Not only can her fellow teachers verify her presence, but there are digital photos and videos all over the Net. Several show Angel smack-dab in the thick of things. Anything else you want to report, Ellie, just in case the CSPD has been lax lately?"

"I never said you were lax, Peter, and I'm sorry I bothered you."

"You never bother me, Norrie," he said, his voice thawing a little. "And I'm very grateful for the information about Rachel. While I've got you on the phone, I don't know about tonight. I might be stuck at . . . make that *in* the precinct again."

"I'll keep the home fires burning, Peter, unless I decide to go to the auditions for *Hello, Dolly!*" she said, but he had already hung up. Without his usual "I love you" and "Will you marry me?"

Perhaps he was so bushed he'd forgotten. No. He wouldn't have forgotten. Besides, his "will you marry me?" had become an automatic substitute for the clichéd "have a nice day."

Meanwhile, she had forgotten to tell *him* about Vincent's quarrel with Sara Lee and the threatening gesture that had followed the quarrel.

In fact, once he had called her Ellie, she had forgotten to tell Lieutenant Peter Miller, *sir,* about her visit to the strip mall and

her conversations with Micki and Theodora.
Accidentally on purpose?

Thirty-Five

The John Denver Community Theatre rented a building that had once been a flower shop run by a dapper man with two black thumbs. The building stood—perhaps a better word would be slouched—in between a bicycle shop and a Salvation Army thrift store.

Ellie knew that the Weight Winners organization had tried to rent the building, but the John Denver Community Theatre had already signed a three-year lease. Inside the shabby structure, JDCT volunteers stored costumes and props. On an improvised stage, directors held their rehearsals.

And their auditions.

As she circled a couple of blocks, looking for a parking space, Ellie thought about her phone conversation with her son Mick's fiancée, Sandra, who had once been a member of the JDCT.

Sandra had said the theatre group was incestuous. They had four directors who cast the same actors over and over again. The JDCT sponsors who contributed the most money were given non-speaking roles, for example, the townspeople in *Our Town.*

"I donated a hefty amount when I received my inheritance from my Grandmother Eleanor, and I've never been cast," Ellie had said. "But then, I've never auditioned."

"That would help," Sandra had said with a laugh.

Yes, Sandra had heard about Sara Lee. Yes, Sandra remembered Sara Lee. The poor kid had desperately wanted a part—

any part. To that end, she had worked the spotlights, painted sets, designed costumes, even joined the makeup crew, until the Peter Principle kicked in. Directors didn't want to cast her and forfeit her backstage expertise. Finally, Sara Lee refused to do any more grunge work. Somewhat reluctantly, a director had given her a part in *Fiddler on the Roof,* one of Tevye's daughters, the Bette Midler Broadway role. The show itself was mediocre but Sara Lee scored a huge success. Audiences adored her. Directors didn't. She had not shown one teensy speck of gratitude . . . or humility. She had thumbed her nose at them and they all had egos bigger than King Kong *and* Godzilla.

Sandra had performed in *Fiddler,* too. She had sung with the chorus and played—make that *vastly overplayed*—Fruma Sarah, which she felt was the director's fault.

Sara Lee, the only cast member to receive rave reviews, had ignored the director's directions.

After *Fiddler,* Sandra moved to Boulder.

"What are you going to sing at the audition, Ellie?" she had asked.

"Sing? You've got to be kidding. I don't plan to sing."

"You'd better. Otherwise they'll ask you to leave."

"Can't people just watch people try out?"

"Nope. JDCT auditions, especially musical auditions, always draw crowds, and they are paranoid about fire laws. If you don't audition, you don't stay."

"Aren't you exaggerating, just a little?"

"No, Ellie. You wouldn't believe how many people want to audition, even if they can't sing and they look dopey. Well, maybe you would, if you've ever watched the tryouts for 'American Idol.' Mick says I should try out for 'American Idol.' "

"Mick's right. Holy cow, Sandra, if I did sing, what would I sing?"

" 'Tomorrow' from *Annie*. Everyone always sings 'Tomorrow,' so the piano player will have it down pat and you won't have to bring sheet music. Unless you know the score from *Hello, Dolly!* That's a plus."

"I know all the songs, but—well, to be perfectly honest, I don't want to be cast in the show. My singing leaves a lot to be desired, my dancing is worse—do the words two left feet mean anything to you?—and my mother would bring all her red-hat lady friends to opening night."

"Then why attend the auditions? Aha! You're sleuthing, right?"

"Yes. I have a feeling there's some sort of connection between the John Denver Community Theatre and Sara Lee's murder."

"One of your gut feelings?"

"Yes, one of my gut feelings. Except I have to tell you, sweetie. My gut feelings haven't been working out too well lately."

Ellie's gut feeling grew stronger as she entered the audition room.

Of course, the feeling in her gut could be hunger. She had been too nervous to eat supper. Instead, she had rehearsed limitless renditions of "Tomorrow." Scout had howled as if she were being tortured, and Ellie had decided the only way she'd get through this audition insanity was to pretend she was singing to her Weight Winners group. "Tomorrow" was a good song for dieters.

To coin a cliché, the audition room was filled to the rafters. To coin another cliché, the noise was earsplitting. If Matthew and Sara Lee had truly planned an assignation, where the bloody hell would they have assignated? Even the staircase that led to a second-floor kitchen and restroom swarmed with bodies, and Ellie suspected that, just like the Olive or Twist, fire laws were being broken right and left.

At the front of the noisy mob, facing the improvised stage, the ferret-faced director and his young female assistant sat behind a long, narrow table. The director stared down at a clipboard while his assistant handed Ellie a form. Aside from the usual contact information, the questionnaire asked for previous experience. Leaning the piece of paper against a patch of wall, Ellie printed: SNOW WHITE AND THE SEVEN DWARFS. THIRD GRADE. I PLAYED DOPEY.

Heigh-ho, she thought as she turned in the form. She hoped her nervousness didn't show, but had a sneaking suspicion her complexion was the color of grapefruit. Pink grapefruit.

She found a seat between a girl who looked no older than eighteen and a man who smelled of hairspray. She smiled at both and said, "Hi, I'm Ellie."

"Tiffany," said the girl. "They call me Tiffy."

"Ray Morass," the man mumbled.

"Angel Zachariah Pitt," said a voice above and behind Ellie.

As she swiveled in her seat, Ellie felt her cheeks flame and her face turn from Tropicana Pink Grapefruit to Ocean Spray Cranberry. Attempting to regain her composure, she looked up at the young woman standing in front of an empty chair and said, "Angel! I was hoping you'd be here."

"Oh, right. Sure you were."

"No, really. I wanted to apologize for my snoopiness last night." She manufactured a fake pout. "And I'm especially glad you're here because I never got a chance to hear you sing the Leonard DiCaprio Titanic song."

Despite her angry eyes, Angel let loose with a chuckle. "You should hear what Cher calls some of the other songs. She calls Grace Slick's 'White Rabbit' the slick bunny-rabbit song, and 'Blue Suede Shoes' that blues song Elvis sings, the one where he says you can do anything you want to do."

As Ellie laughed, the girl seated next to her said, "Hi, Angel."

"Hi, Tiffy."

"What part are you trying out for?"

"Dolly." Angel smiled. "It's one of the few roles where the male lead can be shorter than the female lead."

"You'll get the part," Tiffy said, "now that Sara Lee's not in the picture."

She didn't even simulate a smidgen of sorrow, thought Ellie. Another everybody-didn't-like-Sara-Lee candidate?

"Yes, I'll get the part," Angel said. "Dolly was written with me in mind."

"Don't be so sure," snarled the man named Ray. "Every *girl* in this room wants Dolly."

Angel glared at him. Then she looked at Ellie and said, "What part are you trying out for, Tinkerbelle?"

"The chorus, I guess. But I've never auditioned for a show before, so I don't have much hope."

"Hey, look at it this way. Maybe you'll have beginner's luck." Angel pointed toward the stairs. "Some of my friends are waiting for me over there. Then we're okay, you and me?" At Ellie's nod, she said, "Good. I'm glad. See you later, Tinkerbelle."

Tiffy's gaze had followed Angel's retreat. Now she faced Ellie again. "I thought you said your name was Ellie. Where did Tinkerbelle come from?"

Ellie glanced down at her breasts before she remembered that she had changed clothes, and her Tinkerbelle sweater was now Mick's dark gray WoolEye sweatshirt, whose logo flaunted a wolf in sheep's clothing. "Tinkerbelle is my stage name," she said. "Just one name, like Madonna."

"Cool," Tiffy said.

The ferret-faced director, who looked like the villain in a melodrama, called for quiet. Immediately, the room grew eerily mute. A nervous cough tickled Ellie's throat.

An hour later she was no longer nervous, just bored. This

theatrical gamble had been a complete waste of time. No one appeared threatening, no one had the ambience of a murderer, and as far as she could tell, there weren't any men with large facial moles. Furthermore, her male seat companion's hairspray was making her super-sensitive nose run and her eyes tear.

Her other seat companion, Tiffany "call me Tiffy," was summoned to the makeshift stage. Tiffy announced that she would sing a song by rock star Yogi Demon. The piano player gave it his all, but without a backup band and synthesizer, Tiffy's voice sounded iffy.

Iffy Tiffy, thought Ellie, suppressing the desire to laugh. Damn, she was tired. And hungry. And frustrated. *But the sun'll come up tomorrow,* she thought, letting loose a brief, uncontrollable chortle.

The director obviously liked the girl's legs or bosom, because he convened several male hopefuls and asked them to "sing to Tiffy." Then he told Tiffy to stick around for the dance tryouts.

The hairspray man—Ray—cussed under his breath.

Finally the director said, "Ray Morass, get your butt on stage."

Tall, thin and muscular, Ray had a certain flamboyance. Ellie pictured the frou-frou interior of Reigning Cats & Dogs. Ray wore black jeans and a black turtleneck, but Ellie felt he should have been appliquéd and embroidered like the pet shop's adorable cat blazer. And although she desperately needed a restroom break, she wanted to hear him sing.

She didn't have long to wait. Nodding at the piano player, he said, " 'So Long Dearie.' "

"That's Dolly's song," the director said.

Ray said, "I'm trying out for Dolly."

The director said, "I want you to try out for Cornelius Hackl, the Michael Crawford role."

"I'm trying out for Dolly," Ray said. "A man has never played Dolly. Carol Channing played her on Broadway, then an all-black cast . . ." He paused and took a deep breath. "I'm not suggesting you change Dolly into a man, but we have wigs and gowns in Wardrobe, and a man playing Dolly would be different, innovative."

"We don't want to be innovative," the director said. "We want to sell tickets."

"But we *would* sell tickets. It's my belief that the audience would be intrigued—"

"Are you out of your mind? Sing 'It Only Takes a Moment' or sit down!"

"In Shakespeare's time, men played women's parts."

"This isn't Shakespeare's time," the director snapped. "Either try out for Cornelius Hackl or work the spotlights."

"I can't work the spots. Sara Lee—"

"Is dead," the director said. "Her vote is nullified. We had a quick revote and you can work the spots. Which reminds me." He raised his voice so it could be heard in the back of the crowded room. "Let's have two minutes of silent prayer, people. For Sara Lee."

With a scowl, Ray returned to his seat and bowed his head. Again, Ellie was almost overwhelmed by the smell of his hairspray. Again, the room was eerily mute.

This time she didn't have to cough. Instead, she heard an intrusive sound.

Several people glanced her way with unmistakable malice.

"You're supposed to turn off your cell phone during auditions," Tiffy whispered.

"Sorry," Ellie whispered back, just before she bolted for the exit. She had undoubtedly blown any chance for a *Hello, Dolly!* role, even a small part, but she had finally remembered to tote her cell phone, and only two people would call her after 7:00 p.m. Mick and Peter.

"Where are you?" Peter asked, his voice so low she had to

Denise Dietz

strain to hear him.

"*Hello, Dolly!* auditions, although I don't know why. So far, it's been a complete waste of time, but a seven p.m. JDCT appointment was in Matthew Lester's appointment book and I had one of my gut feelings, so I decided to check it out. Angel Pitt is here, auditioning for Dolly, but since I spoke to you earlier on the phone, I no longer think she had anything to do with Sara Lee's murder."

"What's a JDCT?"

"The initials JDCT stand for John Denver Community Theatre. Sorry, I thought everybody knew that. Where are you, Peter, and why are you whispering?"

"I'm at your house. I was scarfing down your honey lasagna sauce when I heard the doorbell. Your friend Rachel is back in town. A man driving a brand-new Jeep—with a German shepherd mix riding shotgun on the back seat—dropped Rachel off at your house so she could collect Scout. She saw the lights on in the house and my car in the driveway and she figured somebody was home and could drive *her* home. The man skedaddled when I answered the door."

"Have you told her?"

"Yes."

"I'll be right there."

234

THIRTY-SIX

If the JDCT auditions room had been eerily mute, Ellie's family room was as silent as the grave. The only hint of any resonance came from the kitchen, where Peter was preparing herbal tea. Ellie couldn't catch the sound of his sock-clad footsteps but she heard the clink of china and the mournful whistle of the teakettle.

The house smelled of honey lasagna sauce and dog.

Spread out across the patchwork quilt, all legs and legs, Scout gnawed a rawhide bone. Still pointedly ignoring his new rubber mouse, Jackie Robinson played tether ball with the license that swung from Scout's collar.

Rachel wore a sweatshirt and sweatpants and a Colorado Rockies baseball cap. She greeted Ellie with, "A friend bought this baseball cap for me on the way home . . . at a gas station."

Then, as if someone had stuffed a cork into an open wine bottle, she hadn't said another word.

Ellie didn't know what to say, either. "I'm sorry for your loss" sounded so inadequate. "Where the heck have you been hiding?" sounded even worse.

Finally, Rachel heaved a deep sigh. Slicing through the curtain of silence, she said, "I know it's a bother, Ellie, but I want to go home."

"It's no bother—"

"Had I known about my husband . . . had I known what happened, I would have asked my friend to drop me off at home.

He's staying until Monday, but I don't know how to reach him. He said he'd give me time . . . time to face my demons . . . and then he'd call. My cell phone is broken. He . . . my friend has my other number, so I need to be there . . . at home."

"No, sweetie. You'll stay here tonight. I have a guest room and—"

"Please, I want to go home."

"We'll talk about it, okay? I'll help Peter with the tea and be right back. Don't move."

A stupid request, thought Ellie, since Rachel sat motionless on the couch. Ellie had a feeling she could leave Rachel alone for three minutes, or thirty minutes, and when she came back, Rachel wouldn't have moved a muscle.

Inside the kitchen, Ellie said, "Rachel wants to go home, Peter. Is her house still a crime scene?"

"Not really. It's been combed and dusted, but we don't think Matthew Lester was killed inside the house."

"Where do you think he was killed?"

"In the trunk of the car. That's where we found him and that's where we believe he was killed."

"How was he killed?"

"Plastic bag."

"Someone put a plastic bag over his head?" She shuddered at the image. "What kind of plastic bag?"

"What do you mean, what kind of plastic bag? The kind of plastic bag that's made out of plastic."

"Really, Peter, now *you* sound like Tab. Was the bag the kind you can buy in any supermarket? Or was it an industrial bag, like the bags you order in bulk for, oh, say a restaurant?"

"Unfortunately, Norrie, the killer didn't leave us an explanatory note. Or the plastic bag. We're hoping to learn more after the autopsy, but Matthew Lester's mouth was covered with duct tape and his hands were tied behind his back. We have no blood spatters, no fingernail scrapings, no—"

"Have you traced the owner of the car?"

"Yes."

"And that owner is . . . ?"

Peter began to run his hands through his hair. Then he stopped and said, "Sara Lee."

"Sara Lee," Ellie parroted.

"The car is a demo from her husband's lot. Vincent the Chef said she kept her car keys in her apron pocket."

"Are you telling me that somebody killed Sara Lee, stole her keys, stole her car, and stuffed Matthew Lester inside the trunk?"

"Yup. And before you ask, there were no fingerprints. Whoever stole the car wore gloves. There were no obscure clues, either, like you always see on TV, even though the car was full of junk. Water bottles, a hairbrush, a can of hairspray, maps to Nashville and Los Angeles, and . . . why are you looking at me like that?"

"How come Sara Lee's murderer didn't stuff *Sara Lee* inside the trunk of her car?"

"It was daylight when Sara Lee was killed. Plus, we figure the perp was making a statement. He or she considered Sara Lee trash. That's why he or she dumped her in the Dumpster."

Ellie remembered Micki's hostile expression and wondered if the hostess considered Sara Lee trash. Sara Lee was married. Micki didn't sport a wedding ring so she was probably single. Sara Lee was committing adultery and Micki would surely consider that trashy.

Wait a sec. "Peter, what time was Matthew killed?"

"I haven't received the autopsy report yet. And before you ask why not—"

"Remember that real life, or real death, isn't like a TV cop show," Ellie finished.

Micki had worked the lunch *and* dinner shifts, Ellie thought.

Could Micki have had enough time to steal Sara Lee's car keys, steal Sara Lee's car, abduct Matthew, kill him, then bus back to the restaurant in time for the dinner shift? Al had said the restaurant closed at three and opened again at five, so Micki's window of opportunity would have been less than two hours. She was tall enough to strangle Sara Lee from behind, but was she strong enough to overpower Matthew?

Nico's window of opportunity would have been exactly the same.

Ellie didn't know what Nico looked like, but she figured him for a stud. Studs were almost always hunky. Micki had said that Nico carried her from the restaurant to his car, from his car to his apartment. Ergo, hunky! Micki had also said that Nico licked the end of his pen before he wrote down food and beverage orders. Ellie tried to dismiss the image of a hunky thug with a black tongue, pouring vodka, nonstop, down Micki's throat so that he could . . . what?

Suppose—after his lunch shift—Nico had kidnapped Matthew and left him in the trunk of Sara Lee's car? Suppose Nico had worked the dinner shift, then driven Micki to his apartment and plied her with vodka until she passed out? Suppose Nico had left Little Miss Alibi asleep in his bed, gone back to the parked car, and killed Matthew? But why? Because Matthew had found out that Nico was "cheating"?

Chef Vincent might have had the same window of opportunity. He'd worked the lunch shift, but had he worked the dinner shift? And if he had worked the dinner shift, had he stayed until the restaurant closed? Vincent had quarreled with Sara Lee, even raised his fist to her, but why kill Matthew?

Because Matthew had seen Vincent strangle Sara Lee and—

"Earth to Norrie! The wheels are spinning inside your head. What are you brooding over?"

"I'm not brooding, Peter, I'm mulling. I happen to know that

Vincent quarreled with Sara Lee, even threatened her physically."

"Yes, we know about that. Vincent told us right off the bat. He was chastising Sara Lee for the osso bucco she snitched during the lunch shift."

"He yelled and raised his fist because she stole some braised veal shanks?"

"No, because she broke a restaurant rule, and Vincent is very big on rules. Servers can have all the soup, salad and bread they want for free, but not the entrées."

"What about Al?"

"What *about* Al?"

"He said . . . during a TV interview he said he saw Sara Lee in the alley . . . wait, let me think. His exact words were, 'She was rehearsing for the John Denver Community Theatre's *Hello, Dolly!* tryouts and she sounded more like Streisand than Streisand.' Al's not very tall, but you said there was a ladder in the kitchen and—"

"Sara Lee always sang in the alley, and on Wednesday she sang all day, inside and outside the restaurant, rehearsing for the *Hello, Dolly!* auditions. If Al said she sang in the alley, it doesn't necessarily mean he saw her there. Anyway, what's his motive?"

"I don't suppose the stolen osso bucco will fly as a motive, huh? Okay, scratch Al. By the way, where was the stolen car found? The car with Matthew's body in the trunk."

"In a restaurant's parking lot."

"The strip mall's parking lot?" At Peter's incredulous stare, Ellie said, "Sorry, I didn't get much sleep last night. If Sara Lee's car had been found in the strip mall's parking lot, it wouldn't have been stolen. It would have been . . . coffinized. Which restaurant?"

"Some kind of upscale rib joint on Academy, near the Chapel

Hills Mall. It went out of business three months ago—the restaurant, not the mall. A woman didn't know it had gone out of business. She parked her car, opened its door, and her dog jumped out. The dog peed on one of Sara Lee's tires and the woman smelled something in the trunk and—"

"I get the picture."

The Chapel Hills Mall isn't all that far from Uncle Vinnie's, Ellie mused, *so Micki or Nico could have made it back to work on time. Let's say one of them caught Matthew by surprise and—*

"Ellie?" Rachel walked into the kitchen. "All I need is Scout's food and I'll be ready to leave." She turned to Peter. "Let me apologize again for my hysterics, Lieutenant Miller. You've been very kind."

"Ms. Lester, I really think—"

"Please call me Rachel."

"Yes, well, I really think you should stay here tonight, Rachel. I have to leave again and Ellie could sure use your company. And Scout's company, as well."

Clever, Ellie thought. Except she could see by the expression on Rachel's face that Peter's subtle subterfuge wasn't working.

Ellie said, "Peter, why don't I go home with Rachel and spend the night there?"

"Good idea," he said.

"That isn't necessary," Rachel said. "Really it isn't. I'll be okay. I feel much better now."

"But keeping you company will make *me* feel better," Ellie said. "Anyway, I have to drive you and Scout home, so I might as well stay overnight."

As Rachel, defeated, closed her eyes and nodded, Scout nosed Jackie Robinson's belly.

The cat caught Scout's nose between his front paws, claws retracted.

And . . . Jackie Robinson purred.

Ellie felt her jaw drop. The idea of taking Cindy Silberblatt's black and white puppy, Muppet, on board began to look better and better.

Except she really didn't want a dog.

She knew Peter would say it was okay with him, as long as she didn't treat the dog like a furry little person. But, she thought, grinning inside, Muppets *were* furry little people.

Okay, God, here's the deal. If by some miracle I'm cast in Hello, Dolly!, *I'll adopt Muppet. If not, I'll find someone else to adopt her.*

Ellie didn't bother telling God that she hadn't tried out for a part.

THIRTY-SEVEN

If the audition room had been eerily mute and Ellie's family room as silent as the grave, Rachel's house was as silent as a tomb.

Scout settled down on her quilt, happy to be home.

Just like Wednesday night, a storm was brewing. Ellie heard the wind and the muted sound of distant thunder. "Would you like me to check the windows?" she asked Rachel. "Make sure they're all shut?"

"I'll do it."

"Sweetie, please sit down, lie down, drink some tea. When was the last time you ate?"

"I wanted to leave before suppertime, before I changed my mind. We returned my rental car and wrapped up the Pot Luck Gordon to go. It's in my purse . . . or my suitcase . . . I don't remember. So I guess lunch was the last time I ate. We had Zucchini a la Grecque Gordon. The recipe calls for three eggs."

"We, who?"

"I bet I can donate more Weight Winners recipes than Charlene Johnson. Thing is, they're all called Gordon. Quiche Gordon, Eggs Gordon, Pot Luck Gord—"

"Rachel, sweetie, where have you been? You don't have to answer if you don't want to, but I know you weren't in Houston. Or if you were, you weren't taking care of your sick sister."

"You talked to Margee?" Rachel removed her baseball cap

and tossed it toward the living room couch. She had cut her hair.

"No, I didn't talk to your sister," Ellie said. "But I called Murder By The Book and the owner told me Margee was healthy as the proverbial horse. In fact, she was taking inventory. She had just left or I would have spoken with her. Your new haircut looks terrific."

"Thanks. My . . . friend . . . cut it when I insisted I wanted it short. I wonder why they always say that . . . healthy as a horse, I mean. I've seen documentaries about wild horses on TV, Ellie, and they looked starved and skinny and hungry, always hungry, for food, for affection, for *one* kind word."

"If you weren't in Texas, Rachel, where were you?"

Before she could answer or sidestep the question again, the phone rang. It sounded very loud. Rachel snatched up the receiver. As she listened, a smile transformed her face. "I'm all right, Kurt," she said. "No, that's okay. Do your thing with your accountant and I'll see you Monday. Yes, somebody is with me, the friend who took care of my dog. Yes, I feel the same way."

Ellie hummed an off-key rendition of "Hello, Dolly!" to distract herself from what was obviously an intimate conversation.

Rachel hung up the phone and said, "I planned to fly to Houston, Ellie. Instead, I borrowed a mountain cabin from Cee-Cee Sinclair. Do you know Cee-Cee?"

"Yes. I once helped her with a fund-raiser for Canine Companions. Why didn't you tell me about the cabin?"

"I didn't tell *anybody*. I needed to be alone, to think. About Matthew. Matthew and me. I've wanted to leave him for a long, long time but I was afraid."

"Why? Did he threaten you?"

"No. Not physically. I was afraid because of this." She extended her hand. "My fingers claw up. I've seen doctors.

243

They say they can operate, but they can't guarantee success, and there's a fifty-fifty chance I could lose the use of my hand. Matthew made it very clear that no one else would want me with . . . my deformity . . . and that I'd be alone for the rest of my life. My . . . I guess you'd call it my plumbing . . . is cockeyed and I can't have children, but I've always owned dogs. First, Atticus. Then, Boo. Now, Scout. But dogs don't live very long, not unless you count every year as seven years . . ." Rachel shook her head as if to clear it.

"So you borrowed Cee-Cee's cabin to think things out. That was very clever, Rachel. What did you decide to do?"

"At first I decided not to decide, the same decision I've made a hundred times before." Tears stained her cornflower-blue eyes. "I told myself my life wasn't really that bad. After all, I had a roof over my head, food to eat, a generous checking account, and Scout. I planned to cut my trip short and drive home. Then, as if preordained, I met this really nice man—"

"Kurt?"

"Yes. You have to understand, Ellie. Matthew and I haven't shared the same bed for years. I asked him why, once. He said my hand repulsed him. He didn't even sugarcoat it, just came right out and . . ." She paused to wipe away her tears with her sleeve. "He was always cruel, like a sniper. He used words instead of bullets, and I learned not to fight back because . . . well, that would only give him more ammunition. Kurt insisted I ask Matthew for a divorce, but I still couldn't make up my mind, so I asked Kurt what he'd do if he was Lot."

"Lot," Ellie repeated. "The biblical Lot?"

"Yes. I asked Kurt if he'd look back and he said he would. Then he clarified. He stared into my eyes and said if his wife turned into a pillar of salt, he'd look back so he could be with her. It's the most romantic thing anybody ever said to me. So I decided to come home, and then Lieutenant Miller told me about Matthew, and I can't really mourn him. I wish I could, but my only feeling is relief." Face awash with new tears, she said, "And guilt. If I had been here, maybe it wouldn't have happened."

"Rachel, bad things happen. It's *not* your fault."

"Then why do I feel so guilty? I can cry for myself, but why can't I cry for Matthew?"

"You feel guilty because you're human and you'll probably have a nice long cry for Matthew later, when it sinks in. Why don't I put the kettle on and make us some tea and you can tell me about Kurt. Or would you rather try and sleep?"

"I'd rather keep busy."

"When I'm upset, I clean house."

"I cleaned house before I left, but I was about to pay my bills and—why are you nodding?"

Ellie felt her cheeks bake. "I trespassed, Rachel, looking for Scout's missing food. I had a gut-feeling . . . something felt wrong . . . so I checked out all the rooms in your house. That's how I discovered the scattered bills on top of your desk. I didn't look at them," she hastened to add.

"The bills couldn't have been scattered, Ellie. I left them stacked in a neat pile. After I write a check and put a stamp on the envelope, I scribble *paid* and the date across the invoice. Then I file the invoice." Almost yelling, she said, "My CPA sends me a thank-you note every Dopey . . . every Doc . . . every *goddamn* year!"

"Take it easy, sweetie. Maybe Matthew was looking for . . ." Ellie swallowed the rest of her words as Rachel raced toward the study.

By the time Ellie had joined her, Rachel sat at her desk. Although her hand had curled, she sifted invoices through her fingers as if she sifted flour for a cake. No, not invoices. Credit card receipts.

Denise Dietz

"I think you're right, Ellie," she said, calmer now. "I think Matthew was looking for a specific charge. Maybe he bought his waitress a piece of jewelry and—"

"You knew about Matthew and Sara Lee?" Ellie couldn't keep the surprise out of her voice.

"Yes."

"Did you know that Sara Lee was murdered two days ago?"

"No! Oh my God! Oh, that's awful. Did her murder have anything to do with Matthew? Do you know who killed her?"

"I don't know who killed her, and I don't know if it had anything to do with your husband, and—what's the matter, Rachel? You have a funny look on your face."

"Something's fishy." She scrutinized a credit card receipt. "This is from Uncle Vinnie's Gourmet Italian Restaurant. That's not unusual, Matthew eats . . . ate there all the time. But the tip is humongous. Here's another receipt from Uncle Vinnie's. Again, the tip is very generous, nearly fifty percent."

She paused to take a deep breath. "Matthew is . . . was a horrible tipper. When we ate out, I'd make some excuse, return to the table, and leave more money on the tip tray."

"Perhaps," Ellie said, "he was paying Sara Lee for . . . special services."

"No. The server's name on the credit card slip . . . the name on both slips . . . is N-I-C-Q. I wonder what that stands for."

"Nico. He's a waiter," Ellie said, looking over Rachel's shoulder. "The hostess said Nico licks the nib of his pen before he writes. That's why the O looks like a Q. It's smeared."

"Here's another receipt. The server's name on the slip is Lois. The amount is twenty-two dollars and fifty cents and the tip is two dollars. That's more like Matthew. What the *hell* is going on?"

"I don't know. Yes, I do. My brother Tab worked one summer as a waiter. He said another waiter always earned humongous tips and nobody could understand why because he was a worse waiter than Tab—if that's possible. Turns out the waiter ran the customer's credit card through the credit card machine twice. He handed one slip to the customer, who wrote in the tip and signed the slip. Then the waiter filled in a bogus tip on the second slip, forged the signature, and ripped up the first slip."

"Sounds foolproof," Rachel said.

"Not quite. Eventually the waiter at my brother's restaurant got caught by an irate customer who checked his credit card receipts against his credit card bill, but the restaurant didn't prosecute because of the bad publicity. If hordes of people knew about the doctored tips, they'd be standing in line, asking for their money back. And the restaurant, not the waiter, would have to pay. Holy cow, Rachel. Vincent and Al still use the old-fashioned credit card machines. Shame on them. Everything's computerized now. Nico couldn't print out two credit card slips if Uncle Vinnie's used a computer. Of course, he could add any tip he wanted to add into the computer when he closed out the ticket, but at the end of the shift his credit card total wouldn't jive with the computer's total. Owners or managers tend to check both totals against each other, so the scam would be too chancy."

"My goodness, Ellie, how do you know all this?"

"One of my diet club graduates is a waitress at Red Lobster. We went there for lunch one day, after the Friday morning meeting, and we talked about it. I don't remember why. I think I mentioned the crooked waiter my brother worked with. Anyway, getting back to business, is that Matthew's signature at the bottom of the receipts?"

"Yes." Rachel peered at a couple of signatures. "If this Nico person forged my husband's name, he's in the wrong business. He should be forging van Gogh's name. Or Picasso's name. Or Marilyn Monroe's name. He'd make a fortune at auctions."

"Let me see a Nico receipt and a Lois receipt." Ellie stared down at the two slips. "Do you happen to have a magnifying glass?"

"Sure. Doesn't everyone?" Rachel opened a desk drawer.

"Thanks. That's better. I can see the difference now."

"What difference? I swear, it's Matthew's signature."

"Then why would he use one continuous slash to cross every 't' on the Lois receipt, but two separate slashes on the Nico receipt—one slash for Matthew and one for Lester? Is there a Sara Lee receipt? Let me have it. Look, Rachel, one slash, not two."

"Matthew *always* used one slash. The Nico receipt is a forgery." Rachel twisted her wedding band. "I never look at the receipts, Ellie. I never even look at individual charges. I just pay what it says we owe."

"I do the same thing, Rachel."

"So let's say Matthew discovered the discrepancy." She nodded toward the messy pile of receipts. "Then what?"

"My guess is that he blackmailed Nico. How's the real estate business doing these days, Rachel? Was Matthew selling a lot of houses?"

"Yes . . . up until the middle of August. Summer should be the best time to sell houses, but he hit a slump. That's why he insisted I call attorney Jonah Feldman and initiate a class-action suit." She held up her clawed hand and heaved a deep sigh. "Long story."

"I wondered why Matthew had Jonah's name and fax number on his calendar. I was going to call Jonah, but I forgot."

"You've been busy."

Ellie thought Rachel meant busy sleuthing until she pointed toward the Christmas photo of Scout. "Your dog was no problem, Rachel. In fact, my cat, Jackie Robinson, dog-sat. Okay, let's put our heads together and figure this thing out.

Wednesday afternoon Matthew ate lunch at Uncle Vinnie's Gourmet Italian Restaurant. Nico served him. My guess is that Nico pulled his scam."

Peter said there was a huge tip on the credit card and the server was Nicholas!

"Matthew told Tab that Nico was cheating," Ellie continued.

"Tab?"

"My brother. Your husband was setting in motion an investment opportunity, and my brother Tab was involved, but Matthew told him to stop investing because Nico was cheating. Let's say Matthew confronted Nico and threatened to expose the cheat, or con, unless Nico coughed up some hush money. Let's say Sara Lee knew about the credit-card scam. The waitress who found Sara Lee's body said everybody at the restaurant knew about Matthew and Sara Lee, so Nico probably thought Sara Lee had told Matthew during one of their . . . uh . . ."

"Trysts. Go on."

"Nico grabbed some gloves, probably rubber dishwasher gloves, and slithered like a snake through the kitchen and into the alley. He strangled Sara Lee and tossed her in the Dumpster. It wouldn't have taken him very long. He stole her car, followed Matthew home, caught him by surprise, knocked him out, duct-taped his mouth, and stuffed him into Sara Lee's car trunk."

Rachel shuddered and Ellie said, "Sorry. Maybe I should shut up."

"No. Go on. Please."

"Nico drove around, looking for a safe place to kill Matthew and leave the car. But time was running out. He had to work the dinner shift and he had to take a bus to the restaurant because his car was already there, so he left Sara Lee's car in a vacant parking lot. He either taped Matthew's mouth shut or figured Matthew could yell his head off and nobody would hear him. Nico couldn't leave the car in the strip mall lot because after Sara Lee's murder there were too many cops milling around, not to mention that nosy reporter who looks like a monkey. Let's say Nico spent the dinner shift trying to think of a way to kill Matthew and not get caught. He saw some plastic bags in the kitchen and snagged one. He took the hostess, Micki, home with him—to establish an alibi. He plied her with vodka, and when she passed out, he took his car back to Sara Lee's car. He killed Matthew, but he had to leave Sara Lee's stolen car in the vacant parking lot. He couldn't move it to another, more secluded spot. How would he get back to *his* car? Buses don't run that late and walking was out of the question. The wind was almost gale force and it was raining pitchforks."

Ellie felt her cheeks flush. "You probably don't understand half of what I'm saying, but does any of it make sense?"

"Absolutely."

"Then I'll call Peter. I think I have enough ammunition in my arsenal now."

Once she'd outlined her theory, she could practically *feel* Peter's skepticism.

"I bet if you pretend you know everything for a fact, Nico will confess," she said. "Just read him his rights and lie like hell."

"Norrie, that only works on TV."

"The hostess said Nico licks his pen before he writes up tickets, Peter. Tell him you tested his spit and it matched the DNA found on Matthew."

"We didn't find any DNA."

"Lie!"

"Before I can lie, we've got to have probable cause. I'll buy the credit-card scam, Norrie, but why would Matthew Lester shake down Nico? Waiters don't earn big bucks."

"Some do. Tab did, and he could hardly walk across the floor without spilling a beverage on a customer . . . I mean a *guest*. Let's say Nico has a hidden stash and Sara Lee just happened to mention it to Matthew."

"Then why didn't she mention Nico's scam?"

"Maybe she *promised* not to tell. From the photo they showed on the TV newscast, Sara Lee looked like she'd keep a promise through thick and thin, until her dying day."

THIRTY-EIGHT

Saturday

Ellie said, "Nico didn't kill Sara Lee."

She and Peter were snuggled together in front of the fireplace, their butts denting a soft-cushioned sofa, their bare feet atop a coffee table, their toes stretched toward the warmth of the fire.

"C'mon, Norrie," Peter said, glancing toward their celebratory bottle of Spumante Ballatore. "You were the one who figured the whole thing out, the one who caught the bad guy."

She shook her head. "Nico is tall, dark and handsome, but he seems to be one sandwich short of a picnic. He said Sara Lee knew about his credit-card scam, but why didn't he confess to her murder? When you questioned him at the precinct, he admitted he killed Matthew, claimed it was self-defense. So why not admit he killed Sara Lee?"

"With Matthew, Nico can try a self-defense defense. I don't think anyone would buy self-defense when it comes to Sara Lee, who was five-foot-nothing and weighed a hundred pounds soaking wet. Nico wanted to invest in the same computer chip your brother thought was so miraculous. Nico had saved up twenty grand, minus the five thousand to show good faith. Sara Lee knew about the twenty thousand and blabbed to Matthew, who wanted half or he'd tell Vincent and Al about the credit-card scam. Nico swears he didn't plan to kill Matthew, just scare him. But if you believe that, I've got a bridge in Brook—"

"Nico *swore* he didn't kill Sara Lee, and I, for one, believe him."

Peter sighed and wiggled his toes. "Then who do *you* think did it?"

"I don't know."

"Wait. Let me write this down. Then you can date it and sign it. Ellie Bernstein doesn't know—"

"But I've been thinking about it a lot and—holy cow, Peter!"

"What?"

"Hairspray!"

"What do you mean, hairspray?"

"Just a sec."

Barefoot, Ellie walked into the kitchen. Retrieving the telephone directory from the top of her refrigerator, she looked up a number and tapped it out on her phone.

"Oh, I'm so glad you're still open," she said, praying the receptionist—if it was the same receptionist—wouldn't recognize her voice. "A friend recommended a hairdresser named Raymond. Do you happen to have a hairdresser named Raymond?"

"Norrie . . ."

She covered the mouthpiece. "Hush, Peter. We happen to know they have a hairdresser named Raymond." She uncovered the mouthpiece. "You do? What's his last name, please?"

"Norrie, what the hell are you doing?"

"What do you mean your stylists go by first names only? Look, my hair is very important to me and, believe it or not, more than one Raymond cuts hair in this town! His last name is Morass? Thank you. He's the one I want."

"Norrie!"

She held up her hand for silence. "I should book an appointment today? Why? Is Raymond planning to leave town or something?" She laughed, and even to her own ears, she sounded like a donkey. Fake laughs had never been her strong suit. "Oh, I see. He's going to cut down on his shifts because he scored a part in the John Denver Community Theatre's production of *Hello, Dolly!* Good for him. I'll call you back ASAP. Bye."

Peter steered her to a chair. Applying pressure to her shoulders, he helped her sit. "Okay, what was *that* all about?"

"Theodora Mallard, the waitress who found Sara Lee, said—"

"When did you talk to Theodora Mallard?"

"Yesterday. If you ever spent more than five minutes with me, Peter, I would have told you."

"Low blow. I was investigating a homicide."

"So was I. Before she trashed the trash, Theodora saw three beauty salon operators in the alley. Anne Marie, Bruce and Raymond, only he likes people to pronounce it Ray-moan."

"We questioned Anne-Marie, Bruce and Raymond, and everybody else in the strip center."

"If *I* had been able to question Raymond, I would have figured it out sooner."

"Figured what out?"

"Ray Morass, also known as Raymond, also known as Ray-moan, killed Sara Lee. I sat next to him at the auditions, Peter. He *reeked* of hairspray. Holy cow! Didn't you say you found a can of hairspray in Sara Lee's stolen car?"

"Nico stole the car," Peter reminded her.

"Okay, so the hairspray in the car belonged to Sara Lee. Ray Morass reeked because he works at a beauty salon. And he probably went straight from the salon to the auditions."

"If he's the killer, and I'm not saying he is, what's his motive?"

She sighed. "I don't know." She smiled. "Yes, I do. At the auditions, Ray was moody, petulant. He told the director he couldn't work the spotlights for the show, and it had something to do with Sara Lee because the director said that Sara Lee was dead so her vote didn't count. The exact word he used was 'nullified.' Her vote was nullified."

"Are you telling me that Raymond the hairdresser killed Sara Lee so that he could work the spotlights for a local community theatre production of *Hello, Dolly!*?"

"No, Peter. I think Ray wanted a part *in* the production, and I think he thought Sara Lee would keep him from getting one."

"How could she do that?"

"Vincent's brother Al said she sounded more like Streisand than Streisand. Mick's Sandra said audiences adored Sara Lee and—"

"When did you speak to Sandra?"

"In between my snooping at the restaurant and my sleuthing at the auditions. If you ever spent more than five minutes—"

"Go on."

"If Sara Lee was cast as Dolly, she'd probably have enough clout to uncast Ray in any part he got. Or perhaps . . ."

"Perhaps what?"

"Perhaps he wanted to *play* Dolly. He said as much when the director called him up to the auditions stage. The director wouldn't let him try out for Dolly, but Ray didn't know that last Wednesday."

"How could he strangle Sara Lee? He's a *hairdresser.*"

"Actually, he's a stylist. And please don't stereotype."

"I wasn't stereotyping."

"Yes, you were. Ray is tall and muscular, in a wiry way, and—hunky. Can we get a search warrant?"

"You know better than that. There's no probable cause. I suppose I could tell the judge you've solved three homicides and you have a gut feeling, but somehow I think—"

"Okay, let's pay him a visit."

"The judge?"

"No, Peter. Ray Morass."

"Seriously, Norrie, you've got to be kidding."

"Seriously, Peter, I'm not kidding."

"You can't just knock on somebody's door and—"

"You may make fun of my gut feelings all you want, but I have a major one right now. Ray Morass killed Sara Lee, and I need you to come with me. You're more astute than I am, Peter, more experienced. Your instincts are far superior to mine, not to mention your heroic strength."

And your cop's credentials.

He snorted. "Flattery will get you nowhere, especially when it's insincere."

"Insincere? I'm hurt to the quick."

"I'll kiss your quick and make it better," he said, giving her a Groucho leer.

"If flattery will get me nowhere, how about bribery?" She looked at the wall clock. "In a couple of hours *Jeopardy!* will be on." She winked and tried to assume her best come-hither look. "And tonight, my darling, it's the Tournament of Champions."

"You should have called for backup," Ellie said as Peter drove down Ray Morass's street.

"Why do we need backup? I doubt this guy is armed."

"Are you stereotyping again?"

"I wasn't stereotyping the first time. But if it makes you feel better, I called Will McCoy and asked him to meet us here."

"Oh, good." Ellie adored Peter's partner, who possessed more street-smarts and far less stubbornness than Peter.

"If you're wrong about your hairdresser, Norrie, we pay McCoy's bar tab tomorrow at the Dew Drop Inn. That means *you* pay."

"If I'm wrong, and I don't think I'm wrong, you'll have to lend me the money. I saw this adorable appliquéd-cat blazer at Reigning Cats & Dogs, the pet shop where Rachel buys Scout's food. I've decided to buy it, and the cost of one sleeve equals half my food budget."

"Marry me, Norrie, and I'll give you the appliquéd-cat blazer as a wedding present."

"Is that Ray's house, Peter? The little house with the gingerbread trim?"

"Yes." His expression turned solemn. "Norrie, I'm begging you. Don't say anything, not one word. I'll ask the questions."

As they walked up the path toward the front door, Ellie heard music.

The soundtrack from *Hello, Dolly!*

Barbra Streisand singing "Before the Parade Passes By."

As she and Peter drew closer, she heard someone else singing along with Barbra.

Peter rang the doorbell and the non-Streisand voice stopped singing.

Ray Morass opened the door and Ellie smelled hairspray.

Peter flashed his ID and said, "Mr. Morass, would you be good enough to answer a few questions?"

Ray looked around, as if searching for an escape hatch. Then he spied Ellie. "You! You sat next to me at the *Dolly* auditions. I remember because you were so much older than anyone else."

"Tell me, Ray," Ellie said, hiding her internal wince, "did you get the part you wanted?"

"What part?"

"Dolly."

"No. I didn't even get Cornelius. I'm the head waiter."

"Oh, what a shame. That means you killed Sara Lee for nothing."

Once again, Ray looked around. Then he said, "Who said I killed Sara Lee?"

"Theodora Mallard says you strangled Sara Lee. She saw you."

"That's a goddamn lie! She didn't even step outside until after I . . ."

"Killed Sara Lee," Peter finished. "Ms. Bernstein might have been the oldest person at the auditions, Mr. Morass, but she fingered you."

"Really!" Ray turned to Ellie. "Assuming, hypothetically, that I killed Sara Lee, how did I give myself away?"

"I thought from the very beginning that Sara Lee's killer was someone who wanted the part of Dolly. Then, at the auditions, when the director asked for two minutes of silent prayer, you scowled. People kept telling me everybody liked Sara Lee. Obviously, you didn't."

"That doesn't prove anything."

"Maybe it doesn't prove *everything,* but there's an eye witness."

"Who? The waitress, Theodora Mallard?" Ray snorted.

"No, not Theodora . . . Cindy Silberblatt."

"Who the hell is Cindy Silberblatt?"

"The lady who owns the pet shop. She stepped outside into the alley so that Muppet . . . so that her puppy could piddle. She saw you *stalk* Sara Lee," Ellie fibbed. "I know for a fact that your salon receptionist keeps track of stylists on smoke breaks, so all the cops have to do is establish a viable timeline. And then, dollface, you're toast!"

Ray faced Peter again. "May I make a phone call?"

As Will McCoy pulled up to the curb, Peter nodded. "One call, Mr. Morass. My other partner is here now, so I'll trust you not to try an escape."

Ray's smile was wistful. "Where would I go?"

Ellie thought he'd call a defense attorney, but the name she caught had nothing to do with lawyering. It was the name of the monkey-faced reporter.

If Ray Morass couldn't shine in the JDCT spotlight, he'd settle for the lights of a TV camera.

THIRTY-NINE

Sunday

The nondescript man wore a short, nondescript wig. His nondescript car squatted in front of a parking meter. However, it was nighttime, well past six o'clock, so he didn't have to feed the meter. His black Stetson rode shotgun atop the passenger seat.

This morning he had cruised the shabbier neighborhoods in his Jeep, until he found the perfect vehicle, parked half in the driveway, half atop a weedy patch of front yard. The FOR SALE sign in the car's window said $500. Parking his Jeep a few blocks away, he found the car's owner at home and negotiated the price down to three hundred, cash. The nondescript Ford belonged to an elderly lady whose grandson had souped-up the engine. She eagerly accepted the cash offer.

As he handed her the money, he said his name was Bob and he was in a big hurry and he'd be back the next day to complete the paperwork. Since he had pre-paid, the old lady had no objection.

He had parked the Ford in a shopping mall's lot, then walked back to his Jeep. His Jeep was now parked in a movie complex's lot, not far from the shopping mall.

After he finished his job tonight, he'd leave the key in the Ford's ignition and park it in one of the poorer neighborhoods where, hopefully, it would be stolen for parts. If not, and if the cops traced the car back to the old woman, all she could say was, "He's white, his name is Bob, and he had a rather large mole on his face."

Details were important, and "Bob" had always been a whiz at details.

Good thing he didn't have to feed the meter, he thought with a tight grin, because he didn't have any quarters, didn't have any coins at all, just a thick wad of ones, fives and tens from Sara Lee.

He wore nondescript clothes—black leather gloves, faded Levi's, and an old, faded-from-washing gray sweatshirt that, ironically, had once boasted the words COLORADO SPRINGS POLICE ACADEMY. On his feet, dirty sneakers. On his face, a mole that looked like Robert DeNiro's, only much bigger. All eyes were drawn to the mole. If asked for a physical description, people always said, "He has this really big mole." They couldn't remember whether he was tall or short, fat or thin; sometimes not even his ethnicity—just the mole.

And, occasionally, his scar, although he usually covered that up with eyebrow pencil.

His scar was real but the mole was phony. After tonight's job, he'd peel it off.

When he wasn't using his real name for legit business, he pulled one of a dozen aliases out of his cowboy hat. His favorites were Paul Redford and Robert Newman. For the past few weeks he'd been Robert Newman, and when he met pretty Sara Lee at Uncle Vinnie's Italian Restaurant, he had told her to call him Bob.

Through the clean glass of his windshield, Bob stared at the Dew Drop Inn. Its parking lot was full to bursting. So was the tavern. Its marquee read:

SUNDAY NIGHT FOOTBALL
BRONCOS VS RAIDERS

!!!!! FREE SHOTS !!!!!

when the Broncos score

Ordinarily, Bob would be watching the game and rooting for the Broncos, but tonight he didn't care who won. Tonight he needed to score his own victory.

Due to the overcrowded Dew Drop Inn's parking lot, Trent Zachariah had parked across the street. Illegally. In front of a hydrant. He probably thought his football-star status granted him unlimited parking privileges.

That was the attitude he had displayed on the showroom floor when Bob had scoped him out and inadvertently given the muscle-bound ape an alibi. *I'm a football star,* Zachariah seemed to imply, *so if you buy a car from me, you can brag to all your friends.*

As Bob barely tolerated a seemingly endless test drive in what Zachariah called a "new used car," Zachariah talked about his wife. How Sara Lee had trapped him into marriage by pretending to be knocked up. How she, and she alone, was the reason he'd been kicked off the Broncos squad. Why? Because every time he thought about the dirty trick she had played on him, he'd lose his damned temper. Still, he said, the bitch doted on him and he treated her like a queen, even if she *was* a lousy cook.

Sara Lee told a different story, and she had shown Bob the bruises to prove it. She said she'd pay anything to have her husband out of the picture, out of her life. She said she couldn't leave him because he had threatened to kill her. Her tears had nearly drowned the Italian cheesecake she had served Bob for dessert, free of charge.

He refocused on the Dew Drop's entrance. As he did, the front door opened and a couple of bouncers bounced Trent Zachariah, who was dead drunk, just as he'd been Friday night and last night. Friday night he had partied with co-workers, and last night he had slugged down tequila with his sister Angel at the Olive or Twist. But tonight he stood there—make that sprawled there—all by his lonesome. Obviously, the game wasn't over yet. When it came to nursing a drunk bud or watching the fourth quarter of a Broncos football game, friends would let you crawl on your hands and knees before they'd lift a finger to help you cross the street.

Sara Lee had paid all she could afford, five hundred hard-earned dollars, and she had promised to scrape together another five hundred after the hit. It seemed only right to use three of the five hundred to buy the old lady's car. He really didn't need the money all that badly.

Bob narrowed his focus as Trent Zachariah elbow-crawled his way to the curb.

There was no one to witness Zachariah vomiting into the gutter. In fact, there were no witnesses at hand. Everybody was inside, watching the Broncos.

Zachariah stood up on rubbery legs, wiped his mouth on his jacket's sleeve, and began to stagger across the street.

Bob turned the ignition key, maneuvered out of his parking space, revved the car's souped-up engine, and pressed the accelerator pedal with his right foot.

All the way down to the floorboard.

Sara Lee was dead, but one's word was the measure of a man and Bob *always* honored his commitments.

FORTY

Ellie wanted to throttle Peter.

They had planned to watch Sunday Night Football, the Broncos vs. the Raiders, at the Dew Drop Inn, but Peter was stuck at the precinct.

On a Sunday, dammit!

Too much paperwork, he had said.

"You should ask Rachel Lester to organize your desk," she had told him, only half joking.

He had suggested she go to the Dew Drop Inn and he'd join her there later, but she said she'd watch the game at home and cook up some more honey lasagna. He had called again after the game, with a one-liner that sounded like a telegram: "Sweetheart, something's come up, a hit and run, don't know what time I'll be home, will you marry me?"

"Maybe," she said.

Tonight, when he came home, she'd tell him that "maybe" meant "yes."

No, she'd show him.

He had forgotten to say "I love you," but she knew he did.

Restless, she strolled into the kitchen. Jackie Robinson snoozed on his usual chair, and yet the house felt lonely without Scout.

The phone's strident ring interrupted her musings. With a smile, she snatched up the receiver and said, "I love you, too."

"Excuse me?"

"Oh, I'm sorry. I thought—"

"Is this Ellie Bernstein?"

"Yes."

"This is Susan, the JDCT assistant director. We've cast you in *Hello, Dolly!* Rehearsals start next Sunday afternoon at one o'clock."

Ellie's first thought was, *Peter promised we'd go to the Dew Drop Inn next Sunday afternoon to watch the Broncos play the Kansas City Chiefs.*

Aloud she said, "How could you cast me? I never auditioned . . . never even sang . . . please don't tell me you cast me as Dolly."

She heard a snort just before Susan said, "No, ma'am. We gave the role of Dolly to Angel Pitt. We cast you as Ernestina Simple, Dolly's friend. There's no singing. It's a comedic role. Do you want to play the part? Yes or no?"

Ellie pictured the teenage Sara Lee, staring at the camera with a brave *I'm gonna succeed no matter what* look on her face. Prior to Weight Winners, Ellie wouldn't have set foot on a stage. In fact, she would have fled from any trace of a spotlight. She wasn't sure she could hack it now, but maybe she owed it to Sara Lee to play the part of Ernestina Simple, to be the best she could be—and then try to be even better.

As she said yes, she could have sworn she heard a wraithlike, waiflike laugh that sounded like a cross between a puppy's playful growl and wind chimes. A final comment from Sara Lee? Or a gentle reminder from a puppy that looked like a Muppet?

KURT GORDON'S CHEEZY PEROGIE RECIPE

INGREDIENTS:

8 baking potatoes, peeled and cubed
1 cup of shredded Cheddar cheese
2 tablespoons processed cheese sauce
4 1/2 cups all-purpose flour
2 teaspoons salt
2 tablespoons butter, melted
2 cups sour cream
2 eggs
1 egg yolk
2 tablespoons vegetable oil
onion salt to taste (optional)
salt and pepper to taste

COOKING DIRECTIONS:

In a large bowl, stir together the flour and salt. In a separate bowl, whisk together the butter, sour cream, eggs, egg yolk and oil. Stir the wet ingredients into the flour until well blended. Cover the bowl with a towel and let stand for 15 to 20 minutes.

Place potatoes in a pot and fill with enough water to cover. Bring to a boil, and cook until tender, approximately 15 minutes. Drain and mash with cheese and cheese sauce while still hot. Season with onion salt, salt and pepper. Set aside to cool.

Cheezy Perogie Recipe

Separate the perogie dough into two balls. Roll out one piece at a time on a lightly floured surface until it's thin enough to work with, but not too thin so that it tears. Cut the dough into circles using a cookie cutter or a glass. Brush water around the edges of the circles and spoon some filling into the center. Fold the circles over into half-circles and press to seal the edges. Place perogies on a cookie sheet and freeze.

Bring a large pot of lightly salted water to a boil. Drop frozen perogies in one at a time (the perogies are less likely to burst during cooking if they are frozen). Do not boil too long or they will get soggy. They are finished when they float to the top.

ABOUT THE AUTHOR

Denise Dietz is the bestselling author of *Fifty Cents for Your Soul, The Landlord's Black-Eyed Daughter* (as Mary Ellen Dennis), and *Footprints in the Butter*—an Ingrid Beaumont Mystery co-starring Hitchcock the Dog. Denise met her husband, novelist Gordon Aalborg, on the Internet. They wed at a writers' conference and bought a heritage cottage on Vancouver Island. The author of fourteen novels, Denise's most recent mysteries are *Eye of Newt,* starring reluctant witch Sydney St. Charles, and *Chain a Lamb Chop to the Bed,* third in the Ellie Bernstein/Lt. Peter Miller diet club series. The first and second in the series, *Throw Darts at a Cheesecake* and *Beat Up a Cookie,* are available in large print. No animals were harmed in the writing of this book—nor *in* this book. Scout and Ava's humans were the winning bidders at charity auctions, and a portion of the profits from this book will be donated to the BC SPCA. Denise likes to hear from readers. You can contact her through her Web site: www.denisedietz.com.